Look for More Titles by Cassandra Chandler

Court of the Springtime Fae
Jack Frost
Prince Charming
The Oak King

Court of the Yuletide Fae
The Yule Cat
The White Stag
The Krampus

The Department of Homeworld Security
Gray Card
Resident Alien
Business or Pleasure
Tied up in Customs
Entry Visa
Duration of Stay
Duel Citizenship
Invasive Species
Export Duty
COALITION RECKONING
Import Quarantine
Homeworld for the Holidays
Nothing to Declare
Rate of Return
Trade Secrets
THE DEPARTMENT OF HOMEWORLD SECURITY OMNIBUS 1
THE DEPARTMENT OF HOMEWORLD SECURITY OMNIBUS 2

Cygnian 7
NUAR
KRAL
LAR

DORN
BRON
TARN
ROM

The Blades of Janus
PACK
PROGENITOR

The Forbidden Knights
FORBIDDEN INSTINCT

The Summer Park Psychics
WANDERING SOUL
WHISPERING HEARTS
LINGERING TOUCH
THE SUMMER PARK PSYCHICS OMNIBUS

Other Works
CRAFTING A WRITER'S LIFE: Building a Foundation

Coming Soon

The Blades of Janus
PERIHELION

Court of the Summer Fae
The Huntsman
The Green Man
The Big Bad Wolf

Cygnian 7
ZAKARRI

The Yuletide Fae

Courts of the Fae
Book One

Cassandra Chandler

Copyright Page

The Yuletide Fae
Courts of the Fae, Book One
Copyright © 2024 by Cassandra Chandler
Print ISBN: 978-0-9974486-6-5
Digital ISBN: 978-0-9974486-7-2

First eBook edition: December 2024
First print edition: December 2024
10 9 8 7 6 5 4 3 2 1

cassandra-chandler.com
P.O. Box 91
Mission, Kansas 66201

Dedication

For Eliza, who brings so much joy to these adventures.

Don't miss out on any of the magic.
Subscribe to Cassandra Chandler's newsletter at
cassandra-chandler.com!

COURT OF THE YULETIDE FAE

THE YULE CAT

USA TODAY BESTSELLING AUTHOR
CASSANDRA CHANDLER

The Yule Cat

Court of the Yuletide Fae
Book One

Cassandra Chandler

Chapter One

How did everything go so wrong?

The Yule Cat ran along the edge of a roof, calling to the wind to cover his tracks in the dense snow falling around him. The flakes stuck in his silver-white coat, obscuring the dark circles on his pelt. He had no tribute to bring to the Winter Queen. Not once had he returned without a new servant for her Court.

There would be a punishment. He would endure it, whatever it was, as long as she could help him purge this affliction in his chest. His heart was filled with... warmth. His fur stood on end as the skin beneath it crawled from the memory of the child's touch. She had hugged him. *Hugged* him—a fierce snow leopard twice her size with glowing blue eyes, fangs longer than her fingers, and gleaming mist trailing from his pelt.

That tiny mortal had thrown a blanket over his shoulders as if he needed her help. As if a mortal had anything to offer a mighty Fairy Lord, one of the only *two* in the Winter Queen's Yuletide Court. The child had wrapped her arms around him, wanting him to be warm, even though she had so little to warm herself.

The heat in his heart grew stronger, like a fire that had been lit within. A fire he didn't want any part of, didn't know what to do with. He was the Lord of the North Wind, icy and cruel. He tore warmth from others, leaving cold in its wake. He didn't accept it. He didn't *need* it for himself. He didn't want it.

Did he?

The Yule Cat let out a roar like thunder. Around him, the snowflakes shuddered, then paused, spinning in place as he pulled on the pocket of Faerie ruled by the Yuletide Fae. Light burst into being, a spiraling vortex of energy. He charged to the corner of the roof and leapt, arcing his back as he soared through the portal.

The light was so much colder than he remembered. On the other side, he landed in a drift, a shiver coursing through him as he shook his pelt free of moisture. His heat melted the snow clinging to his fur. The portal sealed behind him, the snap of its closure seeming to mark his failure complete.

An unfamiliar dread filled his stomach as he stalked toward the crystalline castle in the distance, rising from the snow and reflecting the verdant aurora flooding the dark sky overhead. When he reached the tall gates, they opened, motes of light threading through their faceted surface. Curious energy tickled his nose and tingled along his back, glowing lights of every color flying close and picking at his coat—pixies and sprites checking him over, as if the child he was supposed to have brought might be hiding in his fur. Their light caught in the hundreds of snowflakes slowly spinning, suspended in the air of the castle.

He hissed as he released his Yule Cat form. Silver magic enveloped him, lifting him to his hind legs. His pelt vanished into the light, replaced with rich sapphire blue silk that swirled around him as it coalesced into a loose shirt, dark indigo pants, and soft black boots that hugged his calves. He lifted his right arm in an arc, summoning the wind to form a silver cloak that swung itself onto his shoulders, anchoring in place with platinum clasps adorned with sapphires, diamonds, and blue topaz.

His heart was still warm. Disappointment surged through him, tightening his throat. He hadn't realized he held hope that his affliction would vanish along with his Yule Cat form. The pixies continued to pick at him, pulling on the ends of his cloak and tugging on his hair. They had never dared treat him that way before. A low growl built in his chest. He lashed out, summoning a harsh, cold wind to scatter them. The snowflakes hanging in the air spun more quickly as they fled. If only those pests were the worst he had to face.

The doors to the main hall stood open before him. He didn't dare hesitate and add showing fear to his shame. Puffing up his chest and drawing himself up ramrod straight, he strode into the chamber. The eyes of his Queen rested heavily on him as he walked to the center of the throne room and dropped to one knee, head bowed. At the edge of his vision, he could see the folds of her intricate dress, the fabric such a pale blue, it was almost white.

"You seem to be missing something, Lord North."

His spine prickled at the sound of his Queen's voice and the power laced through it. A power that was oddly muted. He forced a scowl to hide his surprise. It wasn't enough to conceal his turmoil. Before him, his Queen rose from her crystal throne. He kept his attention fixed to the floor.

"Missing something, but also… gifted something." She glided down the steps toward him, silent as a whisper. "Stand, Cat."

He felt the pluck of the command and his body jerked in response, but didn't rise. Panic flooded him, making the skin on his arms crawl again. A wind picked up in the room as if it wished to envelop him and carry him to safety. The Cat within him stirred, urging him to transform and flee. He could hide in the wintery countryside until he found a way to purge his affliction. His cloak stirred in the breeze and even the skirts of the Queen rippled.

He didn't need to see her face to sense her surprise. His powers had been summoned without conscious thought and dared to affect her. Worse, she had given him a command, and he hadn't obeyed. He didn't know how he had managed it, but he hadn't obeyed.

"Lord North," she said. Magic crackled through him as she summoned the bond of fealty through his name. His skin prickled as though he'd rolled in a patch of nettles in his two-legged form. "Stand."

She lifted her hand above him, power lashing out in tendrils of ice so cold they burned. He pushed himself to stand before her, but couldn't meet her scrutiny. She would see failure in his eyes—the mark the child had left.

"Where is your tribute?" the Winter Queen asked.

"I…" He shook his head. "I have none, Majesty."

"You are the Lord of the North Wind," she said. "The Yule Cat, feared by mortals."

"Not by her."

"Her?"

The word seemed to freeze the blood in his veins, the chill in the air making him shiver, yet, the warmth in his heart prevailed. It beat faster as he considered the danger he had placed the child in through his mistake.

"So, you do have a tribute," the Queen said. "You just *chose* not to bring her to me." The silence stretched on where he felt her intense focus on him heavily. After a time, she said, "Those who are unwanted in the mortal realm, those who are lost and need guidance, find purpose here. Is that not good enough for the child you chose as tribute?"

"My Queen—"

"Am I?" she broke in. "Look at me, North."

Once more, she used her voice of command, forcing his gaze to hers. He could scarcely breathe. His chest had surely turned to stone, his ribs crushing his heart. Her cold beauty crackled through him—skin white as snow, lips red as cranberries, eyes like green emeralds. The contours of her cheekbones were high and sharp, her features all sharp edged like the crystal around her. Like ice. A crown rested on her forehead, its platinum and diamond spikes rising up and contrasting with the pale hair pulled tight against her scalp, revealing her long neck.

He had always thought her beautiful. He had never thought her terrible. His skin crawled at the very idea of bringing the child he had selected as a tribute to this cold domain. The child who had somehow touched his heart with her warmth.

He had always thought the Yuletide Kingdom to be one of stark beauty and endless magic. Now, it looked to him like a wasteland of snow and ice. Unchanging. Unwelcoming. So unlike the child. North knew there was a part of the kingdom that was different—the only bastion of warmth in the realm. But as a subject of the Winter Queen, he would find no welcome there, either.

"I think perhaps you have another Queen," she said. Her attention dropped to his chest and her lips pulled into a frown. "Or at least, there is another who rules your heart."

"Majesty." A deep male voice met his ears.

"Ah, Lord Snow." The Winter Queen turned to greet the enormous man who approached them.

The Lord of Endless Snow towered over him, even though North was over six-feet tall himself. Snow's shoulders were twice as broad and he was packed with muscle. He wore all white—leggings and tunic, with a thick white fur tied at his shoulder and draped over one side. It was easy to see the monstrous Polar Bear lurking within the man before them and to understand the frightening stories of 'the Krampus' that mortals had woven around him.

"I trust your tribute is settling in," the Winter Queen said.

"I've taken him to the kitchens," Snow said. "He'll need a firm hand, but will serve you well in time."

"Excellent." She turned back to North, and said, "Our Lord North has returned alone, though I think he carries his tribute in his heart."

"What?" Snow leaned closer, bending down from his great height to peer into North's eyes. He sniffed loudly, then jerked back, blowing the air from his nose, rubbing at it. He shook his head sharply. "North, you reek of love. A mortal loves you."

"A child," North protested. "She thought I was her gift."

He snapped his mouth shut before more damning words could escape. Enough had already slipped out to deepen his shame. One of the Winter Queen's thin eyebrows rose and Snow crossed his arms over his massive chest.

"She thought the Yule Cat was a present?" Snow said. "The beast who comes on Christmas Eve to steal away children who don't receive new clothes?"

"I see." The Winter Queen smirked. "The little girl wanted a kitty. Does she think you're her pet now? Are you?"

"I am the Lord of the North Wind," North said, stepping closer. Snow darted forward to stand between them, sucking in a deep breath to make his chest even bigger. North lowered his head, trying to stop the growl that rumbled within him.

"Your temper has grown hot," the Winter Queen said. "We cannot have that in the Yuletide Kingdom."

"What are we to do about this?" Snow asked, his voice laced with concern.

"It's an affliction," North said. "Surely, there's something that can purge this warmth from me."

"It is not so easy to remove something that has found its way into your heart," she said. "No, it's much too late for that."

"Then what do I do?" North asked.

"You will return to the mortal realm and stay there until you have found a way to purge yourself of this... warmth," the Queen said with a slight shudder of distaste.

North was stunned. He couldn't believe what he had heard. Banished to the mortal realm? He had no idea how to undo what had been done. He could be stuck there forever.

"Majesty," Snow began. "Please, have mercy. North is…"

His voice trailed off as they stared at each other. North wasn't sure what Snow had been about to call him. Peer? Friend? Brother? The bond they shared was the closest thing to affection that North had known before this night. Now that he knew what true caring felt like, their partnership couldn't compare. Still, North's shame deepened as he realized that Snow would carry the burden of North's duties while he was gone.

The Winter Queen regarded North silently for a moment, then her lips pulled into a cold smile. North's heart pounded and his mouth went dry. His punishment was at hand. What could be worse than exile?

"Fine," the Winter Queen said. "You could not bring your tribute here as a servant, so you will bring her as your bride."

"What?" North recoiled. "She's a child."

He couldn't have heard the Queen correctly. This punishment was beyond anything he had expected. A mortal bride? His humiliation would be eternal.

"She will grow." The Queen shrugged. "When she has come of age, you will present her to me."

"But Majesty—" This time, it was Snow who protested. She silenced him with a sharp wave of her hand, holding her arm up before him.

"I don't know anything about winning a mortal's heart," North said.

"That is not my concern," she said. "If you can win her heart by Christmas day of her twenty-seventh year, I will forgive your failure tonight. If not…"

North's blood pounded in his ears loudly enough to nearly drown out her words.

"Your exile will be permanent," she said.

Chapter Two

Ice and snow managed to get into every slight gap in Melanie's clothes, chilling her neck and chest. The thick flakes swept into her eyes, half-blinding her. She was absolutely crazy to be doing this. Then again, she'd be crazy to let the opportunity pass. As long as the private baking lesson she had won didn't take too long, she'd be home in time for her own Christmas tradition—sitting by the tree at midnight as the Eve ticked over to the Day, waiting for someone who would never come. Who wasn't even real.

She probably shouldn't have gone ahead and dressed up for the occasion. Warmer pants would have been better. Or any pants, instead of a dress and woolen leggings. But it was Christmas Eve, and she always dressed to celebrate, even if she was spending this one with a complete stranger —at least the next few hours of it. How long did it take to bake a batch of cookies or whatever the owner of the Yuletide Bakery had in mind?

The storefronts on either side of the road were lit with gorgeous lights of every color. Fluffy flakes of snow caught the lights and glowed like a magical Faerie landscape. A pang threaded through her as she wished she could pause and enjoy it more, but frostbite was not on her agenda for the evening. The snow had driven everyone inside early, it seemed. She pulled the lapels of her dark blue peacoat closer to the silver-and-blue scarf she had knitted last year, then pulled the matching hat down farther over her ears.

Most of the buildings were dark inside, their owners at home celebrating with family. For once, Melanie didn't feel sad at the thought that she had none. She was too excited about what the evening held. She had taken a risk and shared something deeply personal in a writing contest and won first prize—an evening being tutored by the owner of the Yuletide Bakery. The bakery was in a cozy part of town she had somehow never explored. She had read up on it after winning the contest, and it sounded absolutely magical.

The owner's theme was "Christmas Year-Round." She loved that. Christmas was her favorite holiday, even if she spent it alone. She still went all-out decorating her apartment, hanging up lights, and dressing a beautiful tree. The tree was the most important part, because she always held out hope that one day, *he* would come back to her. She even hung a stocking for him filled with toys and treats—which was ridiculous on so many levels.

Melanie shook her head hard enough that snow

dislodged, sliding down her back and making her jump and squeal. It served her right. She'd made a promise to herself and was not about to break it. When faced with the choice of staying home alone and waiting for a fictional beast that she *had* to have imagined as a child to crawl out from under her tree or having a private baking lesson from one of the most successful bakery owners in town, she did the only sane thing.

Trudging out into the snow to spend an evening with a man I've never met in a place I've never been, knowing I'll then have to trudge back to my apartment in the middle of the night. Yeah. That's sane.

She scoffed at herself, but kept pressing onwards. Someday, she would have her own bakery. This was an amazing opportunity. A *real* opportunity. And she would still be home in time to wait by the tree. She walked faster, just in case.

Ahead of her, golden light spilled out onto the snow, cast from the plate glass windows of a storefront. It was bright enough to illuminate the street in front of it and somehow made the air seem warmer. A sign hung above the door, decorated with a flowing script that said, "Yuletide Bakery—Where Christmas is Eternal." Smiling despite the cold, she hurried forward to look inside.

Tables with the chairs stacked upside-down on top of them dotted the floor, letting her know it was a cafe as well as a bakery. The heavy-duty espresso makers along the far wall—brick with just the right amount of weathering—would have clued her in as well. In front of the coffee machines, glass display cases were filled with sparkling gold and silver lights that curled around empty trays. She wished she could have come earlier and seen them when they were full. There was still plenty to catch her eye.

Dark mahogany shelves lined the wall to the right of the display cases, adorned with ropes of evergreen and filled with books, mugs, and sculptures. A staircase wound around one corner, heading to a door on the second floor. Beneath it, a huge Christmas tree was nestled near a stone fireplace with a blazing fire within. Three stockings hung from the mantel, one green, one white, and one blue. The tree was covered in glittering silver and gold ornaments that complemented the lighting perfectly. She had never seen anything so beautiful, except maybe for her fictional childhood 'friend.'

Her breath caught as her gaze was drawn to movement right beneath the window. A man was stretched out on a window seat, his chest rising and falling with each slow breath. He was tall, his long legs crossed at the ankles, and his hands clasped over his stomach. His brown hair was long enough to dust his shoulders, with bangs that fell across his eyes. Dark stubble dusted his strong jaw, showcasing his gorgeous lips, slightly parted in sleep.

Was *that* the owner? Her heartbeat spiked at the

thought of spending Christmas Eve with the most beautiful man she'd ever seen. He lifted his arm, crooking it so that he could rest his head on it. Blue-green eyes like arctic depths stared at her as his lips pulled into a smirk. For a second—only a second—she would have sworn his pupils were slitted. Like a cat's.

"The view is even better from inside," he said, his voice somewhat muted by the glass. "You coming in or would you rather stand out there and freeze to death?"

Her cheeks prickled with heat at being caught gawking at him, though she scowled at his teasing tone. Apparently, he was one of those guys who knew exactly how gorgeous he was. Good. That would make him less appealing.

She headed to the door. Snow was piled up in front of it. This might not have been as good an idea as she thought. Would she even be able to get home at the rate the snow was coming down?

She shook her head again and pulled the door open. A blast of warmth and the most amazing scents wrapped around her the moment she did. Sweet cinnamon, earthy nutmeg, and the beautiful scent of chocolate and coffee overwhelmed her senses. She closed her eyes, taking a deep breath and savoring each smell, trying to sort them all out.

"Mind closing the door?"

She jumped at the man's voice so close. She hadn't heard him approach, his footsteps absolutely silent. He was even taller than she'd thought, and with her being shorter than average, that meant he towered over her. One long arm stretched above her and the other rested on the door jamb, boxing her in as he continued to smirk at her. She needed to duck around his side to enter the bakery, but she took a deep breath and did so, pulling the door shut as she did.

He chuckled and turned to lock the door in one smooth movement. Why did he lock them in? It must be because the store was closed. She had been thorough in her research and knew that the bakery had held a contest like this every year for the last seven years. There had never been any complaints about him. Then again, with how gorgeous he was, a lot of people probably wouldn't mind his attention.

"Let me get your coat for you," he said.

She took off her hat and gloves and shook the snow from them, then tucked them into her coat pockets before unfastening the large black buttons. He watched each movement, his smirk firmly in place. His cocky attitude made her scowl deepen. Just because he was utterly gorgeous didn't mean she was going to throw herself at him.

Probably.

She stomped her feet on the carpet just inside the door to dislodge the last of the snow, then slid her coat off. He lifted it from her arms and hung it on a peg near the door.

As he moved near her, the scent of cinnamon rolls flowed off of him.

Definitely not throwing myself at the gorgeous bakery guy who smells like cinnamon rolls.

His shirt was a deep sapphire blue, unbuttoned enough to give her a tantalizing view of perfect collarbones and a glimpse of his smooth, muscular chest.

"It's Melanie, right?" he said, pulling her attention away from his physique. His voice had a nice, low timbre.

"Yes," she said. She waited a few moments for him to give her his name before giving up. "What do I call you?"

"North."

"North? That's it?"

"That's it." He shrugged, his smirk deepening. Was that a dimple? Oh crap, he had dimples. She had a weakness for those. And for strong hands with long, artistic fingers, which she also noticed he had.

"You're chilled to the bone," he said. "The ovens will warm you right up."

Melanie balked as he gestured toward a door behind the counter next to the biggest display case. For some reason, images from fairytales she'd read as a child filled her head —stories about children being popped into ovens.

She was being completely ridiculous. How was he supposed to give her a baking lesson without using ovens? She cast a nervous smile at him and nodded, then headed for the kitchen and whatever else the night held.

Chapter Three

This was the most delicious looking mortal North had ever seen. 'When Snow had insisted that North host a woman every Christmas Eve, trying desperately to find the bride that North had 'lost track of,' he hadn't been too keen on the idea. Snow thought it was because North didn't want to have to endure an evening with a mortal, but he had been living among them for two decades now. North had learned to appreciate the mortal realm and all it had to offer.

Spending his days sleeping in his apartment above the bakery while his employees ran around downstairs, using the night hours to make the most magical pastries in town, filling the place with warmth and sweet fragrances that lured in the most wary customer, had become his own private paradise. Over the years, he'd grown accustomed to the warmth in his heart. Liked it, even. He only had to make it through one more day without finding his bride and he could stay here forever. He had done everything he could to make sure that would happen.

Minutely studying the tasty morsel in front of him, a

shiver of doubt trailed down his spine. Her hair was too dark and straight. The child's had been curly and much paler. She had the same piercing eyes, though—blue as the ice in a glacier. It wasn't a common color, but that didn't have to mean anything. The woman, Melanie, was tiny. He had at least a foot on her in height. She wasn't wiry like most of the wealthy women who came into his bakery. No, Melanie had curves. Very ample curves. His height gave him a fantastic view.

He leaned over her to open the door to the kitchen when they reached it. Her skin was pale, but there was a flush of color around her collarbones, neck, and cheeks. It might be from the cold, but judging from the looks she kept casting his way, it might be from something else. His smirk deepened as she crossed into his kitchen.

"Oh wow…" she said.

The breathy sound to her voice hit him like a blow to the chest. He rubbed the spot, wondering what the hell that was. She spun in a circle, eyes wide and smiling lips somewhat parted. With a little distance between them, he could see that she wore a dress of deep blue with an ivy pattern woven onto the fabric in silver thread. The hairs on the back of his neck rose. Those were his colors. It had to be a coincidence that she was wearing them… Right?

Her pale eggshell-white leggings were tucked into dark blue boots trimmed with silver fur at the top. The dress hugged her waist, flaring out at her wide hips and showcasing her figure perfectly. Heat rushed through his body at the sight of her. Apparently, it didn't have the same misgivings his mind did.

"This is amazing," she said. "You even decorated your kitchen to look like Christmas."

He grunted an affirmative, trying to get himself under control. What the heck was wrong with him? His heart raced and his skin prickled with goosebumps. His fingers curled and uncurled, as if trying to summon her into their grip. Three minutes in her company, and he already wanted this woman with an intensity that honestly frightened him.

Another shiver of doubt coursed through him. Could she be the same person who had shown him his first kindness? His first taste of what it was to be loved? No, she couldn't be. This wasn't even the same town where she had lived.

He had settled on the other side of the continent—after visiting her foster family in his human form and ensuring the child would receive better treatment than the neglectful way they'd been raising her. He was certain after that conversation, she had enjoyed a much better childhood. He had made sure she would want for nothing, casting a gaes compulsion spell on her foster parents to care for her after giving them enough gems to provide for her. She would never have to work a day in her life, thanks to him. He just wanted her to live that life far from himself.

Keeping his distance was how North helped her. The Kingdom of the Yuletide Fae was no place for someone so warm and caring. At least, not in the Winter Queen's court. Once Christmas Day arrived, he wouldn't have to worry about returning—or condemning the child to an eternity of winter's cold. Perhaps, some day he would seek her out to thank her for how she'd changed his life. Some day *after* tomorrow.

"I can't believe I'm here." Melanie smiled at him, cherry-red lips beaming and sending another jolt through him.

"Are you okay?" she asked, stepping closer. Again, his body heated in response, his energy coiling as if waiting to wrap around her and pull her close.

"Yeah, I'm fine."

He needed to get the baking lesson over with and send her back to wherever she'd come from as quickly as possible. Luckily, he'd prepared all of the ingredients before she arrived. Everything was measured out in individual cruets and bowls, just waiting to be combined in the right order.

"This looks amazing," she said, surveying the table where the prep work had been laid out. "What would you like me to do first?"

A whole slew of ideas flooded his mind. None of them involved baking. She stared up at him, her eyes bright with anticipation. Anticipation about *baking*. He needed to get his head in the game.

"I have some dough chilling in the fridge for my own take on Chocolate Crinkle Cookies," he said, rounding the table to stand beside her. "We can make a dough for Cocoon Crescents and start the Crinkles baking while the Crescents dough sets up in the fridge. It doesn't need to chill as long."

"Wow, sounds like you have this all sorted out."

He leaned a little closer. "I have done this a time or two."

She laughed and nodded. His heart gave a little skip at the sound. Laughter that sincere wasn't common. It was captivating. *She* was captivating.

She reached into a pocket hidden in the full skirt of her dress. "Shoot," she said. "I think I left my pen at home."

She pulled out a small, spiral bound notebook that had a deep blue cover with a snowflake pattern on it and flipped through it. He caught glimpses of pages filled with neat, flowery handwriting, but she turned them too fast for him to read. The strength of his curiosity about her surprised him. He wanted to know what was on those pages.

"You planning on stealing my secret recipes?" he asked, his voice gruffer than he'd intended.

"No." She cast a teasing scowl at him that had him leaning closer again. "Your secrets are safe with me."

He felt another shiver at her phrasing. What were the

odds that out of everyone in the world, on the final night before his exile became permanent, *she* would show up in his bakery? After he'd taken steps to make sure it never happened. He stared at her intently, trying to see a trace of the girl he had met. No, Melanie was too young to be the same person. She looked like she was just entering her twenties and that girl would be twenty-seven.

Melanie lifted her book and sort of waved it at him strangely, as if she were using it to pull something from him. "I won't steal your secrets, but before I leave tonight, I need to suck everything I can out of you."

He paused, angling his head to the side. The shiver from that statement was a heck of a lot nicer than the one before. Her face immediately turned scarlet. He could practically see steam coming off her cheeks and struggled not to laugh. His misgivings vanished in the heat brought on by her words.

"Learning," she quickly added. "I need to learn all I can."

"Sure," he said, not bothering to hide his smile.

"I wasn't going to write down ingredients or proportions or anything," she said, talking quickly and not making eye contact, "but I figure you have plenty to teach me. Like, for dough that needs to be chilled, how long do you leave it in the fridge?"

"Depends on the cookie." He rested his hand on the edge of the table, inching closer as he cast a charming smirk at her.

The flush darkening her cheeks spread over her chest as she smiled and glanced at him briefly. She was definitely interested, but this one… She would need to be warmed up if anything was going to happen between them, and he had to admit to himself that he was starting to really hope something would happen between them, even with his concerns.

Most of the women he'd entertained on previous Christmas Eves had all but thrown themselves at him. A couple literally had, pretending to trip and fall against him. He'd gotten rid of them as quickly as possible, as he had intended to do with Melanie. Now, though… Now, he wanted her to stick around. She fascinated him. He just hoped that saying about curiosity and cats wouldn't apply to him.

"Oh, I found it!" She pulled a midnight blue pen from her pocket, her smile brightening the entire room. How could someone be so happy over a pen? And why did it make his heart skip a beat to see that smile?

"You sure do love blue," he said.

"It's my favorite color."

She beamed at him with those ice-blue eyes. He couldn't stop himself from staring into them. Despite the color, there was so much warmth there—along with traces of the attraction he knew he was stirring up in her. The attraction he shared. Her smile faded and her lips parted.

He could hear her heartbeat pick up as she leaned toward him. But then she sort of shook herself, pulling back.

"We should get started," she said, laughing nervously again.

"I suppose we should." He turned back to his prep work, quite a bit more keen on the evening than he had been before.

Chapter Four

Melanie was going to melt the dough at this point. They wouldn't need to preheat any ovens, North could just hand her the cookies, and they'd bake from the heat she was putting off. Even his name gave her a shiver. The image of her plucking some of the dough from the bowl and sensuously feeding it to him popped into her head.

Her cheeks tingled with embarrassment, as if he could hear her thoughts. She was being ludicrous. She would never do such a thing. Besides, he was epically hot and probably wasn't interested in her. And no one should eat raw cookie dough.

She glanced over at him as he started talking about the different ingredients in their little dishes, his profile just as striking as seeing him head-on. Who was she kidding? She would hand-feed him anything that he wanted if he was interested.

Shaking her head again, she turned back to the ingredients, hoping to distract herself. She threw the softened butter into the stand mixer, then added the sugar and started it up to cream them together. When they seemed mixed enough, she added the vanilla and started on the other ingredients.

"Wait, I know what these are," she said. "These are Wedding Cookies."

"I prefer to call them Crescent Cookies."

"Aww, what's the matter?" she teased. "Are you afraid of commitment?"

Where the heck had that come from? Her cheeks prickled with heat again as she looked away, a stupid smile on her face that she couldn't get rid of. North leaned against the edge of the table and crossed his arms. The movement opened the collar of his shirt wider, letting her see more of his tempting chest.

"Right now, I'm more concerned about getting my recipes poached by a ringer," he said.

"What?"

Her eyes widened as she realized what she was doing. She was supposed to be getting a baking lesson from a master, and here she was, throwing his ingredients around and using his equipment without asking.

"I'm so sorry." She backed away from the mixer. "I didn't mean—"

"Relax," he said, following her retreat.

He told her to relax, but the way he moved and the intensity of his stare made her feel like he was about to serve her up instead of cookies. Not that she would even mind at this point. Except she would. Of course she would.

It didn't matter how attractive he was, she didn't just hook up with strange men.

No, I sit in front of a Christmas tree every year by myself waiting for a magic cat to show up. That's so much healthier.

That was who she had been up to now, but this Christmas was different. She could feel it, ever since she won the contest—since she decided to make a change. How many more new things could she push herself to do? How many new incredible experiences could she have if she got out of her own way?

"It's kind of a nice surprise to have someone with me in the kitchen who knows what they're doing." North leaned over her, his smirk deepening those entrancing dimples. "Most of the people who enter the contest seem more interested in tasting than baking."

She licked her lips reflexively and his eyes followed the movement. Her nerves flared up, the hair along her arms standing on end. Slowly, his smirk faded as his expression became filled with heat. His eyes almost seemed to glow. The light was familiar. Two bright spots of blue beneath her Christmas tree when she was a little girl. The eyes of the Yule Cat. She had thought he was the gift she had begged for and worked to earn for as long as she'd been with those foster parents.

All she had ever wanted was a cat to be her companion. The Yule Cat had seemed like something beyond her wildest childhood dream. She had lavished him with love when he'd crawled out from under the tree—an enormous snow leopard putting off a cold, white mist. At the time, she'd been young enough to believe in magic, and the experience had made it hard for her to stop, even when she was supposed to 'grow up' and move on from such things.

She had covered the Yule Cat with the blanket she brought down with her from her bed and wrapped her arms around him as much as she could to warm him, even though she herself was bitterly cold. He had felt so real, the softness of his fur, the rumbling growl that turned to a purr the more she promised to protect him, love him, and take care of him forever. Thinking about it now, it seemed insane. It always did, until she was sitting in front of her Christmas tree on Christmas Eve, wondering if there was any magic in the holiday that could bring her first friend back to her.

She'd researched the Yule Cat, and knew about the stories where he ate naughty children. The stories where he took children to Faerie were the ones she believed. Somehow, she knew that he had come to snatch her away from all the disappointments of her reality. Except he hadn't taken her. He had left her where she was, with foster parents who hadn't seemed to want her up to that point. If he really was the friend she had wished for, wouldn't he have come back for her by now?

Her foster parents had changed after that night. They

were more attentive, but there was always a layer of fear beneath their interactions. They had been so relieved when she moved to the other side of the country for college. Their behavior made it harder to believe the Yule Cat *wasn't* real. She had convinced herself that he had let her stay where she was to protect her, and had even intervened with her foster parents to make them be nicer to her.

She had watched for him under the Christmas tree every year since, just as she still planned to do tonight. She hadn't dressed up for North, she had dressed up for the Yule Cat. How pathetic was that? Now, she was standing in front of the most gorgeous man she'd ever seen, who inexplicably seemed interested in her, and still she was thinking about how she needed to be home before midnight just in case this was the year that the Yule Cat returned to take her to a magical wonderland.

Unless she was done waiting. Unless it was finally time to move on and grab what was real and in front of her, even if it was only hers for a brief moment.

North didn't seem like the kind of guy to settle down. Why would he, as gorgeous and charming as he was? He gave off definite 'player' vibes. Maybe this once, she was ready to play.

He was still staring at her, very much like he wanted to eat her up. She stepped forward, hoping he would. His warmth seeped into her as he swayed in place, his gaze filled with uncertainty.

She took another step, closing the distance between them. He started to lean down when her stomach let out a huge growl. Her eyes widened as her hand flew to her abdomen, mortification chilling the heat from a moment before.

"I'm so sorry," she said. "I was in such a hurry, I think I might have forgotten to eat dinner." She reached into her pocket and pulled out a granola bar.

"What the hell is that?" he said, his voice lower and rumblier than before.

"This? It's a granola bar."

"I know it's a—" He let out an exasperated gasp. "That's not dinner. That's… sawdust."

"It's good enough for now." She gestured to the stand mixer and said, "We have baking to do."

He made a disgusted snort, then turned around and flipped up the top of the mixer. After detaching the bowl quickly, he pulled out some plastic wrap and covered the dough. With his long legs, it only took him a few strides to reach one of the big fridges in the kitchen. He tossed the bowl inside and turned off the oven on his way back to her.

"What are you doing?" she asked.

"You're hungry."

She laughed, trying to hide her embarrassment. "I'm okay."

"I'm not. I can't have you being hungry and I sure as

hell am not going to let you eat that dry piece of—" He took a deep breath and let it out slowly, visibly working to calm himself down. "I'm cooking you dinner."

Dinner? He cooked, too? And wanted to cook for *her*? Her stomach did a little flip, then let out another loud growl. She actually scowled at it, then turned her frown at him.

"That's too much to ask," she said. "It's okay, really."

"It's not okay and I don't recall you asking for anything. As a matter of fact, neither am I."

She wasn't sure what he meant by that until he ducked down, planting his shoulder against her hips, then stood, taking her with him. She ended up draped over one shoulder, feet and arms flailing on either side of him. Her face was just above his butt. The view was so good, some of the fight went out of her. She still shimmied in his grasp, prompting a swift swat to her rump.

She went still, and said, "Did you just *spank* me?" her voice incredulous.

"Stop wriggling."

Let's see how he likes it.

Impulsively, she reached out and swatted his butt. He stood straighter as he sucked in a quick breath. His grip on her waist tightened and he let out a sound that she swore sounded like a purring growl.

"Harder next time," he said.

Melanie let out an indignant gasp, even though her

body had a very different reaction. Goosebumps raced across her skin as heat built within her.

"You're going to eat some real food, and that's final," he said.

She was so flustered, it took her a moment to respond. "Fine."

"Yeah, fine."

He made a disgruntled 'hmph' sound. She expected him to set her down, but instead he walked back into the main bakery area, then carried her up the staircase that wrapped around two of the brick walls. The view was dizzying, with all the lights and decorations, so she fixed her gaze on a single point. The closest thing was his backside. Her cheeks must be scarlet. By the time he reached the second floor, her stomach was fluttering for a very different reason than the dizzying changes of view.

North opened a door and carried her into a darker section of the building. He paused and closed the door behind him, then toed off his shoes. With her still dangling over his shoulder, he reached up and pulled one boot and then the other from her feet before dropping them on the floor near the door.

"Granola bar," he murmured. "Like I would let you eat that crap in my bakery when I could make you some decent food."

Part of her screamed that she should be worried. This guy was manhandling her and carrying her to who-knew-where. He had taken off her boots—not that she minded—and he hadn't even asked first. But a stronger part knew he would never hurt her. That he would take care of her and protect her. She had no idea where that belief was coming from, but it wasn't just her attraction to him.

There was goodness, familiarity, and yes, a whole lot of hotness in him. She could tell that this had the potential to be the start of the biggest adventure of her life. As he walked down the hall, deeper into what appeared to be his apartment above the bakery, she relaxed against him, eager to see what the rest of the night held in store.

Chapter Five

Had he gone crazy? What the hell was he doing, carrying this woman into his den?

I know just what I'm doing. I'm going to feed her and then we're going to spend some... quality time together.

He shook off the images that assailed his mind. No, he was just going to feed her, then finish the baking lesson and send her on her way. Into the dark, cold, snowy Christmas Eve night.

Yeah, like that's going to happen.

They passed through his living room on the way to his personal kitchen, soft Christmas music playing on speakers cleverly hidden near the ceilings. Another tree stood in the window, decorated with blue ribbons and silver lights—his colors from the Yuletide Kingdom. The fireplace sprang to life as he entered the room, motion sensors kicking in and turning on gas pipes that had the fake logs inside glowing in seconds. A large, comfortable couch sat in front of it. She could sleep there. Or she could take his bed and he'd sleep on the couch. Hell, he could transform and curl up on the huge, gray faux fur rug in front of his fireplace while she slept wherever she wanted.

Another image coalesced in his mind—of Melanie joining him by the fire and curling up against his back. That thought was even less welcome. It reminded him too much of the little girl who the Winter Queen had declared must become his bride. North didn't want a bride, he wanted a lifemate. And he would be the one to find her, to choose her. He wasn't about to let himself be forced to spend eternity with a woman that had been chosen for him by someone else.

Melanie... He could already see himself spending eternity with her. She had handled herself like a pro in his kitchen. Fit right in. And she was handling his 'enthusiasm' for feeding her better than he'd expected. Other women might have screamed for help or yelled at him to put them down or, hell, tried to cop a feel while his goods were right in reach. More than one of the women he'd had to spend Christmas Eve with had spent the night chasing him around the table instead of paying attention to what he was trying to teach them. He'd let a few catch him, but sent them packing as soon as they were done. When he imagined being in bed with Melanie, the fantasy went all the way to waking up next to her in the morning.

This was dangerous. Not just how strongly he was drawn to her, but that it was happening on the last Christmas Eve that he needed to get through before the Winter Queen's edict ended. He should be hiding out in his bakery, not carrying around a soft, warm, lusciously-curved woman. Then again, if this was his last chance to enjoy a night with a mortal, he couldn't think of someone he'd rather be with than Melanie.

What if the Winter Queen somehow found his bride and summoned him back to Faerie forever? His odds would be worse if she set Snow after the bride. The Krampus was a fierce tracker and had never failed to find his target. But Snow had visited North frequently in the mortal realm to check up on him and had only asked about *North's* efforts in finding the woman. Snow hadn't mentioned going after the bride himself.

If North had met Melanie the next day, he wouldn't be so worried. They could take their time and explore each other and see if there was something between them without the specter of his Queen's gaes hanging over him. It wasn't just a command, but a spell that the Winter Queen had cast over him. He was bound to take his bride to Faerie—if he found her before the spell lapsed. He had only barely managed to evade the part of the spell that demanded he seek her out, using the contest and these Christmas Eves with mortal women to satisfy the essence of the spell while avoiding its purpose.

He had escaped. He had done everything right to keep the spell at bay. This would be the last night he would ever have to worry about returning to Faerie again. He was going to enjoy it, then see what his life had to offer when he was truly free.

He glanced at Melanie, her skirts bouncing as he walked. Taking off her boots had actually made the warmth in his chest grow. It had been intimate without being sensual. The feeling was oddly… domestic. She seemed to just fit next to him, like she had worked seamlessly at his side in his bakery. But if anything was going to happen between them tonight, he didn't want her distracted by hunger.

"Are you going to put me down, or are you planning to cook with me draped over your shoulder like a Neanderthal?" Melanie's sharp voice brought him back to the room. They had reached the kitchen, and he was just standing there staring off at nothing.

He brought his free hand up to her waist to steady her as she slid down his front. That had probably been a bad idea. His body lit up wherever they touched, the spark between them burning brighter than ever. Her blue eyes were wide as she stared at him, lips parted as she gulped in air. He had followed her descent, bending his head close enough that he would barely have to lean forward to kiss her.

Her stomach growled again.

Dammit.

Her lips snapped shut and she stepped back, her blush deepening. "Sorry."

He should have let her eat the damn granola bar. But

no, he wanted her to have a proper meal. The idea of her being hungry brought back memories of the neglected child that he had spared so long ago. The child who had taught him what it felt like to be loved. Shaking his head, he pushed thoughts of her out of his mind. He wanted to focus on the here-and-now. He wanted to focus on Melanie.

"Don't worry about it." He felt his lips pull into a smile.

Her eyes widened again as she stared at them, her brow furrowing slightly. She shook her head and turned around. Had she seen something that unsettled her? He ran his tongue over his teeth and found that his canines had sharpened without him realizing it nor willing it to happen. Melanie was bringing out the beast in him. He needed to be careful.

"How can I help?" She crossed to the stove, putting more distance between them. He stifled a growl. He wanted her close.

"No need," he said. He headed for the fridge and started pulling out ingredients, setting them on the counter.

"I *want* to help." She shifted closer, leaning against the counter. "I like to cook, too."

Warmth spread from his stomach up through his chest. If she was as good at the stove as the oven, this might really be something. He had never met anyone he wanted to share his love of everything kitchen-related with before.

He pulled out a cutting board, one of his favorite knives, and set them up, then handed her a head of cabbage that he had washed earlier.

"Oh, fun," she said. "How do you want it?"

He almost choked at the question. Thoughts ran through his mind that he absolutely could not voice. '*I want the damn food to be cooked so we can eat and I can move us on to dessert.*'

"Sliced?" She rolled the head of cabbage on the cutting board, staring at it intently. "Julienned?"

"Diced, actually. We only need a quarter of it."

"Interesting," she said, smiling over at him. She cut what she needed, then put the rest of it back in the bowl and handed it to him. He watched while she started to work, admiring her skill and precision. She really did know how to cook. This was still going to take too long.

He rested his hand on the counter, pushing a bit of his magic out through the air of the kitchen. Everything would cook faster, taste better, and they'd be ready to eat in a fraction of the time. Melanie gave a little shudder as the magic-filled breeze swept past her.

"It's a little drafty." She glanced up at him briefly, smiling again. Her cheeks were still flushed.

"Let me help with that." He turned on the oven and the burner he planned to use, then reached up to grab his favorite skillet that hung from the high ceiling and set it on the stove to warm.

Melanie kept at her work. She fit right in next to him. Being with her was easy. That was new, too. The warmth in his chest flared again. At this rate, it wouldn't matter if he had to go back to the Yuletide realm. The moment he set foot in the place, he'd melt it and be sent right back to his beloved exile. With a chuckle, he turned back to the fridge to get the rest of what they needed.

Chapter Six

What was happening? Her baking lesson had transformed into the most romantic date she'd ever had. Not that it was a date. But it sure felt like one.

North's personal kitchen was as amazing as his professional one, just in a different way. The exterior walls were exposed brick and the interior painted a deep red that matched it. High above her head, every kind of pot, pan, or skillet she might ever need hung on racks mounted on the ceiling. Off to her right, another rack held wine glasses hanging above an impressive wine rack that was taller than she was. She would need a stepping stool to get anything down. Or, she could just ask North to give her a boost.

She imagined him reaching past her for a bottle, but then grabbing his face for a long, deep kiss. Again, her skin erupted in goosebumps, heat blazing through her. If she knew her stupid stomach wouldn't distract them with more growling, she would have pounced on him right then.

He put away the rest of the cabbage, then brought out a package wrapped in brown butcher paper. She still wasn't sure what they were having. After adding a tiny bit of oil to the skillet, he slid the meat from the package into it. The sizzle and pop made her mouth water even before the heavenly aroma reached her nose. Had he already seasoned it?

She glanced over and saw that it was already turning a nice brown. That was fast. He added some butter and diced onions, then reached for the cutting board with her cabbage. After she handed it to him, she carefully rinsed the amazing knife she had used and blotted it dry on a towel hanging near the sink. His smirk was closer to a smile when she looked back to him.

"What?" she asked.

"It's just nice to see that you know how to take care of a good knife."

Her stomach did a little dance at the compliment. "What else can I do?"

"How about you grab us a bottle of wine off the rack?"

"Sure." She crossed to the rack, staring at all the bottles and trying not to think of her daydream from a moment before. There were so many bottles, she didn't know which to grab. Some of them looked really old. All of them looked expensive. "Which one?"

"Third row down from the left and two over. Grab some glasses while you're at it."

She counted out the rows and stacks and pulled out the bottle. The label had a polar bear on it along with dozens of snowflakes. She couldn't read the language. It didn't even look familiar. Stumped on that front, she glanced up at the wine glasses. Even if she jumped, she doubted she could touch them.

"Um, problem," she said, turning back to North.

He glanced up from the skillet and laughed. "Sorry about that. How about we switch?"

"Okay."

She hurried back to the stove. As they passed each other, their arms brushed, and more molten heat flooded her. She had never been so attracted to anyone nor had such chemistry. If she was imagining that he felt something similar toward her, she would be mortified. The lingering gaze he cast at her as he passed reassured her. She set down the bottle, then picked up the spoon he'd been using to stir the contents of the skillet. Her mouth watered at the aroma floating up from it as she set to work.

"This smells amazing." She was certain this was a stuffing for something. "What is it for?"

North placed a large cookie sheet that held several small squares of dough next to her. "Runzas."

"No way!" She looked up at him with a huge smile. "I've always wanted to try those."

He leaned a little closer, his warm breath fanning her face. "Well then, tonight's your lucky night."

She really, really hoped so. Her cheeks prickled and she felt the flush run down her neck. Their gazes locked as an unmistakable heat sparked in his eyes. His lips looked soft. They were so close, she could rise on her tip-toes and kiss him if she wanted. She would have to be careful of his teeth, though. His canines had looked wickedly sharp earlier. Almost as if—

She turned back to the skillet quickly, pushing the thought away. This was not the time for fantasies. There was a real, solid, gorgeous guy inches away from her and very obviously interested in something happening between them. She wouldn't mess this up.

"How about that wine?" she asked.

"Sure." He opened the bottle, chuckling as he did so. "I kind of feel like I should ID you."

Melanie snorted. "I get that a lot. I'm older than I look."

He paused turning to stare at her as his smile faded. "How old?"

"You're not supposed to ask," she said, casting a playfully disapproving frown his way. At least, she hoped she managed to pull that off.

He poured the wine and placed a glass next to her, but kept his distance. She wasn't sure if she'd offended him by not answering. Maybe he had a thing for young women and was afraid she was older than he wanted? She wasn't entirely sure she cared. She didn't want anything to ruin this evening. Besides, it was just one night. She never had to see him again after this if she didn't want to.

The thought felt like a weight in her heart. Not seeing him again after one Christmas Eve wasn't what she wanted. But she had thought her loneliness was over before, or at least, she had dreamed that it had been. The Yule Cat had left her. Would North do the same?

"You're letting the meat get a little scorched there," he said.

"Oh, sorry." She scraped at the skillet, loosening the bits that had become stuck. It didn't seem too crispy, thankfully.

North came to stand behind her, his arms wrapping around hers as he covered her hands with his. "You need to ease into it."

His chest was flush against her back. She closed her eyes and leaned into him, feeling him enveloping her. He nuzzled her hair, his breath causing it to tickle her neck. The scent of pine wrapped around her, mingling with the amazing aroma from the food. If her stomach growled again, she was going to... To do something to it.

"That looks about ready to me," he murmured against her ear, his voice low and provocative.

"Yeah." Shivers ran all along her arms at his closeness. She wished she hadn't worn a long-sleeved dress. She wanted to feel more of him.

"Why don't you let me take over?" He took the spoon from her, turning her toward the counter. "Get yourself some wine."

She nodded, heading straight for the glass filled with dark red liquid. His was already almost empty. She took a sip and flavor exploded on her tongue. It was as if she was drinking a molten cherry cordial, but without being cloyingly sweet or thick. She took a deeper drink, shivering as the wine burned its way down her throat to her stomach.

"Go easy on that, now," he said. "At least until you've had something to eat in you."

She turned back to him, wishing she had the guts to make a suggestive quip, but only let out a little choked noise. The runzas were already filled, formed, and coated in a light egg wash.

"How..." She pointed at the tray. "Don't those need to rise again?"

"Not the way I do it."

Warmth rolled through the kitchen as he opened the oven door. He lifted the cookie sheet and placed it inside, then sealed them in and set a timer. Wiping his hands on a towel, he approached her, caging her body against the counter with his. If she wanted to, she would barely have to move to touch him. And she really, really wanted to. She wanted *him*—more than she'd ever wanted anyone. He set down the towel next to her and kept his hand there, using his free hand to take her wine glass and set it aside.

"Besides," he said, leaning close, "things don't take long to rise again around here."

She started to laugh at the cheesy line, but then he suddenly leaned forward, capturing her lips with his. Everything within her felt as though it had caught fire. Her abdomen filled with heat, burning through every thought until all she had left was need. His hands gripped her hips, lifting her easily onto the counter. She wrapped her legs around his waist, delighting in the taste of the sweet cherry wine lingering on his lips.

Heat built within her even as a cool breeze sprang up around them. It only heightened the magic of the moment, of giving herself over to the experience of this—of him. He moved his kisses to her neck and nuzzled her hair, his breath warm.

"Woman," he murmured against her skin. "You are going to ruin me."

Chapter Seven

His woman was still hungry, but North was starving.
Not for food, but for more of her. Her scent, her smile,
everything about her drew him in. Most of all, how easily
she fit into his life, sliding in right next to him as if she'd
always been there. He had never felt comfortable around
someone else before. Not like this. He couldn't wait to see
if they were as compatible in other ways.

He needed them to get to the bedroom as quickly as
possible. For that, the runzas had to be done. He turned to
the oven and opened it, barely remembering in time that he
needed to use a hot pad when mortals were present.
Melanie might not be as attracted to him if she realized he
was a magical, shape-shifting Fae. At the very least, she'd
have questions, and he didn't want anything delaying what
he hoped would be the next activity of the evening.

He pulled out the tray and set it on top of the stove,
then leaned forward and blew on them, his head angled
away so that she couldn't see what he was doing. A little
bit of the North Wind's chill, and these would be ready to
eat immediately. His breath came out in a fog, swirling

around the runzas and cooling them off.

He stepped back and gestured to them. "Eat. Quickly."

She blinked heavy-lidded eyes, then laughed. "I'll burn my face off."

"It's okay." He picked one up and took a big bite. The flavors had turned out better than he had hoped. The savory filling held a hint of sage that made the sweetness of the dough that much more pleasant. As soon as he managed to swallow, he held another up to her lips. "A drafty kitchen is good for cooling things off."

He doubted even the full freezing power of the North Wind could help him, though, especially when she licked her lips, then leaned forward to take a bite of the runza he held up for her. He groaned inwardly as her eyes rolled shut. Stepping closer, he fed her another bite, then another, watching her expression with rapt attention. Everything she did fascinated him.

"Oh my God," she said. "These are so good."

He handed her another, then finished his own in one bite. How many would she need to be full? He snatched another for himself, eating it as quickly as he could. When he turned back to her, she was sitting with her eyes closed, cradling the half-eaten runza near her nose. She let out a contented sigh, lost in his cooking. His chest tightened. Cooking for others had always pleased him, but he had never experienced such happiness while watching someone enjoy his food—not even previous lovers.

Could he use that word for the women he'd slept with before? Lovers? After being with Melanie, even for just a stolen moment of passion in his kitchen, he wasn't sure. 'Hook-ups' seemed more appropriate for what he'd experienced before this. Brief shared physical pleasure, then moving on with his life.

He didn't want to think about moving on beyond Melanie. He didn't mind thinking about moving with her. Especially to the bedroom.

"Melanie," he said, taking a step toward her.

She opened her eyes, her soft smile gutting him. A flurry of energy rose within him, flooding his abdomen with warmth and settling in his heart like a kaleidoscope of butterflies. He wanted to drop to his knees and ask her to stay with him forever. That would be certain to scare her off. It was too soon, for her at least. Mortals needed time to accept their emotions. Immortals... not so much. The depth of his feeling for her, of his attraction and comfort was all he needed to know.

In that moment, North knew that she was his 'forever.'

"Do you need more?" he asked.

She nodded, leaning back, and bracing her arms against the counter. A thrill shot through him at the thought of taking her right there, but he had to be sure her other needs were met first. He wanted to satisfy her in every way possible, so thoroughly that she wouldn't question for a moment that they belonged together.

He chuckled and said, "I meant the food. Are you still hungry?"

"Not... Not for that."

Thank the Gods.

Heat exploded in his chest. The idea that she wanted him as much as he wanted her was headier than the wine he'd downed earlier. There would be no more waiting. He practically leapt forward, grabbing and kissing her again. She clasped his arms, meeting his kiss as if she were as desperate for him as she was for her. Surely, that wasn't possible. He wanted her with an all-consuming fire that threatened to melt his world.

He trailed his kisses along her neck, delighting in the goosebumps that rose beneath his touch. All of this was a prelude to what he had planned for them next.

"God, North," she said. "You've already ruined me."

"I'm just getting started," he whispered.

He lifted her from her feet and carried her to his bedroom, laying her gently on the bed. For the next little while, she became his world. All thoughts of the Yuletide Kingdom and his exile vanished. There was no future and no past. Nothing besides the two of them and this blissful union. A union he would never let go of.

"You are mine," he said, when they were finally taking a moment to catch their breath.

She swallowed hard, then traced her hands along his back, pulling him closer into her embrace. Her next words sealed the bond between them.

"Only if you're mine, too."

Chapter Eight

Melanie woke up blearily, trying to remember the last night. She didn't want to forget a single detail. She wasn't sure when they made it back to the bed. It was sometime after the couch, the shower, the rug in front of the fire, and in the kitchen during a midnight snack. Christmas Eve had come and gone, and it was Christmas Day—the first Christmas Day that she wasn't spending alone since she'd left her foster parents' house. She stretched out along North's warm body, a huge smile on her face.

She half-sat up as she started to roll over, but then yelped, pulling the covers up to her collarbones. An enormous man was standing at the foot of the bed. His dark hair was cropped close to his scalp, shorter than the stubble on his wide jaw. His arms were crossed over the biggest chest she'd ever seen. He must be seven feet tall at least and was packed with muscle that strained against the fabric of his clothing. He was dressed in a white uniform with gold and red trim that looked like something a fairytale prince would wear. A cape of thick white fur was slung over one shoulder. His eyes were such a warm brown, they almost looked red as well. It had to be a trick of the light.

He cast an oddly familiar smirk at her and said, "Good morning."

Melanie reached over and grabbed North's shoulder, shaking him hard. He mumbled something incoherent, then wrapped his arms around her waist, pulling her closer.

"Stop that," she hissed. "Someone is in the room with us."

"What?" North blinked sleepily and let out a huge yawn.

"Damn, North," the stranger said. "Did you guys bother to get any sleep last night?"

North's eyes widened as he bolted upright. "Krampus? What are you doing here?"

At least they knew each other. Melanie's apprehension lessened a tiny amount. It was still weird that this guy thought he could just walk into North's bedroom and—

"Wait, did you say *Krampus*?" she asked.

"You can call me Snow, if you'd rather," the giant man said.

"Snow," she repeated.

He shrugged, that infuriatingly cocky smirk deepening. It was just like North's, only where North exuded swagger, this guy had a quiet confidence that scared the crap out of her. There was no doubt this guy was the toughest person in the room, and he was absolutely aware of it. Heck, he was the toughest person she'd ever seen.

"Time to go," Snow said. "Come on, the Queen is waiting. You've left your duties for too long."

"Queen?" Melanie looked back at North. His face was drawn and pale, his lips pressed in a thin line. The newcomer was dressed like a prince. Did that mean... "Are you royalty or something?" she asked.

"Or something—and not anymore." He wouldn't look at her as he spoke. With a broad gesture to Snow, North said, "It's Christmas Day and I missed the deadline. My exile is permanent now."

"Exile?" Melanie said. "North, what is going on?"

Finally, he turned to her, shaking his head. He took her hand in his and said, "Nothing. Nothing you need to worry about."

"'Nothing.'" Snow snorted, then laughed. "Sure. There's nothing anybody needs to worry about because everything is taken care of now." He inclined his head toward Melanie and said, "Merry Christmas, by the way."

"Merry... Christmas." She half-smiled as she turned back to North, trying to find a clue to what was going on in his expression. She'd be a lot less nervous if he didn't look so upset. And if she had clothes on.

"Come on." Snow clapped his massive hands together. "Time to go."

"We're not going anywhere," North said though gritted teeth.

"Of course, we are." Snow chuckled again. "Now get moving." He reached for the blanket and tugged on it.

"Hey!" Melanie slid off the side of the bed to her feet, dragging the covers with her. She glanced back at North, who was just crouched on the bed, staring at Snow as if he were about to pounce on the huge man. Naked. She had to help him.

"We're not going anywhere," she parroted.

"Not like that you aren't." Snow lifted one massive leg and stomped it on the floor hard enough to make the pictures on the walls shake. A glowing snowflake appeared under his boot. With the sound of crackling ice, more snowflakes formed, darting toward her over the dark hardwood floor in a line that extended from his foot.

Melanie yelped again, jumping back as the snow reached her feet. It spread so quickly, there was nowhere she could go to escape it.

"Hey!" North leapt from the bed, landing in front of her, but the snow already had her in its grip.

Aching cold spread up her legs and body, coating her in the feeling of pins-and-needles. The crackling turned into the swishing of fabric as the snow covered her body, coalescing into a velvet and silk dress in deep sapphire blue with intricate silver embroidery. The smooth skirts plumped around her legs as she felt a petticoat form underneath it, and the bodice laced up snug along her ribs, lifting her chest in the perfect décolletage. The sleeves were tight along her upper arms, then flared out along her forearms and wrists.

Ice wound around her fingers, solidifying into rings of white gold with channel set sapphires. More crept along her neck and up through her hair, lifting it from her neck. She shivered as the cold ran along her scalp, pulling her hair into a chignon. A heavy weight settled on her chest and she glanced down to see a huge sapphire surrounded by diamonds and suspended by a gorgeous platinum chain around her neck.

Her freezing feet were wrapped in warm boots that lifted her slightly as heels extended from their soles and stockings snugged against her legs. A whirlwind of snow swept over and around her, then suddenly dropped to the floor, and vanished. She gaped up at Snow to see his arm stretched toward her, his fingers splayed wide. His lips pulled into a huge smile.

"So?" He dropped his arm to his side as he looked at North. "What do you think?"

Melanie thought she might be having a mental breakdown. She dropped the covers she'd been holding onto so she could fully see the gorgeous gown she was draped in, then lifted her hands to look at the jewelry on her fingers. She briefly lifted the skirt's hem to study the dark blue, soft leather boots peeking from under her skirts. It all felt so real.

Just like the night when the Yule Cat had visited her.

"What is happening?" she said, her voice a tight whisper.

"Dammit, Snow," North said. "Leave her be."

"I can't do that." Snow shook his head. "I have orders to take you both back to the Yuletide Kingdom. It's time for you to come home."

Chapter Nine

This was a nightmare—worse than a nightmare because it was actually happening, and because Melanie was caught up in it with him. Was Snow willing to take whatever woman North had slept with on the last Christmas Eve of his exile back to the Winter Queen and just say that she was his bride? The Queen would see through any ruse they tried. She would know that Melanie wasn't the girl that had sparked warmth in his heart all those years ago. But the Queen might decide to keep Melanie as a servant, the very fate that North had tried to avoid for the girl who had given him his first glimpse of love and caring.

"She's not my bride," North said.

Snow laughed. "Of course, she is. Don't be stupid."

North stood, working his own magic to conjure clothing around himself—the dark blue button-up shirt and jeans he preferred. Melanie made a little choked gasp. Her eyes were wide enough to show the whites all around their irises. His heart tightened at the thought that this was driving her away from him. Surely it had to.

"How did you do that?" she asked, her voice quavering.

"I can explain." North knew he was stalling. He had no idea what to tell her or how she would react. They hadn't known each other long enough for him to have time to even consider telling her about him. He didn't know what to say or do. He reached for her and she jerked back. The movement felt like she'd stabbed him through the heart with ice.

"You can figure this out later," Snow said. "I know you've been messing around in the mortal realm for a long time, but some of us still have responsibilities. I'm on a schedule and you're underdressed."

Once more, Snow thumped his foot on the floor. The snowflake pattern darted toward North, then swirled up his legs and torso and flowed down his arms. He was left in indigo velvet breeches and a sapphire jacket with two rows of dark blue buttons running straight up along his torso in formal rows. Snow had even pulled North's hair back with a tie.

"How did you do that?" Melanie nearly shouted, this time at Snow. At least she wasn't cringing as much as she had been. A bit of hope sparked in North. Maybe he could salvage this after all. "And what do you mean, 'mortal realm?'"

Then again, maybe not.

"This is all just a misunderstanding," North said. He took a step closer to Melanie, and this time, she didn't back away. "Don't worry, I won't let him take you anywhere."

"What did I just say about being stupid?" Snow laughed and shook his head, but the skin at the corners of his eyes tightened.

North knew his friend well enough to see the signs of his patience fraying. 'Let sleeping bears lie' was an understatement when it came to Snow. He put both hands on his hips and took a deep breath, his scrutiny intensifying as he stared at North.

"You are both going to appear before the Winter Queen." Snow's words were carefully measured as he spoke, and utterly calm, which was more unnerving than anything else he'd done. "Are you coming with me or am I *taking* you there?"

"Snow, please," North said.

"What is wrong with you?" Snow shook his head. "You should be thrilled to be coming home—and bringing your bride with you."

"I can't go back there and I sure as hell am not taking Melanie." North took a step closer, his voice pleading. "The Yuletide kingdom has become locked in a joyless, unchanging winter since the Queen established her own domain. Don't you remember the colors of autumn? The warmth of summer or the flowers of spring?"

Snow snorted. "I'm the Lord of Endless Snow. What do I care about spring? I'll tell you what I do remember. I remember that I can kick your ass and that your time is up."

Snow took in another huge breath. As he did, a whirlwind of snow flew up around him, coating his body in bright white light. North knew what was coming. If he could distract Snow long enough, maybe Melanie could escape. It didn't matter what dreams North had dared to entertain about her. He wouldn't condemn her to an eternity in an icy wilderness just because Snow was intent on bringing North back with a 'bride.'

He turned to Melanie, and said, "As soon as you can, run."

"What? No." She shook her head sharply, concern etched in her expression—not for herself, but for him.

In that moment, North knew that his heart was forever lost. He would do anything to protect Melanie—even if it meant losing her.

"I won't leave you," she said.

His chest constricted, his heart was shattering like a fallen icicle. He knew how she would most likely react when she saw him transform. Mortals didn't adjust well to their first view of magic.

"You will," he said.

He turned back to Snow, readying himself for a battle he knew he couldn't win. Snow wasn't boasting when he said he could kick North's ass. North was smaller, more agile, and definitely faster. He could keep Snow busy while Melanie escaped.

Snow's face elongated as his skin turned as white as his namesake, fur began sprouting everywhere. His fingers curved into huge clawed paws, his nose darkened to black, and his ears pulled up into round crescents on either side of his head.

North didn't wait for him to fully transform into his polar bear form. Coiling, North pulled forth his Yule Cat form. Silver fur with black spots sprang from his skin as a whirl of light enveloped him. His teeth lengthened as well as his ears, his face pushing forward into a muzzle. His claws gripped the crumpled blankets Melanie had dropped on the floor, their shared scent blooming around him as his senses intensified.

A shrill screech jolted through his heightened hearing, throwing him off balance. He hissed in response, turning toward the source of the sound. Melanie had pressed herself against the wall, eyes wide with terror as she gaped at Snow. It wasn't enough that he was fully transformed into his polar bear form. Mist and snowflakes swirled around him, sending a chill through the air that made even North shiver. Snow covered his ears with his paws, the mist and snow dissipating as he shrank back to his human form.

"Gods, is she always this loud?" he said, still covering his ears with his hands.

This was North's chance. He wouldn't have a better

one. He coiled his body, preparing to leap as Melanie's scream suddenly cut off. The change was so abrupt that he turned to her, ears perked forward. Her eyes were still wide, but instead of fear, shock and confusion flooded her features. She took a step closer, than another. How could she not be afraid of him?

"You," she said, lifting a trembling hand toward him. She shook her head suddenly and pulled back. "This isn't happening. This can't be real."

"You know it is," Snow said. "You studied the lore in college."

"How…" She swallowed hard, her focus riveted on North, though her head angled toward Snow. "How do you know what I studied in college?"

North wanted to hear the answer as well. His stomach tightened as foreboding swept through him.

Snow arched an eyebrow and grinned. "Who do you think paid for it?"

"I got… a scholarship," she said, haltingly.

"That you won because of your essay on 'The Night I Met the Yule Cat.'" He made air quotes as he said the last bit.

North's heart started to pound. Melanie couldn't be… Could she?

"I had my subjects go through most of the submissions after telling them what to watch for," Snow said. "Finalists from all over the world were invited here, to North's town, for a full-ride scholarship plus room and board at the local university—provided they study folklore. You'd be surprised how many that weeded out. I figured you would stick around after school. Then I just needed to get you and North in the same room to let the magic take its course. Hence the 'My Most Magical Christmas Eve' contest that you won this year."

"No," Melanie said, shaking her head.

"You sure as hell didn't make any of this easy." Snow turned to North and said, "Either of you."

"This isn't possible," Melanie said. "It can't be real."

Snow laughed. "It's right in front of you. The Yule Cat. *Your* Yule Cat. And you are his bride."

Melanie backed away from them both. The turmoil in her eyes tugged at North's soul. Was she really that same person he had met and spared so long ago? The girl who had first shown him kindness?

If she was… their fates were sealed.

Chapter Ten

There had to be an explanation for this. People didn't just turn into gigantic polar bears and then back again like it was no big deal. They didn't turn into... into... Melanie swallowed past the lump in her throat, her eyes still locked on the snow leopard crouched in the blankets at her feet. He stared back at her with blue eyes that were so familiar. North's eyes. And earlier...

The Yule Cat.

Her ribs ached from the punishing beat of her racing heart—and more, from the fact that he had left her. Now he was sitting in front of her as if nothing had happened. As if he hadn't left her alone all those years, questioning her sanity, questioning her worth. Why had he left her behind?

"You can't be here." She pointed at him as her voice grew more shrill. "It's not right. Not now. Not right when I decided to stop waiting by the Christmas tree for you every year. Not when I finally realized it wasn't worth it."

The Yule Cat—North—flinched, a low hiss escaping his muzzle. He lowered his head and backed away.

"Don't you dare run away from me again," she screamed, her eyes burning with tears. Her entire body began to shake as rage and the shock of seeing him took hold. She took a step after him as he retreated. "You left me. You *left* me. You were supposed to be mine. I wasn't going to be alone anymore. But you made me more alone than I had ever been."

Light swirled around North. He rose on his back legs, his fur retreating into his skin and his face reverting to the human features she had lovingly traced with her fingertips and lips just hours before. His eyebrows were knitted together, the skin around his lips pulled tight in despair.

"I'm so sorry, Melanie," he said.

"For what?" She scoffed. "For freaking me out with your giant bear friend? Or not telling me that you're a shapeshifting Yule Cat? Or for leaving me on my own to wonder if I was crazy for most of my life?" She took a step closer and jabbed her finger against the hard muscles of his chest at the last question. "Or the worst of it—giving me a glimpse of a magical world just beyond my reach, one that I had dreamt about and longed for, and then leaving me here with nothing and no one."

"I didn't leave you with nothing," he said. "I gave your foster parents money. I ordered them to take care of you."

She snapped her mouth into a tight line. So much made sense now. Before that night, her foster family had always seemed to have enough, though her foster parents hadn't really shared much with Melanie beyond what was expected. After the Yule Cat came to her, they had showered her with gifts, clothes, and toys. They had also been even more stand-offish than before. They had taken care of her, but not cared for her. Now, she realized they must have been terrified. She had no doubt that North had used his magic to convince them to become 'better parents.'

"I was still alone," she said. "More than ever because I knew no one else had experienced anything like the things that I had. I couldn't talk to people about it without sounding crazy."

"Melanie—" North stepped forward, reaching for her. She jerked back reflexively. It would be too easy to give in if he touched her. Too easy to forget the years of isolation that he had helped to cause.

But, did he really?

She had always been strange. How many seven-year olds would think a mystical snow leopard twice her size and glowing with a misty light was a safe companion? She had lived with one foot in a dreamworld, only giving enough attention to reality to function. She had wished for him so fervently because she was already alone.

What really angered her was that they could have been together all those years. But if they had been, would they have come together as they had last night? As lovers instead of companions? She had to admit it was unlikely.

By staying away, he came to her as a prospective partner, not a caretaker.

"What would have happened to me if you had taken me with you that night?" she asked, her voice more level.

He winced, lines of strain appearing at the corners of his eyes. "I would have taken you back to the Yuletide Kingdom as tribute. You would have become a servant to the Winter Queen's court. One of my subjects."

Melanie prickled at the thought. The dreams she had built up around the Yule Cat were nothing like the reality that he would have offered her.

"You make it sound so terrible." Snow's low voice startled her. She had almost forgotten he was there with them. "It isn't. We only take children who are unwanted or who aren't cared for."

"I had a family," she said.

"You were a decoration," Snow said, his voice surprisingly gentle.

She flinched as if he'd struck her. It wasn't his words, though, but the truth behind them.

"Had you ever received clothing on Christmas?" he asked. "New clothing just for you. Not ill-fitting hand-me-downs or dresses you hated but that made you look pretty for pictures they could use to appear as a family?"

Her eyes filled with tears, but she tilted her chin up defiantly, blinking them back. "Just because they didn't give me clothes, that doesn't mean they didn't want me."

Snow nodded. "Yeah, they did. But for their own reasons. Their own purposes. I looked into them when I did your background check. It wasn't love or caring. It was all about appearances."

Her eyes cleared for a moment as the tears she'd been fighting spilled down her cheeks. "So you just judge people and take their kids? What gives you the right?"

"We give them a home," North said, his voice so quiet, she almost didn't hear him.

"In a dreary, winter-locked kingdom?" she said. "How is that better?"

"It wasn't always that way." North shook his head, a haunted look entering his features that made her want to reach out to him. She kept her arms tight to her sides. "There used to be seasons. There used to be spring."

"What about him?" She nodded toward Snow. "The Krampus eats naughty children."

Snow let out a disgusted rumble. "Gods, I wish people would stop saying that. The children I help will never get what they need from this world. They are the unwanted who fall onto the path of darkness. I take them to a world of winter, yes, but also one of light." He lifted his hand and a swirl of snow rose from his palm, forming a tiny Christmas tree, covered in lights of every color. "The people of my kingdom were once just like the children I bring as tribute. We guide them and help them find purpose."

She didn't know what to say. She turned to North and said, "Why didn't you take me as tribute then? If you were helping children, why didn't you help *me*?" She hated how small her voice became as she spoke.

"You wrapped me in your blanket, even though you were freezing," he said. "You promised to take care of me. You loved me." He shook his head. "And then I knew that I was a fraud. I told myself I was helping all those children, that they were better off in the Yuletide Kingdom. But when spring left our world, so did love. I didn't know until that moment what we had really lost. I didn't know what it was to be loved. And I couldn't condemn you to a life in that world." His voice cracked with strain as he forced out the next words. "As I had condemned all those other children."

Her heart broke for him. The pain in his words, his face, his bearing. She had been so caught up in how him leaving her behind had affected her and had never thought of what it had done to him. He had mentioned being exiled. Did that mean he could never go back to his home again? And what had happened to his 'subjects' then? The people—grown or otherwise—who he had brought to that land?

"North…" She took a step closer, but he looked away.

"You're right," he said. "The things I've done. How selfish I've been, even now." His eyes glittered in the light and his voice was hoarse. "I'm not worth it."

She closed the space between them and wrapped her arms around him, just as she had that first night when they met. Pressing her face into his chest, she said, "Giving up my life to wait for the Yule Cat wasn't worth it. But you are."

Chapter Eleven

"If you're both done crapping on our kingdom, it's time to go," Snow said.

North would have to smooth things over with his friend later. At the same time, he had meant every word. Melanie was so ready to give up her life for him. He wasn't quite as eager to let go. He would miss his bakery so much, and seeing the crocuses push through the snow in the spring, feeling the warmth of the summer sun and watching the trees turn to orange and gold in the fall.

If he was going to go back—and take Melanie with him as his bride—things had to change. The Queen would want him to resume his duties, but he couldn't go back to just taking children. There had to be a better way. Maybe his love for Melanie and her love for him could be examples to others. The people of the Yuletide Kingdom could have children of their own, if they learned how to love each other.

Winter might be eternal there, but he could fill it with comfort. Hot cocoa and cookies. Stories by the fire, music and song. There was so much to celebrating the winter season that he had learned in the mortal realm. It would be worth anything to keep Melanie safe and happy. He knew that she would only be happy if the others in his domain were as well.

He pulled back from her far enough that he could gaze into her eyes. "Will you come back with me?"

She smiled, her eyes sparking with excitement as she nodded. "Of course."

"Not really a choice," Snow said. "Like you guys were listening at all."

He shook his head and turned his massive back to them, murmuring complaints that turned into an incantation. Lifting his arms, he swirled them in a circle. Snowflakes filled the space he outlined with his hands, growing thicker and broader until it had become an ellipse floating above the floor large enough for him to step through. He moved to the side and gestured toward the vortex.

"After you," he said.

Melanie glanced at North, worry obvious in her features. He nodded, taking her hand in his as he led her to the portal.

"Are you sure about this?" he asked. "Once we're through, there's no coming back."

"I just… I want to be with you," she said.

Snow leaned closer, hovering over the pair. "Again, not a choice," he said, before straightening.

Melanie actually ignored him. North chuckled at the

way Snow's eyebrow arched and the appreciative glint in his gaze.

"That's all I've ever wanted. Having someone special in my life. And this—" Melanie looked him up and down and smiled. "This is so much better than anything I ever dreamed. My very own fairy prince."

"Ugh, I think I'm going to be sick," Snow said. "And it's Fairy *Lord*. Gods. Just jump through the portal before I toss you through."

Melanie laughed and smiled up at Snow. North had never seen the Krampus look taken aback, but his brows were knitted together in confusion and he leaned back, as if trying to put distance between them. He lifted a massive hand to his chest and rubbed the spot above his heart. If North wasn't mistaken, Snow had just received his first taste of love as well.

Maybe this wasn't a terrible thing at all. Melanie was North's very own spring. With her at his side, anything was possible. He pulled her close, wrapping his arm around her waist.

"You ready?" he asked.

She nodded, her smile brightening as she grabbed onto his waist and held tight. He leapt through the portal, holding her close against his chest. Behind them, North sensed Snow jump through the portal. A moment later, it snapped shut. There was no going back.

The cold was worse than he remembered. Melanie

shrieked as they fell through the perpetual midnight sky, surrounded by auroras of deepest green. North pulled her closer, summoning a zephyr to slow their descent. In the mortal realm, it would only have been perceived as a gentle wind. Here, it took the shape of a beautiful horse, translucent as the misty wind and glowing like the auroras around them. She gasped as it galloped beneath them, sweeping them toward the ground at a less intense angle. It set them down right in front of the castle's doors before dissipating into the air.

"What was that?" she asked, breathless.

"One of my servants," North said. "I'm the Lord of the North Wind."

Her eyes widened. "That was really cool."

A huge drift of snow swept past them, the Krampus riding on top of it. He pulled himself to his feet, shaking off the excess snowflakes from his clothes.

"I'm the cool one," he said. "Lord of Endless Snow." He hooked a thumb toward his chest and then pointed a finger at North. "And that was a dick move."

North tried to suppress a grin as Snow pushed the huge double-doors open and stomped into the castle, mumbling, "Zephyr for two. Yeah, Snow can break his own fall and make his way to the castle."

Melanie pressed herself into North's side and said, "I think you hurt his feelings."

"He's just working through some stuff. I've been gone

a long time."

"You went into exile because of me," she said.

North had wondered if she had picked up on that. He nodded, and said, "It didn't turn out to be the hardship I expected. I mean, the first few years were rough, but then I opened the bakery. Bringing all that warmth to people, making them happy through my baking…" He shook his head. "Honestly, it's kind of addictive. Taking care of people."

"And now you're giving up your exile for me," she said.

"That's not a hardship either. You're worth it." He spun her around to face him. "Besides, I'm hoping we can bring some of that warmth to the Yuletide Kingdom."

"Me, too." She gazed up at the castle walls around them. The clear crystal of the outer walls caught and reflected the lights of the auroras beyond while the interior lights radiated an intense white light, glowing from within. "This place is amazing."

A swarm of pixies flew toward them, their sparkling lights bringing an even bigger smile to Melanie's face as she gasped and ran forward. She spun in a circle, surrounded by the pesky things, looking at them as if they were the most miraculous creatures in existence. They plucked at her hair, pulling strands free and wrapping them into curls around their glowing bodies. Melanie laughed with delight.

"What are these?" she gasped. "Are they alive? Do they understand me?"

"Those are pixies." North stifled a growl, wanting nothing more than to swat them away. He figured that would upset Melanie, though. Plus, the little terrors might take it out on her.

"Pixies!" She turned back to the lights still whizzing around her and reached out a hand.

"I wouldn't do that if I were you," North said. If one of them bit her, it would be over. He would crush them all beneath his boots.

"They're just being friendly." She cupped her hands together beneath a pixie that glowed bright gold. "I'd love to be your friend."

The light hovered over her hands for a few moments, then coalesced into the form of a tiny, lithe, androgynous humanoid with huge eyes and fluffy antennae. Its gossamer wings continued to buzz against its back as it landed on her palms, head cocked to the side curiously. Melanie's eyes widened and she gasped, her body held perfectly still as if she were afraid she would scare a swarm of pixies. A mortal.

"You are utterly beautiful," she whispered, her voice filled with awe.

The pixie jerked back, buzzing into the air for a moment.

"I'm sorry, I didn't mean to offend you," Melanie said.

"You're just... amazing."

It hovered near her face, as if scrutinizing her. Perhaps it was looking for signs of deceit. It wouldn't find any from Melanie. She was the most earnest person North had ever met. It was part of what had let her make her way into his heart. He wondered if the pixie had experienced something similar, as it settled back onto her palm, this time dropping to its knees and letting its wings fold against its back as it stared up at her.

"You are precious," Melanie murmured. "Thank you for this time with me."

Even North felt an odd tug on his heart as he watched the pair. He never thought he could have such gentle feelings for a pixie. Melanie had a way about her. She brought tenderness out of people. He should have known she was the same person as the little girl he had met all those years ago. They both had the same warm heart. Would it survive the cold of the Yuletide Kingdom? Would it survive the harsh judgment of his Queen?

There was no more putting it off. North rested his hand on her back and said, "We'd shouldn't keep the Queen waiting. It's time."

Chapter Twelve

Melanie's heart was beating in her throat as they approached a huge archway that led off from one side of the even bigger hall. She felt like she was walking through an incredible movie set. She could scarcely believe it, but she was walking through an actual fairytale. Snow stood by the open arch, his arms crossed over his enormous chest as he scowled at them.

"Took you long enough." He turned and headed into the room.

North urged her to follow, their arms linked. She rested her hand on his elbow as well. She needed to feel like she could grab onto him if she needed. Truth be told, as much as she'd dreamt of something like this, now that she was living it, she was terrified. She had read the original fairytales as well as the modern revisions. The stories had started off incredibly dark. Even the stories about North and Snow had their frightening versions, more sinister ones where the children were taken away to Faerie to be served in a stew, or gobbled up right in their bedrooms.

A shiver raced down her spine as they walked down a long staircase. The cold of the place seeped into her, making her bones ache. She clutched North's arm tighter, remembering the heat from their passion the previous night. The more she thought about him holding her in his arms, the less she felt the cold. She was blushing by the time the stairs opened out into a room the size of an amphitheater. North followed Snow toward one side, where a raised dais dominated. In the center of the dais was a throne, and on that throne had to be the Winter Queen.

Her white-blonde hair was pulled back in a tight bun covered with a web of intricate platinum chains. On her slight frame, she wore a silken dress of blue as pale as a colorless sky. A crown rested on her forehead, spires of platinum set with diamonds as long as Melanie's forearm seemed to be shooting up toward the sky. Her skin was almost bloodless it was so pale, heightening the red of her lips. As cold as the rest of her was, her eyes were large and as green as a lush spring meadow. They were haunted by sadness and shadowed in pain.

Melanie almost let go of North's arm as she took a step forward, wanting to do something for the Queen, to take the burden that weighed so heavily on her heart. The Queen stiffened in her seat, her lips pulling into a deeper frown. North tightened his grip on Melanie's arm, keeping her at his side. He bowed formally and Melanie gave the best curtsey she could manage.

"My Queen," Snow said, bowing low. As he stood, he

gestured toward North and Melanie with a broad sweep of his hand. "As promised, I bring you Lord North and his bride, Melanie of the Mortal Realm."

North was still bowing, so Melanie held her curtsey. Her calves started to twitch, threatening to cramp. Time seemed to creep to a halt as she waited for someone to say or do something. All she could hear was the blood rushing in her ears until the Queen finally spoke.

"Lord North, your bride is infested with pixies," she said.

North finally stood, pulling Melanie along with him. She tried not to wince as she straightened, discretely stretching stiff muscles.

With an incline of his head, North said, "They do seem to be rather taken with her." He placed his hand over hers where she clutched his arm. "As am I."

"Scatter them," the Queen said.

Melanie spoke without thinking. "They're not hurting anything." She snapped her mouth shut as North tensed beside her. Even Snow's eyes widened as he looked between Melanie and the Queen with misgiving. Melanie's stomach clenched and her heart raced even faster.

"They are bothering *me*," the Queen said.

"Majesty." North nodded, then half-turned toward Melanie.

A cold breeze lifted her hair. She felt the pull of tiny hands holding on, and reached up to gently loosen them, trying to give the pixies a reassuring caress as they were swept away. She did her best to hide her anger, lowering her eyes to the floor. Whatever else this Queen was, she was a bully. Melanie couldn't stand bullies.

"You do not like having those who place themselves in your service being removed from your side?" the Queen said.

"What?" Melanie's gaze snapped up at that. "They aren't my servants, they're my friends."

"Oh, are they?" The Queen angled her head at Melanie, then rose to her feet. She was taller than Melanie realized, the crown adding even more to her imposing height. "You have been in my kingdom for only a few minutes, and already you claim them as friends?"

"I don't claim anyone," Melanie said. "That's not what friendship is about."

North hissed in a breath, his grip on her hand becoming almost painful. Melanie had a feeling she was not making a friend of the Queen. Then again, she wasn't sure she wanted to.

The Queen shook her head as she stepped closer, her movements as smooth as if she were skating across ice. "You poor thing. If only North had brought you to me as a child." Her voice hardened as she said, "I could have taught you proper manners."

Melanie opened her mouth to respond, but a warning squeeze from North helped her hold in her comment.

"I see now that I was wrong to think that a mortal could have a place among us as caretakers of this land." The Queen glanced at Snow and said, "Take her to the servants' quarters. Lord North and I have important matters to discuss."

Melanie's heart felt as if it was about to jump out of her chest. Was she going to be separated from North? Would they ever be allowed to be together again? The room felt like it was spinning as she contemplated an existence in this cold world without him near to warm her heart.

"What?" North pulled her closer against his side and she knew that if they tried to take her away, it wouldn't be without a fight.

"Majesty." Snow surprised her by stepping forward. "This was not the arrangement. Melanie is North's bride. It is done."

"The gaes binds you, too, my Queen." North said, a low growl tracing his words. "Your spell was clear. I was to bring Melanie back as a servant *or* as my bride. I have brought her as my bride."

"She is a disruption," the Queen said. "She has already cost me twenty years' service of one of my most trusted Lords, not to mention the tribute that you would have brought in that time. Do you know how long it has been since the North Wind has carried children to this land? There are so many that we could have aided while you selfishly chased this girl."

Melanie knew that North felt guilty about enjoying his time in the mortal realm. She wasn't about to let the Queen use that guilt against him.

"You are the one who sent him there," Melanie said. "If you want to be angry with anyone, be mad at yourself."

Snow's eyes widened as he stared at her. A slight tremble shook North's body. That was probably not the best thing to say, but Melanie was not going to stand by while someone hurt the man she loved. She stepped closer to him, straightening her spine and raising her chin as she stared defiantly at the Queen.

"Such insolence," the Queen said. "She cannot stay. Remove her from my kingdom."

"Majesty," North bowed.

"Not you." She gestured toward Snow. "The Krampus shall take her back to the mortal realm."

"She is my bride—my mate," North said, wrapping his arms around her. Melanie clung to his side when she had to release his arm. "Wherever she goes, whatever fate befalls her, it's mine to share as well."

"Fine, then you can both go to the servants' quarters," the Queen said. "You will stay there, Lord North, until you learn that mortal love does not last."

Melanie wanted to take her to task for that sweeping statement, but she was too busy worrying about North. She knew she could make the best of whatever the servants' quarters were like. She'd been in bad situations before.

But she wasn't sure if North could stand it. Maybe if he could serve by cooking or baking, he could find some glimpse of happiness, but he would still be trapped in a world he hadn't wanted to return to. After meeting the Winter Queen, Melanie could see why.

"My Queen, please." Snow stepped between the Queen and North. His voice was pleading. "We need him."

"Do we?" She scoffed. "We have functioned well without him all these years. His subjects are grown and his seneschals well trained. They can run his domain with or without him."

"But his duties as Lord of the North Wind—" Snow began.

She cut him off. "Can be handled by Frost."

Snow recoiled. "Frost? *Jack* Frost? He's an insufferable di—"

"He is loyal to me," the Queen said. "As North should have been."

North seemed frozen in place beside Melanie. He stared straight ahead at nothing, a muscle in his jaw twitching.

"Please, I didn't mean to cause any trouble," Melanie said.

"It's rather late for that, don't you think?" the Queen said. "You have been causing trouble for me since you were a child."

"I only wanted to love him," Melanie said. "To care for

him. You can't punish him for that." Dread flooded her as she realized that she had once more spoken out of turn—and that this being was quite possibly the most powerful person she'd ever encountered.

The Winter Queen drew herself up to her full height. Ice and snow gathered in a swirling cloud above them. Freezing rain pelted Melanie, stinging her skin wherever it was exposed. North pulled her against his chest, wrapping his arms around her to shield her from the cold just as she'd done for him the first night they had met. A drift of snow began to form around her and North, quickly rising past their knees. Her teeth chattered and her body shook from the cold.

"I am the Winter Queen," the Queen said. "This is my domain and I will do as I wish."

Melanie was sick of her crap. She shouted over the growing maelstrom so that the Queen would hear her words. "North told me this was a place of safe harbor for children who needed a home. You said you wanted to help me as a child, but now you're fine with hurting me as an adult? Is that your idea of a better place than the mortal realm?"

"My Queen, please." Snow trudged toward them, lifting the fur cloak over Melanie to shield her from the worst of the biting wind.

"North must recommit to me," the Queen shouted. "I will not lose another."

Melanie felt North's chest expand as if he were about to speak. Was he going to offer himself back to the Queen to save Melanie? He would be doomed to remain in this winter land forever, without Melanie at his side to warm him. She couldn't let that happen.

She reached up and grabbed his face, then pulled him down for a kiss. His skin warmed hers, his love flooding into her as he deepened their embrace. She kissed her way to his ear and said, "Whatever fate is mine you will share and I will share yours. I won't leave you here alone."

He claimed her lips again, kissing her so passionately, the cold around her vanished. When he finally pulled back, she saw that the maelstrom had ended. The floor and air around them was clear. The Queen stood several feet away, anguish twisting her features. She schooled her expression, folding her hands before her.

"So be it," she said. "Your fates will be shared. North. You are Lord of the North Wind no more. You will live out your pitifully short life in the mortal realm—as a mortal." She gestured toward Snow, and said, "See to it."

Snow's mouth hung open and his eyes were wide as he stared back and forth between the Queen and North. Finally, he clamped his mouth shut and nodded.

"As you command," he said.

Chapter Thirteen

North felt Melanie tense beside him. He bowed low enough that he could pull her with him into something like a gesture of respect, then immediately stood and headed for the stairs. He glanced down at her, hoping she would see the urgency in his gaze. She started to speak, but he shook his head as discreetly as he could, squeezing her arm again. Her lips tightened into a thin line as she straightened and fell in step beside him. They made their way from the throne room as quickly as he dared. He could hear Snow's sullen footsteps behind them.

North's chest hurt from how long he held each breath. At any moment, the Winter Queen could change her mind and order them to return. He wouldn't be able to relax until they were in the mortal realm. Melanie also seemed to be holding her breath, but he thought it might be more that she was keeping back her words. That was absolutely for the best. He would have to thank her for trusting him when they were safe. Or at least, safer than they were in the Yuletide Kingdom.

As soon as they exited the castle, Snow made a portal again. North didn't hesitate a moment once it was formed.

He lifted Melanie from her feet, holding her tight against his side, and leapt through. They landed in his bedroom on the very spot where they had left. He guided her away from the portal as Snow leapt through, landing heavily on the floor.

The moment the portal snapped shut, Snow let out a huge roar. The glass in the pictures on the wall nearest him cracked from the sound. North kept Melanie clutched against him as she pressed her hands over her ears.

"This is bullshit," Snow bellowed. "We did as we were told. She was supposed to—"

"Snow, please." North reached out and grabbed Snow's arm, hoping to calm his friend before he said something that could get him in trouble, too.

"She's overstepping," Snow said. "She doesn't have the right to transform you into a mortal."

Keeping his voice soft, North said, "I gave her that right when I pledged myself to her."

"No." Snow shook his head fiercely. "No, this isn't right."

"Listen to me." North squeezed Snow's arm. "I'm okay with it. I *want* this."

"But he's right," Melanie said, still rubbing her ears. "She's being unfair and a jerk."

North chuckled darkly. "You've read the lore. Fairness isn't part of the Faerie realm. We were lucky she let us go."

"Only to make an example out of you," Melanie said.

"It doesn't matter why." He wrapped his arms around her and kissed the top of her head. "A mortal life with you sounds wonderful. I wouldn't want to go on forever without you."

"North..." She reached up and stroked his cheek, her fingertips light as the wind.

He grasped her hand and pressed a kiss into her palm, then turned back to Snow. North had never seen such a fierce frown on Snow's face. His brow was knitted tightly, deep furrows between them, and the huge muscles along his jaw flexed and jumped as he ground his teeth together. His hands were clenched in such tight fists, North was afraid he'd draw blood.

"North..." Snow said.

"It's okay." He stepped away from Melanie and nodded. "I'm ready. Do it."

Snow's upper lip curled back from his teeth. He lowered his head and shook it. For a moment, North thought that meant he was going to defy the Queen. That wouldn't end well for any of them. But then, Snow suddenly snapped his head up, his arms stretching wide as he pulled on North's power. North's clothing whipped against his skin as a gale blew forth from him, the intense cold making his bones ache. He had never felt the cold of the North Wind before. But then, he was no longer its master as Snow drew the power into himself.

North staggered as the last bit of it left him. Melanie jumped forward to help catch him, as did Snow. Her warmth comforted him, but there was something more. Something that remained.

"Snow—" North began.

Snow cut him off with a sharp shake of his head. "You are no longer Lord of the North Wind, as my Queen has commanded. I took back what *she* gave to you."

He angled his head for a moment, as if willing North to understand the full meaning contained in his words. North didn't need an explanation. He could feel it. The Yule Cat was still within him. The backs of his eyes burned at the gift his friend had left him, though he didn't know how he could handle being immortal while Melanie wasn't. Snow grabbed North's shoulders and pulled him into a hug that enveloped him. He pressed his cheek against the top of North's head.

"We are as we always were," Snow whispered. "As we always will be, brother. I'm not giving up on you."

North's throat was too tight to speak. He nodded against his friend's chest. Snow gave him a last bone-crushing squeeze and stepped back, releasing him. He summoned another portal, a mix of wind joining his snow. North felt only the slightest pang of loss. He wasn't the Lord of the North Wind anymore, but he was still the Yule Cat, as he always had been and always would be, as Snow had said.

Snow pointed at Melanie and said, "You promised to take care of him and love him forever on that first night when he came to you. I'm going to hold you to that."

"I will." She stepped back to North's side and wrapped her arm around his waist. He draped his arm over her shoulders and hugged her close.

Snow nodded. "Keep the outfits. You might need them later. Merry Christmas."

"Merry Christmas," North and Melanie said together.

Snow stepped through the portal and it snapped shut behind him. They were alone once more. Melanie stood next to North, quietly holding him for several moments.

Finally, she said, "Are you okay?"

North turned to her and smiled. "I'm better than okay. I get to be with the woman I love."

Her eyes widened and she smiled back at him. "I love you, too."

"I know." He smirked and said, "You told me the night we met."

She laughed, stepping closer so that her chest pressed against his. He bent down and claimed her lips gently at first, but then deepening into a long, sensual kiss. She was breathless when they parted.

He left their foreheads touching and said, "Keep telling me."

"Every day," she whispered. "I love you."

"I love you, too. Forever."

He kissed her again, the need to feel her close overwhelming him. They were wearing too many clothes —she was especially. He reached toward the laces of her bodice just as the bell in the shop downstairs rang. Breaking off their kiss, they looked at each other.

"Isn't it still Christmas Day?" Melanie asked. "Are you even open?"

"No, and I locked the door after you came in last night."

"We should see who it is. Maybe they need help."

North took her hands and walked backwards toward the door, pulling her after him. "Maybe they need cookies."

They both laughed as he turned so they could walk through his home together. *Their* home now. He went first down the stairs just in case whoever had arrived wasn't friendly. He had a feeling they were, though. Warmth and happiness coursed through him, even stronger than what he felt when he was with Melanie. He glanced over at her, and from the rosy flush of her cheeks and the bright smile on her face, she felt the same way. There was magic at work that he hadn't experienced before. Magic that he liked.

At the bottom of the stairs, they surveyed the room. Snow was piled up against the door, and the locks were still in place. What had set off the little bell above the door, then? Movement near the tree caught his eye. They turned, and North's breath caught in his chest, his stomach doing flips. A man was bent near the tree, pulling packages from a sack in his hand. He wore dark red jeans with black boots peeking out beneath them and a red jacket. White hair dusted his shoulders as he rose and turned to face them. His cheeks and jaw were covered in a thick snow-white beard.

Melanie made a bunch of odd half-choked sounds, then bellowed, "Santa?"

He laughed and smiled at them, the skin around his eyes crinkling. The warmth North had felt grew a thousandfold. It was almost enough to calm his nerves. Melanie gasped and stepped forward. North couldn't bring himself to move to stop her.

"You're real?" Melanie asked.

Kringle angled his head to the side as he gestured toward North. "What, you believe in the Yule Cat but not Santa?" He laughed again.

"I didn't even think of that," Melanie said. "But... But..."

She looked back and forth between North and Kringle, her brow furrowing. She stepped closer to North and took his hand, her face flooded with concern. It was enough to snap North out of his shock. He placed his hand over his chest and bowed.

"Lord Kringle," North said.

"Oh, please." Kringle winced and shook his head, waving at the air as if trying to dissipate the title. He smiled again, and said, "Call me Kris. Or, Kringle, if you must. I always liked 'Father Christmas,' too." He let out a big chuckle, and said, "Hey, you can call me 'Dad.'"

North sucked in a breath that went wrong and set him into a fit of coughing. Melanie patted his back, still holding onto him with her other hand. He had a viselike grip on her. He was terrified to let go. Kringle was second only to the Winter Queen in power in the Yuletide Kingdom. They were forbidden from speaking of him as he was left to his own work in the farthest reaches of their domain. The only place that still held warmth.

"How about Kringle?" Melanie said. "I think we'd all be comfortable with that."

Kringle chuckled and shrugged one shoulder. "Fine with me."

"May I ask why you're here?" Melanie asked, her earlier wonder replaced with caution.

"I heard about your visit to our kingdom," Kringle said. "I just thought I'd pop in and check on you both. Make sure you're okay."

North felt his eyes grow wide as his eyebrows hitched up his forehead. Was Kringle making a play for North so soon after the Winter Queen cut him loose? What use did he have for the Yule Cat, though? Kringle was all about the joy and giving of the season. North was about consequences—and redemption. Was this his chance to be redeemed?

"I think we're okay." Melanie looked up at North, a question in her expression. He nodded and she smiled.

"Yeah," North said.

Melanie's eyes suddenly widened, and she said, "Cookies! We never finished those cookies." She smiled a bit sheepishly, and said, "You know... Because 'Santa.' Unless that's not—"

Kringle lifted a hand in a reassuring gesture. "I would love some of North's cookies."

"There are plenty in the fridges." North nodded toward the door to the kitchen. "Would you mind grabbing some?"

"Sure." Melanie glanced between the two of them, then hurried from the room.

Kringle looked around, and said, "This really is wonderful. You've created so much joy here."

"I... I suppose," North said. "I just wanted to make it feel like home."

"And you did." Kringle laughed softly as he stepped a bit closer. "You made it feel like home for many, many people."

North hadn't really thought about that when he'd designed the place. He'd wanted it to be as comfortable as possible for himself. If others enjoyed it, too, that was just a bonus.

"I wasn't really trying to make a place for others," North said.

"But you did," Kringle said. "Good deeds don't have to be done consciously for them to bring more joy into the world. You did it without even trying. I wonder what you could accomplish if you actually set your mind to helping." He winked at North and turned back to one of the shelves, staring at an ornate sculpture of a snowflake.

Was he trying to recruit North to his section of the Yuletide Kingdom? North wasn't sure how he felt about that. He had only just gained his freedom from the Winter Queen. Maybe Kringle felt some sort of bond with North now that he had also been removed from her inner circle. But the Winter Queen hadn't taken away Kringle's title. She had left him be in his corner of her Kingdom, free to continue to use his powers as he pleased.

Melanie returned with a big tray full of cookies and three large glasses of milk. North would have to wait to ask any more questions. It was probably for the best, since he needed to sort his thoughts. He would talk to Melanie as soon as Kringle left and get her insight. As Snow kept saying, she had studied the lore.

"Oh, that looks delightful," Kringle said, beaming at her as he picked up a sugar cookie shaped like a bell along with the milk. He took a bite of the cookie and closed his eyes, making happy sounds as he chewed. Melanie kept staring at him as he did. He dusted some crumbs from his beard when he'd finished it.

"Sorry about that," he said. "Hazards of the job."

She smiled and actually giggled, then blushed and pinched her mouth shut. North would have to explain that Kringle had that effect on people, too. He brought out the child in everyone. He also brought out their best. What would it be like to work with him? Not as a subject, but as a colleague? North wondered if that could happen. With Kringle as an ally, anything seemed possible.

Chapter Fourteen

"I can't believe you stopped by on Christmas Day," Melanie said. "Aren't you incredibly busy?"

He shook his head and smiled at her. *Santa* smiled at her.

"That was last night," he said. "Christmas Day is when we all get to relax and spend the day celebrating all we've accomplished. Which reminds me, I should be heading back. But first, if you don't mind..."

He lifted the tray from Melanie's hands and set it aside on a nearby table, then reached into the big pockets in his jacket. He pulled out two perfectly wrapped gifts—one in gleaming gold and the other sparkling blue paper. The gold he handed to Melanie and the blue to North.

"What is this?" North asked.

He had seemed withdrawn ever since Santa arrived. Was there some kind of rivalry going on there between Santa and the Winter Queen? Melanie knew who she would side with, especially after how mean the Winter Queen had been.

"They're gifts." Santa gestured toward them and said, "Open them."

Melanie beamed at North, then lifted her box to her ear and started to shake it. It made a little squeaking sound. Was there a mouse in there? Santa reached out quickly and gripped her arm, stilling it.

"Um... I wouldn't shake that one," he said, winking at her.

Melanie tried to stifle her smile. Santa was touching her arm! She carefully tore through the paper. A beautiful wooden box was inside, ornately carved with an image of the Yule Cat on it.

"Oh look, it's you!" she said, holding it up for North to see. She pulled her lower lip between her teeth and opened the box. A bolt of golden light burst out of it as she did, spinning around her head before landing on her shoulder in its humanish form.

"My pixie friend!" she shouted. "How did you..."

Santa lifted a finger to his lips, and said, "Christmas secrets," then winked at her.

She grinned and nodded. She couldn't believe that she was standing there having a conversation with Santa on the best Christmas Day ever. Melanie set down the box, then lifted a cookie from the tray and offered it to the tiny pixie on her shoulder. Did pixies need to eat? How would she know how to take care of it? The idea of a pixie on a sugar rush didn't seem wise, but by the time Melanie had that thought, the little fairy had already grabbed the cookie from her hand and was happily chomping on it.

North would help her. Together, they would figure everything out. Melanie was more certain of that now than ever. After all, Santa had come to visit them. They were friends now. Her stomach did happy flips as she thought of how amazing her life had become in such a short time. She smiled at North, but he didn't return it. He was staring at the present in his hands.

"You should maybe open that one after I leave," Santa said. He glanced at the tray of cookies and said, "Wedding cookies. My wife always loved these." He looked up to North, his warmth subdued, and said, "Do you mind?"

"Not at all." North gestured toward the pile of cookies. "Take the whole plate."

"One is plenty." Santa patted his surprisingly flat stomach and chuckled as he winked at Melanie again. "I don't want to embody the stereotype." He lifted the cookie and held it, a soft smile pulling at his beard. He tucked the cookie into his pocket and said, "Well, Merry Christmas to you both. If you need anything, just drop me a letter in the mail. I'll be sure to get it."

Melanie felt her eyes grow wide. Santa could get mail? Of course he could get mail. Had he read all the cards she'd sent him as a child? Was he the one who had sent the Yule Cat to her when she'd asked for a kitty over and over again?

A million questions—as well as some squees of joy— bubbled up inside her. She pinched her lips between her teeth and clutched her hands in front of her chest to keep them from bursting out. Santa just laughed, then walked over to the fireplace.

"I'll see myself out." He placed his finger next to his nose, then burst into a million motes of golden light that swirled up the chimney and were gone.

Melanie couldn't hold it in any more. She practically shouted, "Oh. My. God. That was Santa!" She jumped up and down to get out some of her excitement, but stopped when the pixie on her shoulder made a little squeaking sound of protest. "Oh, sorry."

North was still staring at the present. Melanie reached out to him and squeezed his arm.

"Are you okay?" she asked.

"I don't know." He shook his head. "Kringle is the Winter Queen's counterpart in the Yuletide Kingdom. She's still the ruler, but he has an incredible amount of power. For him to come and visit us now... I don't know what it means."

Melanie angled her head to the side. "Maybe it means that he's happy for us. That he wants us to make this work."

North chuckled and nodded. "I suppose that's possible."

"This is the first day of spending the rest of our lives together," she said. "And it's Christmas. Anything is possible."

North finally smiled and nodded. She stepped closer and grasped his wrists, lifting the present closer to his face.

"Go on," she said. "Open it."

"Fine." He peeled apart the paper, revealing another beautiful wooden box. This one had a heart carved into it.

"Aww," Melanie said. "Maybe that's supposed to represent me since my box had a Yule Cat on it?"

"Maybe." North opened the box and gasped, his eyes widening.

"What? What's wrong?"

He shook his head. With trembling fingers, he lifted a small vial from inside the box. It was filled with a swirling silver light. He clasped the glass in his hand and held it close to his chest, closing his eyes as he smiled softly. Whatever was in that vial, it was making him very happy. He opened his eyes, then held the vial out to her.

"It's for you," he said.

She peered at the beautiful light held in the vial. "What is it?"

"Immortality," he said.

Her eyes widened. A moment ago, she had thought anything seemed possible. But this?

"I thought the Krampus made you mortal," she said. "I don't want to be immortal without you, either."

North's eyes widened, then he grabbed her and pulled her in for a deep kiss. The pixie fluttered from her shoulder and squeaked at them angrily. North broke off the kiss and laughed at the little fairy.

"Sorry about that, little fellow," he said. He turned back to Melanie and said, "I just… I've never felt as loved as I do when I'm with you. I want that forever."

"But if you're mortal—"

"I'm not. Snow only took the powers of the North Wind from me—which the Winter Queen gave me when she asked me to join her court. I've always been the Yule Cat. My immortality is my own."

Melanie felt her eyes widen as she realized what it was North was offering her. "Then we can really be together forever."

"If you'll have me."

"Of course, I will!"

North laughed, then lifted her in a huge hug and spun her around. Endless possibilities flowed through her mind. Everything their life together could hold. Magic and adventure, baking, cooking, and making love. Celebrating holidays, inviting Snow for dinner. Maybe having a cup of cocoa with Santa from time to time. North set her back on her feet and claimed her lips in a deep kiss. She wrapped her arms around his shoulders and held on as tight as she could.

The night they met, she had promised to take care of him and love him forever. She would spend every day of the rest of eternity doing just that.

Epilogue

Snow trudged back to the throne room alone. His friend was trapped in the mortal realm, but at least not in mortal form. For once, Snow did not agree with the Winter Queen's judgment. He didn't like how it felt. He dropped to one knee and lowered his head as she regarded him from her throne, hoping to hide the turmoil in his soul.

"Is it done?" she asked.

"He is Lord of the North Wind no more."

Snow hoped she wouldn't see through his evasion. If she did, she didn't mention it. He felt the heavy weight of her gaze on him. She rose from her throne and strode toward him, pausing at the edge of the dais.

"You were commanded to bring the Yule Cat back to us," she said. "You have failed me in that task. His home is with *her* now. We have lost him."

"My Queen…" Snow lifted his eyes to her at last, knowing that the blazing fires of purpose would burn away any evidence that he hadn't done exactly as she asked. "I will find a way to fix this. I promise you. North will be with us again."

"Careful, Krampus," she said, her voice so cold, it

made his skin crawl. She turned back to her throne and sat down, staring at him with an icy glare. "Do not make promises that you cannot keep."

This was North's home. *They* were his family, even if Melanie now was as well. His friend was just confused from living so many years in the mortal realm. Snow would show North that he needed to return to them. Whatever it took, Snow would find a way to bring them all together again. This wasn't just wishful thinking.

Wish...

The word was a seed in his mind, quickly growing into an idea. A plan. *A hunt.*

He rose, his hands curling into fists as he said, "It will be so."

—

Thank you so much for reading *The Yule Cat!* This project came on suddenly and would not let my muse go. Writing it was an absolute delight and I'm so grateful for the chance to share it with you. I adore Melanie and fell in love with North from the very moment he appeared in my mind. And they aren't the only ones in this world who have stolen their way into my heart.

The magic continues in the next book of the trilogy, *The White Stag.* Read on to see what the Krampus is up to as he tries to find a way to bring his best friend out of exile (and don't worry, Krampus's story will finish out the trilogy!).

COURT OF THE YULETIDE FAE

THE WHITE STAG

USA TODAY BESTSELLING AUTHOR
CASSANDRA CHANDLER

The White Stag

Court of the Yuletide Fae
Book Two

Cassandra Chandler

Chapter One

The lights from the Christmas tree cast rainbow patterns on the polished oak of the cabin walls. Sylvia pulled her blanket closer around her shoulders as she stared at them. She should probably take the decorations down, since it was almost New Year's, but they were a reminder that she had made it through her first Christmas Day as a single woman in years, even if she'd spent it at the same cabin where she and her ex, David, had always celebrated.

He had accused her of claiming the cabin out of spite, but she honestly just loved the place. The outside of the dwelling looked rustic, with rough-hewn timbers, but inside, the walls were smooth with panels stained to bring out the wood's rich golden hue. A giant fireplace made of natural stone took up most of one corner of the cabin, the multi-hued granite absorbing heat from the fire and keeping the cabin cozy on all but the most frigid days.

The front door had beautiful stained glass in rich purples, reds, and greens, depicting a forest scene that Sylvia had designed herself. Though there weren't too many other windows, they were placed to make the most of what natural light could filter into the cabin through the lush forest outside. The trees weren't thick enough around the cabin to block the solar panels that gave her electricity or to keep rainwater from being collected in the clever reservoir the architect had built into the cabin's design, but they still left her with a feeling of being embraced by nature.

She gazed at the great room that was both comfortingly familiar and achingly empty. How many nights had she spent in the loft staring out the highest windows at the stars peeking through the canopy beyond? How many hours had she spent in the open kitchen, cooking while their friends sat at the stools surrounding the island that sectioned off that space from the rest of the great room?

Now it was just her. She was grateful that they hadn't had kids or pets. That would have made their already painful divorce so much worse. He could have the house in the city and his fancy car—and their friends, most of whom he'd been sleeping with, it turned out. At least, the female ones. The guys had all apparently known about his conquests and cheered him on from the sidelines.

All Sylvia really wanted was this cabin and everything in it—the designs she had made and the items she selected to make it feel like a home. All she needed was the beautiful forest surrounding it, teeming with wildlife. The nearest neighbor was miles away. It had been a draw at first, but she had to admit she was now getting a little lonely. And cold.

She reluctantly let the blanket fall to the couch, then went to the fire and added a few more logs. While they caught, she hurried upstairs to get more blankets and pillows. This was going to be a night for sleeping in front of the fire, it seemed. She looked out the window in the loft area, barely able to make out the trees through the driving snow in the fading light. They had definitely received their white Christmas—and then some.

She shivered as the cold hit her, then grabbed all the blankets that were piled on the bed and pulled them into her arms, along with several pillows. She could barely see the steps as she made her way back downstairs. At least her armful of fluff would cushion her landing if she tripped. When she made it to the fireplace, she dropped everything on the plush faux fur rug in front of the safety screen, then grabbed the poker to stir up the blaze.

She had just finished banking the fire when a tremendous crash reverberated through her cabin. Pictures shook on the walls and the many bookshelves tilted back and forth precariously. She fell backwards, luckily landing on her blanket pile.

"What the heck was that?"

It had almost sounded like an explosion. She quickly put the poker back in its place and set the fire screen in front of the hearth to keep the blaze she'd worked up safely behind it. She had really been looking forward to cozying up with her pile of blankets and pillows. Hopefully, whatever this was, she'd be able to proceed with her evening as planned, after investigating.

She ran to the front door and grabbed her coat, hat, and gloves. Even a few minutes outside would freeze her solid, and she wasn't in the mood to turn into a snow person. She pulled everything on in record time, then grabbed her go-bag and hurried outside, shutting the door behind her as quickly as she could to keep the warmth of the cabin inside.

Dusk was falling over the forest, but she still had enough light to see. The large flakes of snow coming down in a steady stream worried her a lot more than the darkness. She grabbed the emergency sled she kept by the door, just in case she needed it, and headed toward the sound of the crash. The crunch of snow beneath her feet was the only sound in the forest. All the wildlife had long since hunkered down for the storm, and the snow itself muted any ambient noise.

Before too long, evidence of... something began to show around her. The trees above had broken branches and piles of snow and pine needles beneath where everything that had been stuck to their limbs had been dislodged. It was almost like a meteor had come through. Bits of broken twigs and needles dotted the ground, already being covered by the falling snow.

"That's not good," she said. "Then again, neither is talking to myself constantly." She'd gotten into the habit after staying in the cabin alone for so long.

Maybe she was about to have an encounter with little green men. As long as there wasn't any probing involved, she'd be fine with making new friends. Heck, if the guy looked like the sexy aliens on the covers of some of those Scifi Romances she'd seen at the bookstore last time she went into town...

"I really have been alone too long."

She checked her GPS to make sure it was still working and she could find her way back to the cabin even after dark, then trudged deeper into the forest. More damage led the way for her. Whole trees had been felled. Her meteor theory was gaining ground. She skidded down an incline, pausing in a level spot that seemed to be the edge of the event horizon.

The light was fading, but she could still see well enough. Even better, the area was slightly shielded from the heavy snow. Scanning her surroundings, all she saw was white drifts punctuated by the occasional branch sticking through them. What could have caused all this damage, though? Had it already been covered in snow?

"Well, that was a waste," she said. Hopefully, the fire would still be burning nice and hot when she returned to the cabin. At least it hadn't taken too much time.

A sudden movement in her periphery caught her eye

and she froze. It wasn't the wind or snow. One of the branches had moved. She was sure of it. She should just turn around and keep heading back to her cabin and leave things be, but what if it was some animal that had been hurt when whatever this was had happened?

"Dangit." Cautiously, she made her way closer to the branch.

It stirred again as she grew closer. The way the branch had grown didn't look quite right. She wasn't sure what was off about what she was seeing until she was almost on top of it and realized that it wasn't a branch at all. It was an antler. An antler attached to the biggest, most beautiful stag she had ever seen.

His coat was completely white, blending in almost perfectly with the snow covering his body. The antlers caught the light oddly, gleaming like gold in the fading sun. They were also caught in a bunch of other branches and debris. It almost looked like the poor thing had crashed through the trees.

"Oh boy," she said. "You look like you're in a predicament."

She glanced up at the trees and froze. Standing right next to the stag, she could clearly see the line of damage that led straight to him. But it started at the tops of the trees. It started in the sky, as if *he'd* been the meteor.

"Okay, this is very weird."

She turned back to him and gasped. As the sunlight

faded even more, she could clearly see that his eyes were glowing, casting a soft gold light on the snow in front of him. Weren't there legends about a white stag? Like, if you caught him, he had to grant you a wish? There were so many things Sylvia would wish for. World peace—could he manage that? Happy homes for children and honestly everyone who needed them. Enough money to try to make a difference in the world, if he couldn't grant wishes that big.

He let out a sigh and looked up at her, his eyes filled with such sadness. Who gave a crap about wishes? This being—whatever he was—needed her help. She had to focus. They had already lost almost all their daylight.

"Sorry," she said. "This is kind of a new experience for me."

But only kind of. She had rescued animals and even people before. That's why she had the sled. It was big enough for a person, but she wasn't sure about the stag. She started digging out the snow around him, sweeping it away with her gloved hands. The snow darkened as she did. Had he stirred up some dirt as he fell? That didn't make sense. The ground was frozen.

Cautiously, she dusted the snow away from his body. She hissed in a breath as she saw four long gashes marring his white coat from his neck down to his shoulder. They weren't bleeding anymore, but they looked painful and deep. She reached out to gingerly touch the skin around the area. The stag didn't flinch, but he watched her with wary eyes.

"I promise I won't hurt you," she said. She peered more closely at the injury. "What did you face off with? A giant grizzly?"

The stag closed his eyes, his head lowering as much as it could with all the debris restraining his antlers. How was she ever going to get him out of this? Now that she had cleared some of the snow from around him, she could see a large branch that was way too heavy for her to move— and the snow was still coming down. She would need a chainsaw to get him out of this and a tent or awning to keep the area clear while she worked. Even if she did get him free, he wouldn't fit on her sled. He was at least twice the size of any stag she'd ever seen.

"I don't know what to do," she said, resting one hand on his chest and the other on his antlers. "You're so tangled up, it'll take me hours to free you. Not that I'm not going to try," she quickly added. "I won't give up on you. I just... I wish I could help you more right now."

The antler she was holding onto warmed against her glove. She gasped and tried to pull away, but her hand was frozen in place. Not from the cold, but from something else. The antler glowed bright gold, the light was spreading over the stag and illuminating his entire body. He put off so much warmth, the snow around them melted.

She squinted against the brightness he was putting off,

trying to see what was happening. It looked as though his entire body was turning into pure light. She finally had to close her eyes against it, but she could feel him rippling and shifting under her hands. The antler she was stuck to shrank and flattened, the shape of his chest changed as it heaved with quick breaths. She heard him take in a huge gasp, like someone surfacing from water after too long below, and opened her eyes.

The most beautiful man she had ever seen was sprawled before her on the ground. His hair was pitch black, shorter on the sides than the top. Dark stubble coated his jaw. His eyebrows were also dark and strong, resting above thick lashes that surrounded amber-gold eyes. His soft lips were parted as he took in deep breaths.

Her scrutiny strayed over the rest of him, her eyes widening the more she saw. Broad shoulders and sculpted chest, rows of abs stacked on each other, muscled thighs... Goosebumps raced along her skin, and not because of the cold. In fact, she was starting to feel quite warm—in certain places. Her eyes had to be popping out of her head. He was beyond perfect.

No one can be this hot.

Sylvia shook herself as she noticed four angry red lines that ran from his neck down across one shoulder. His wounds had healed incredibly, but they were still there. Whoever—whatever—this guy was, he needed her help, not for her to be lusting after him. And hadn't he just been a deer? Unless she had hallucinated that whole thing. That would make more sense, but she couldn't bring herself to believe it. No, this guy was some kind of... deer shifter. Yeah, that made sense. Like in the Paranormal Romances she'd been devouring since she had arrived at the cabin.

He was a super-hot deer shifter and she was going to plop him on her sled and take her back to her cabin. Where she would be respectful of his boundaries and not lust after him. Not at all.

Yeah, good luck with that.

Chapter Two

How was he so cold? Suddenly, transforming himself into a human didn't seem like such a good idea. He wasn't even sure how he could change back. All he knew was that the Krampus was hunting him, and this human had given him the perfect opportunity to escape. The Krampus was after the White Stag not... this human guy.

"C-c-cold," he stammered.

"You can talk? Great." The woman pulled a large orange sled alongside him. "Can you understand me?"

He nodded, still getting his bearings in this new form. Everything around them was so dim and white. The air was thick with falling flakes, obscuring both his vision and hearing.

"That'll make this a lot easier," she said. She pulled off her backpack and opened it, getting out a shiny silver packet from inside. With a shake, it unfolded into a blanket that she draped over him. "I need you to get on this sled so I can get you back to my shelter. Okay?"

He nodded again. The woman helped him roll onto the sled, which was somehow even colder than the ground. He hissed in a breath, curling himself up in a ball to try to stay warm.

"I need you to lay straight," she said. "I'm sorry the sled is so cold. The blanket should help with that."

He let her straighten his legs and then she tucked the blanket around him. It helped, but he still shivered violently. How could he become so cold so quickly? How did humans survive like this? He felt as though he'd never be warm again. The woman stared at him with a grim expression, then shook her head.

"This is going to suck," the woman said, but she seemed to be talking to herself.

She took off the long, thick coat she wore, then draped it over him. His body desperately soaked in the warmth stored in it—*her* warmth. But now, she would be the one who was freezing. He wanted to say something, to object, but his jaw was clenched shut from the cold. Once her coat was in place, she quickly pulled straps from the sled and secured him to it, then hefted her backpack onto her shoulders again. There were two longer straps attached to the top of the sled above his head. She looped them around herself and started pulling him through the snow. He managed to let out a laugh at the absurdity of it.

"What's so funny?" she said, grunting as she carted him up a steep incline.

Through chattering teeth, he forced out, "Y-you pulling me. D-don't humans usually use animals to p-pull them around in the snow?"

"Last I checked, you were a dude," Sylvia said.

He laughed again. "I g-guess so. I'm still ad-djusting to it."

"So, you're not a shifter then?"

"No. I'm j-just the White Stag. At least, I w-*was* the White Stag." His chest constricted. He didn't know what he was now or how to change back. At least the Krampus would leave him alone. In this form, there would be no granting wishes.

"What do I call you?" she asked, her voice winded.

"I don't c-care."

"Okay." She was quiet for a few moments, then said, "How about Buck?"

"Don't c-call me that."

"I thought you didn't care what I called you."

"That was before I knew you were thinking of calling me B-buck."

She snickered, the sound warming him somehow, and he smiled. She didn't seem like someone who laughed often. He wondered why and how else he might make her laugh. As a being who granted wishes, making others happy was something he truly enjoyed, as long as their wishes weren't harmful. Unfortunately, that was rarer than he would have liked.

A wave of sensation swept over him, his stomach tightened and his heart was beating faster. She had been given a wish, and she used it to help him. *Him.* Was that on purpose, or did she not know the meaning of capturing the White Stag? In all his time, he'd met many giving souls, but never one who thought of him. Some of the biting chill dissipated at the thought.

The sled paused for a moment. Now that he wasn't on the verge of freezing himself, he wondered how she was faring. She had given him her coat. Humans didn't have thick pelts or magic to keep them safe in the cold. What had she been thinking?

"Are you okay?" he asked, glad to find that his teeth had stopped chattering.

"Yeah, just adjusting the s-straps."

"Take back your coat," he said.

"No t-time. We're almost there."

He tried to move his arms to loosen the coat and give it to her, but she had strapped him in so tightly, he couldn't move. Panic reared up in him. He hated feeling trapped. It was like the many times he'd been captured as people sought him out for wishes. He closed his eyes and took slow breaths, the cold air burning his nostrils as he calmed himself. The chill passed from his lungs through his body, making him shiver harder again. Just how muted was his magic in this form?

Reaching out with what magic he had left, he found he could still sense the woman's heart. Warmth immediately suffused him and he gasped in a breath, struck first by her single-minded purpose and then by the intensity of her desire to help him. That was truly all she wanted in this moment, all she had wanted since finding him. In her heart, he was a being who needed help that she could offer. There was no question, no doubt, no glimpse of hesitation that she should give him that help. It was at the very core of her nature.

The sled started to move again. She made a few grunting noises, but the trees above him passed more quickly. Aside from the crunch of snow beneath her feet, all he could hear was her heavy breaths. The light was almost gone, and with it the last of the sun's warmth— what little of it there was. He tried to reach out with his magic to warm her, to ease her path, but felt a resistance between him and that aspect of his power that he couldn't pierce.

"Let me walk," he said. "I'm getting some of my strength back."

"You're still naked," she huffed. "We'll be lucky enough if you don't have frostbite by the time we get there. Oh, I see it. The cabin's just ahead. Hang on."

What did she mean by that? How was he supposed to hang on to anything when she had him wrapped up tighter than a caterpillar in a cocoon? She picked up speed, the sled moving fast enough to worry him a little. She had given him her wish, though. And her coat. She was risking her own wellbeing to help him. Beyond her actions, he had seen her heart. He knew he could trust her.

"Gonna get bumpy," she said.

"What?"

The sled suddenly angled upwards, a series of thumping sounds matching the sled being jostled as she dragged it up a short flight of stairs. She paused for a moment, then beautiful gold light and warmth washed over him. She dragged the sled inside the shelter and slammed the door shut behind her.

Thank the Gods that part is over.

Except the sled started to move again. It scraped across a wooden floor as she pulled him further into the cabin. From his limited vantage point, he could tell the place was still decorated for Christmas. He loved it when people left their decorations up after the holiday. It made the darkness of winter so much cheerier.

He still couldn't believe that the Krampus had been hunting him since just after Christmas day, the horrible wish in his heart reaching out with claws as sharp as the ones he had used to try to grapple with the White Stag. The Lord of Endless Snow, or just Snow, as Krampus was known in the Yuletide Kingdom, was supposed to gather tribute for the Winter Queen on Christmas—in the form of 'naughty' children who he claimed for her. Krampus was supposed to stick around and help them settle in after they had arrived. What was he doing hunting down the White Stag instead?

The Stag was part of the Yuletide Court, but he was considered a free agent. He had always felt more of an affinity for Lord Kringle than the Winter Queen, focusing on joy wherever he could. Many of the people who caught the Stag wished for things that he couldn't bear to grant, and he could sense that the Krampus's wish, whatever it was, would be among them. The White Stag had become wily over the millennia, learning to twist those wishes against the few who managed to catch him. No one had ever wished for something as straightforward as, 'I wish I could help you.'

And this woman *was* helping him, more than anyone ever had in his long existence. She was backing up her wish with action, was willing to work to make it come true. She had sacrificed for him without thought for herself, without hesitation. He could see in her heart the goodness there. And also a recent pain.

She thumped her feet, then removed her gloves and hat and tossed them out of his line of sight. From the sound of it, her boots followed shortly after, landing heavily on the floor near the door. She bent over him, undoing the straps with shaking, bloodless fingers.

"Sorry," she said. "I think I've gone a bit numb myself."

"It's okay," he said.

"Lucky for you, I just built up the fire and brought down a stack of blankets."

She leapt over him, toward the main source of warmth in the room. From the flickering lights on the ceiling, that must be the fireplace. He heard fabric rustling, then the sled shifted again. Her face appeared above him, his first good look at her.

Warm brown eyes stared intently at the straps as she worked to loosen them. Her hair was bright red, a complete mess from the snow and wearing her hat. She had a small, pert nose, round face, and full lips. He had the oddest urge to reach out and brush his fingertips over them, but his arms were still pinned to his sides.

"Dangit," she said. "Oh, here it goes."

She undid one strap, then another. Each one calmed him. She could have held him prisoner and demanded more wishes. That had happened before, too, but the Stag could grant only one wish per person. She had used hers. He wondered if she would mind.

The moment he was free, she took her coat from him and threw it aside. He was about to thank her when she hooked her fingers on the edge of the sled and flipped it over, dumping him onto a mix of blankets, pillows, and a thick faux fur rug. He let out a yelp that was muffled as she folded an immense pile of blankets over him. The weight of them was so much that he could barely breathe, but at least he was getting warmer.

The woman paced back and forth in front of the fire, rubbing her hands together. She looked like she was freezing. Her pantlegs were soaked through, as well as her shirt and the ends of her long hair. She hugged herself, patting her arms as if trying to restore feeling to them.

"What's your name?" he asked.

She stopped, eyeing him warily. That pain he had sensed earlier was rising up in her, mixed with a heavy dose of mistrust.

"It's okay," he said. "I'm not the kind of fairy that uses names against people."

She pinched her lips together, their corners lifting slightly. Was she about to laugh again? He wondered how he could push her over the edge into that lovely sound.

"But you *are* a fairy?" she said.

"I am."

"Never seen a fairy look like this before," she muttered.

He laughed and she froze again, eyes wide.

"Sorry, I'm not used to company," she said. "I've gotten into the habit of talking to myself. It weakens the filters."

"Your name," he said gently. "Please."

She hesitated for another beat, then said, "Sylvia."

He smiled. "Well, Sylvia, I'm not the only one on the verge of freezing. You need to get out of those wet clothes and get yourself warm."

He lifted the edge of the blankets. As he did, her eyes grew even wider, till he could see the whites all around them. She shook her head and took a step back. Was she afraid of him?

"I don't want you to be distressed because of helping me," he said. "I promise, I won't hurt you."

She snorted and murmured, "I've heard that one before." She snapped her mouth shut, glaring at him as if she expected a retort. When he didn't respond, she finally said, "Don't look."

He remembered that humans had issues with being seen naked and nodded, covering his eyes with his hands. The soft sound of her clothing moving over her skin made a strange sensation sweep over his own. It was probably just the cold.

More of the odd tingling covered him as he felt her shimmy under the covers behind him. He had the strongest urge to turn around and wrap his arms around her, but didn't think she would like that. Perhaps she had her own fears of being trapped. He let the blankets drop as she settled next to him, content to bask in the warmth of the fire and of the intriguing woman who had rescued him.

Chapter Three

Isolation had finally driven her mad. Sylvia's stubborn insistence on staying in the cabin was coming back to bite her. How else could she explain the events of the last hour? It had to be some kind of delusion or hallucination. At least it was a gorgeous hallucination. She only wished she wasn't so cold.

Another bout of shivers wracked her body. The guy craned his neck over his shoulder to look at her, his brow furrowing. She had hunkered down under the covers as much as she could, but she didn't seem to have any heat left to trap. At this rate, she was going to go into shock or become hypothermic or something. She should have packed two thermal blankets in her emergency bag.

"You're freezing," he said, rolling over to face her.

"You are t-too." Her teeth wouldn't stop chattering.

"I'm better, thanks to you."

He shimmied under the blankets, getting closer. She wanted to pull away, but when he lifted the covers separating them and his glorious heat rolled her way, she instinctively shifted toward him. He wrapped his muscled arms around her and pulled her close. Then closer.

Her heart started to pound as he lifted himself on his elbows and rose over her. He was naked and she was just in her underwear and a sports bra. What was he planning to do?

What wouldn't I encourage him to do?

Where the heck had that come from? She hadn't been with a man since leaving her husband a year ago—and she wasn't even sure this guy was a man. He had all the right parts in all the right places, but he had been a deer not long ago. A magical deer, but still.

"What are you d-doing?" she forced herself to ask.

"Moving you closer to the fire."

She shook her head. "N-no, you n-need if more than I d-do."

"I'm immortal," he said. "The cold couldn't kill me."

"N-now you tell me," she muttered.

He smiled gently, using the arm that was still beneath her to pull her closer to the fireplace. Once she was where he had just been—luxuriating in the warmth of the blankets in that spot—he settled in right behind her, his body pressed to hers. She would have protested, but he was so warm. He must be magic to have recovered so quickly. Besides, he felt too good tucked up next to her for her to resist.

His arm was beneath her head so that she was using his bicep as a pillow. Her ex would already be complaining about her big head pinching his arm and putting it to sleep. Instead, this guy was tucking the blankets around her body to trap every bit of warmth he could. When he was satisfied, he draped his other arm over her stomach, pulling her tight against his body.

There was no trace of arousal coming from him, which was a relief. Her cheeks prickled as she realized it was a disappointment as well. She had definitely been alone too long. She shouldn't be letting herself think such things about him. He made it all too easy, though, as he held her against his firm chest, sharing his warmth with her. Immortal or not, he had been through an ordeal.

"What happened to you?" she asked, trying to distract herself.

"The usual. People hunting me."

"Do they usually run you down with bears?"

His chest stilled as he held his breath a moment, his arms tensing around her. Slowly, he relaxed. His voice was guarded as he said, "You saw the claw marks."

She nodded. "Looked like a grizzly based on the spread. A huge one at that."

"Are you a hunter?"

She snorted. "Hardly. I used to want to be a vet tech."

"What happened?"

"I got married." She shrugged, then bunched herself deeper into the covers.

"Why would that make you stop wanting to be a vet

tech?"

"I just—" She let out an exasperated sound. "We're not talking about me. We're talking about you."

"O…kay."

"So, it was a bear?" she prompted.

"A polar bear."

"Wow."

She could imagine all too easily the white stag and the white bear battling it out. The stag wouldn't stand a chance. But it wasn't a normal fight. The stag had fallen from the sky—and not straight down. They hadn't been running around on a cloud or some celestial landscape. From the angle and trajectory, their fight had involved flying.

"So, it could fly, too?" she asked.

Again, he stiffened. "How do you know that?"

"The trees." She sniffed, her nose finally starting to thaw. "They were broken on the tops at an angle. I thought I was tracking down a meteor at first."

"If only."

She wasn't sure what he meant by that, but the bitterness in his tone was clear.

"I'm sorry that people hunt you," she said. "And I'm glad I was there tonight to help."

He was quiet for a few moments, then he said, "Me, too."

He tightened his embrace, almost as though he was

willing his heat into her. Maybe he was, because her shivering stopped. She wiggled her toes and found that the feeling was returning to them.

"I've read stories about the White Stag," she said. "But never a magical flying polar bear."

He snorted. "You'd know him as the Krampus."

Krampus... She'd heard that name before. It was a Christmas legend about a monster who took away naughty children and ate them. Her stomach felt like it flooded with ice and her skin prickled.

"Krampus is real?" she said, gasping.

"Yeah."

"Oh my God. That is terrifying. Does he actually eat children?"

"What? No." The disgust in his tone was reassuring, until he went on. "He takes them to the Yuletide Kingdom to become servants to the Winter Queen."

"That's not much better."

"As someone who nearly got their head ripped off by the Krampus today, I can tell you that it is decidedly better."

She couldn't argue that point. "Why is he after you? Did he want a wish?"

Again, the deer-guy tensed. It was easy to tell when it happened, with how close he was holding her. This time, he sucked in a breath, too.

"They always do," he said softly.

"I'm sorry." She reached up and clasped the arm that was bent under her head. "That's no way to live."

"It's the only thing I've known for... eternity. I can't remember a time when it was different. Except for tonight."

"Because you turned into a man?"

"Because you gave your wish to me. No one has ever done that before."

"I wasn't thinking," she began.

"You were. I was confused at first, but I sensed the wishes brewing in you. When it came time to put your heart into it, all you wanted was to help me." He nuzzled the back of her head, then pressed his forehead to it. "Thank you."

Her cheeks heated. She had considered other wishes, but how could she not wish to help a living being who was in as much distress as he'd been?

"I still don't know what to call you," she said, eager to change the subject.

"Anything you want." After a brief pause, he said, "Except Buck."

Laughter bubbled up in her chest and spilled out. She was too tired and cold to stop it. Besides, she didn't want to. He joined in with her, and something tightly coiled unwound in her chest. The sound made her feel lighter than she'd felt in months. She rolled onto her back so that she could look at him, which... was a mistake.

He was so beautiful. His dark stubble made his straight teeth gleam whiter in contrast. The skin at the corners of his eyes crinkled when he laughed, their amber depths glowing with a soft golden light. She wanted to reach up and trace his cheekbones, his brow, his jaw. She wanted to… to kiss him.

Being held in his arms made her feel safe for the first time in so long. Maybe forever. She swallowed hard, reaching for a better topic to distract herself from his closeness and warmth. The stories she had read about the White Stag were in a book on Irish folklore. Something Irish, maybe.

"What about Aidan?" she said.

A crease appeared in between his dark eyebrows. "What about him?"

She scowled, then said, "For a name."

He laughed, grinning sheepishly. "Yeah, I figured. Aidan sounds good. May I call you Sylvia?"

"That's my name." She let out a little snort and rolled her eyes.

Smooth. Real smooth.

"It's a beautiful name." His smile softened as he looked down at her. "And it's nice to meet you, Sylvia."

Her heart started to pound at the sound of her name in his low, rumbling voice. Heat built deep within her, chasing away the last of her chill. She stared up into his golden eyes and wondered just what she had gotten herself into.

Chapter Four

"So, the Krampus, huh?" Sylvia said. "How worried do I need to be that he's going to show up and wreck the cabin and finish us both off?"

Aidan didn't know how to answer that. He didn't want to frighten her, but he didn't want to mislead her, either. He sighed and shook his head.

"I'm not sure," he said.

"Okay, I'll just add that to my list of worries."

"You have a list of worries?"

"Doesn't everyone?"

"I suppose mortals do," he said.

She snorted. "And immortals have nothing to worry about?"

"Until today, the only thing I worried about was the kinds of wishes people would try to get me to grant."

A small crease appeared between her eyebrows. He wanted to run his thumb over it gently and ease it away.

"I don't understand," she said. "You can't control what people wish for."

"True..." He looked off to the side and half-shrugged.

When he gazed back at her, he knew he had a wicked grin. "But I can usually twist the outcome."

"What do you mean?"

She scooted closer to him, her body pressing tight against his and causing an oddly pleasant sensation to sweep over his skin. It took him a moment to remember what they'd been talking about. He shook his head, as if that might clear it.

Right. Wishes.

"I try to pay attention to what's happening in the mortal realm," he said, "both in nature and among people, so that I can minimize any damage wishes might cause. Like, there might be someone who wishes for riches—that's a really popular one—but I can see in their heart that they would use their wealth to dominate people and cause grief and hardship to others."

"You can see what's in their hearts?"

He shrugged again. "Yeah. It's part of who I am."

She looked pensive for a moment, then said, "What would you do in that case?"

"I'd give them what they want, but I would make sure they regretted it."

"How?"

"People aren't usually very specific with their wishes." He smirked and said, "I once gave a guy five million dollars. He didn't bother asking where it was from."

The corner of her lip quirked up. "And where was it

from?"

"A bank vault," he said. "The police were very grateful for the anonymous tip they received about the location of the stolen money. Which was not easy to manage, what with me being a deer and all."

"That is fantastic."

She laughed and shifted next to him again, bringing their legs closer. Her feet were like ice and he gasped.

She flinched away and said, "Sorry."

"It's okay. You really did freeze out there. Let me help you."

"I don't want to get my cold feet on you." She looked away from him, a deep frown pulling at her lips.

Though his powers were muted, he could still sense the huge spike in emotion within her. It went beyond concern for him or self-consciousness. Someone had tried to break her spirit. The scars of it pulled at his own heart as he sensed the pain in hers.

"Sylvia." He reached to tilt her chin toward him. Her skin was still cold, but softer then he had expected. Defiance burned in her eyes, as if she was prepared to fight him—or she thought he was going to try to start a fight with her.

He kept his voice gentle, and said, "I'm fine now, thanks to you. But you're *not* fine, because you helped me. I'm not okay with that. Please, let me help you."

Her lips parted for a few moments, then she pressed

them together tightly. She turned away, as he expected, but then she scooted back so that her body was pressed against his chest, her legs flush against his. He wrapped his arms around her, pulling the blankets more tightly to entrap the heat. He even brought his mouth beneath the covers for a few breaths, giving her as much of his warmth as he could. She sort of shimmied in his grasp when he did so, a tremor running through her.

"Are you okay?" he asked.

"Yeah, I'm fine." Her voice had reverted to the crisp, efficient tone that she'd used when she first found him— after he'd turned into a man. She had been gentler when she thought she was dealing with an animal and not a magical, immortal being.

"What do I need to know about the Krampus?" she said. "How do I fight him if he comes back for you?"

His heart gave a tug. She still wanted to protect him, even against the Krampus. Most people would run in terror if they saw Krampus in his polar bear form. Aidan had a feeling that Sylvia would stay at his side. She was not 'most people.' He pulled her closer, tangling his feet with hers to try to warm them.

"Aidan?" She looked back at him over her shoulder. "I'm not afraid. Tell me what to do, and I'll fight him."

"I believe you." Aidan lowered his head. "That's what scares *me*."

"Death is nothing to be afraid of," she said. "Living a

half-life is worse. Living a lie." Her eyes pinched at the corners as she spoke. She turned back to face the fire.

This woman...

Aidan's heart did another leap in his chest as his admiration for her grew. He had felt something similar in his deer form a few times when observing people, but this was deeper. The feeling reverberated throughout his entire body, as if his very soul was reaching for her, wanting to pull her closer however it could. He tightened his arms around her ever so slightly. Her body might be cold, but her heart was filled with so much warmth, it flooded through him, granting him an energy he'd never experienced before.

"The Krampus," she prompted, bringing him back to their conversation.

Aidan let out a sigh. "I'm honestly not sure what to tell you. He's always been focused and efficient. He runs several corporations in the mortal realm."

"Seriously?" she said.

"Yes. And then there are his holdings in the Yuletide Kingdom. He's known as Snow there, since that's his dominion."

She glanced at the dark window. Snow had stuck to the glass in thick clumps, illuminated by the fire and the Christmas lights. A thick coating of frost obscured their view of the night sky.

"Any chance this is his doing?" she asked.

"It's very likely. He was probably trying to bury me in snow, then hunt me down at his leisure."

"What an ass." She sucked in a small breath, her body stiffening, then said, "Sorry."

Aidan laughed. "Why? He's being an ass."

After a few moments, she relaxed against him again.

"He might succeed in burying you," she said. "Just in the cabin instead of the woods."

"Yes, but when he goes hunting for the White Stag, he'll find nothing."

"Because you're a guy now."

He laughed again. Sylvia had a way of making him laugh. He wished he could do the same for her more often.

"Yes, thanks to you," he said.

"Can you change back? I don't want to think I've trapped you."

His stomach tightened. He had been so intent on getting away from the Krampus, Aidan hadn't really considered how he would change back. There were members of other Faerie Courts he could approach or mortal witches and wizards, but they would all want some form of payment. With his abilities as the White Stag, he could grant them power beyond anything they should have access to. Lying here with Sylvia, basking in the warmth of her body, heart, and mind, he wondered for a moment if he even wanted to turn back.

Sylvia was still waiting for an answer. He could tell by

the way her muscles tensed in his arms. She was ready to act, ready to help. Her heart sang of that so clearly. It was as if her very nature was to help others. His own heart warmed as it basked in the beauty of her soul.

"We'll figure something out." Without thinking, he nuzzled the back of her head once more. She stiffened a bit, her heart thumping against his chest where she was pressed against him. More of that pleasant sensation swept over him.

"So, a guy who can transform into a flying polar bear and has the power to bury us in snow might come knocking on our door any moment," she said. "I'm guessing my shotgun won't have any effect on him."

"The iron pellets will hurt him, but not enough to slow him down. It'll just make him mad."

"I wonder what he wants from you anyway," Sylvia said. "If he's already so powerful and well off, what more could he need?"

Aidan shivered and pulled her closer against his chest. "I sensed the core of his wish when he was chasing me. He wants me to destroy something." It was becoming clearer the longer he was away from their battle as he had time to reflect back on what he had felt.

She tightened her grip on his arm, pressing her body tighter against his instinctively. "What does he want you to destroy?"

"Love." Aidan's own heart ached at the thought.

She tensed, and half-turned in his arms. "What, like all love?"

"No, he's focused on just one loving heart. But any diminishing of love is horrible. At least, to me. The world needs more of it, not less. I can't be part of that."

Her eyes softened and her lips parted. They looked so warm. For a brief moment, he sensed her heart open in invitation. His own leapt in his chest in response. He started to lean closer just as she turned back toward the fire, her expression shuttering.

"You're a good man," she murmured. "Deer. Entity."

Aidan chuckled, pulling her closer again. He thought back over his fight with the Krampus. There was no way Aidan could ever defeat the Krampus in battle, but the way he had fought didn't seem right. Aidan would have expected the Krampus to tackle him or wrestle him to the ground. He'd never expected to have his blood spilled. His shoulder still stung where the Krampus's claws had torn through his flesh before Aidan could turn and take flight.

Take flight...

The Krampus shouldn't have been able to fly after the White Stag. His powers only affected snow. Aidan thought back over his own flight, replaying the moments he had dared to glance behind himself at the raging polar bear chasing him down. There had been snow swirling around him, but not enough to carry him through the sky. That was a power carried by a different Fairy Lord.

What was going on?

Chapter Five

"What is it?" Sylvia asked. Aidan had tensed around her. It was hard not to notice, since he had pretty much enveloped her with his body.

She was definitely heating up in many ways. It had been a long time since anyone had held her close. Honestly, she'd never been held like this. She could practically feel Aidan's desire to bring her comfort and... keep her safe? That was new. She had always felt like she was on her own in that regard. Having someone to watch her back, to focus on her happiness as well as their own—

That was not something she should let herself think about. She sure as heck shouldn't let herself rely on anyone. They always let her down. At least, all the mortals she knew. Maybe Aidan was different.

The stories she'd read portrayed fairies as flakey and mischievous. If anything, they should be even less reliable than humans. Aidan didn't seem like any of the fairy tales she'd read, though. Especially feeling his rock hard body behind her.

Well, not all of it's hard.

The disappointment she felt at that stunned her. Did she actually hope something would happen between them? Her cheeks prickled. She should *definitely* not be entertaining thoughts about *that*. What she should be doing was gathering more information about the magical flying polar bear that might be after her house guest.

"Aidan?" she said, realizing that he hadn't spoken in a bit.

"I was just thinking."

"And I am just asking you to share your thoughts with me." She sucked in a breath, waiting for his response. David wouldn't have appreciated that tone. He would have punished her with emotional distancing or cutting comments. Aidan pulled her closer, resting his chin on the top of her head. Goosebumps swept over her at the tenderness of the gesture.

"The Krampus is one of the two main Fairy Lords in the Court of the Yuletide Fae," Aidan said. "The Winter Queen made him the Lord of Endless Snow. That's where he gets his snow powers."

"Who's the other Lord?"

"The Lord of the North Wind."

She shivered. "It's a good thing you didn't go up against him or we really would have frozen."

"Yeah," Aidan said, his voice pensive.

"What is it?"

"I just... Something isn't right. The Krampus can't fly.

Not like he did while chasing me. That's a power of the North Wind."

"If their powers can be given to them, can they be taken away? Like maybe he took the Lord of the North Wind's power?"

She couldn't believe she was seriously talking about this. It all sounded so crazy. What was even crazier to her was that Aidan was actually listening. She had forgotten what it was like to be taken seriously.

"I can't imagine the Krampus doing that," Aidan said. "He and Lord North are close. Like brothers."

She snorted. "Do they hang out at the North Pole with the Yule Cat?"

"Lord North *is* the Yule Cat. Just like Lord Snow is the Krampus."

Her brain kind of stopped at that for a moment. The Yule Cat was real. The Yule Cat. How was that so hard for her to believe when she was being held in the White Stag's arms?

"The Winter Queen must really like animals," Sylvia said.

"They're shifters. They can appear as humans or in their animal forms at will."

That… put a different spin on things.

"But you can't?" she asked, looking over her shoulder at him.

"No. It took your wish to turn me human. I've never

had this form before, although I've always been curious about it."

"What do you think so far?"

He angled his head from side to side as if thinking, then smiled at her. "I think I like it. Especially this part." He tightened his arms around her. "I've never been able to hold anyone. It's nice. Really nice."

A few choking noises escaped her throat when she tried to respond. Her cheeks heated and goosebumps erupted all over her skin. 'Nice' did not begin to describe what it was like for her to be held in his arms.

"Glad you're enjoying it," she managed at last. That smile of his had her melting. Everything about him did. "When I turned you into a person, did I change who you are?"

"Well, I was always a person. I just used to also be a deer," he said. "But no, this is who I am. Why do you ask?"

Her stomach clenched. What could she say to cover her impulsive question?

Because you're the kindness, gentlest, most tender man I've ever met and that is why you don't seem possible, not the whole 'being the White Stag' thing.

"I'm just trying to get everything straight," she said. It wasn't a lie. Not really. She needed to understand what she was dealing with. "So, the Yule Cat, the White Stag, and the Krampus are all real?"

"Yup," he said.

"What about Bigfoot?"

"I've met a couple in my day," he said.

She scoffed a bit at how nonchalant he sounded. They were mostly talking about beings related to Christmas, so she asked about the most obvious name that came to mind.

"Santa?" she said.

"Of course," he replied.

Her heart beat faster. "Really? Santa is real?"

"Yeah."

"What about Rudolph?"

"Him, too."

"I've always loved Rudolph," she murmured.

He tightened his embrace ever so slightly and leaned close to her ear. "Do I need to be jealous?"

"What? No. I mean—"

"Relax, I was only joking." He laughed, his breath fanning across her neck and sending shivers down her spine. "You're taking this all so seriously."

"I don't want to make any mistakes," she said, only a slight defensive cast to her tone.

"Everyone makes mistakes," he said.

She scoffed again, an odd awkwardness rising in her. "'I'm only human,' right?"

"*Everyone*, makes mistakes," he repeated. "There are wishes that I've granted that... I wish I had tried harder to stop them."

She couldn't believe that he was admitting such a thing. The regret in his voice tugged at her heart. She reached up and squeezed his arm.

"You're doing everything you can," she said. "It's on them, what they wished for. You were bound to grant it."

He was silent for a while, then she felt him press his forehead to the back of her hair.

"Thank you," he said.

She squeezed his arm reassuringly, then let out a huge yawn, unable to stifle it. The weariness she felt went bone deep, her muscles felt rubbery, almost as if they'd already fallen asleep without waiting for her brain.

"Sorry," she said, once she could close her jaw again.

"Don't be. You must be exhausted after dragging me all the way here."

"Yeah, you, too, after fighting a flying, magical polar bear." She chuckled and rolled her eyes. "There's something I never thought I'd say."

He joined her light laughter and a feeling of weightlessness suffused her body. She realized that she didn't have to explain herself to this man. Or worry that he would take offense at her reactions in ways she couldn't understand or predict. He was so different from David. Whatever else Aidan was, she was certain that he was kind.

I've been wrong before...

The past year on her own had helped her reconnect

with strengths she had forgotten she'd had. She drew on that to push the doubts aside. She'd always had a gut instinct about people in the past. When she ignored it, that's when things turned out badly, like the years she'd lost to her initially way-too-charming ex-husband. Right now, every fiber of her being was telling her that Aidan was a decent person. Even if he'd recently been a deer.

"I'm actually more relaxed than I've ever been in my existence," he said. "For the first time, no one is hunting me. I have no wishes to grant. Nothing to offer."

"Don't say that." She spoke with more emphasis than she thought she could muster, considering how tired she was. "Just because you can't grant wishes, that doesn't mean you have nothing to offer."

She felt his quick intake of breath and how his chest tightened as he held it, but then he relaxed and pulled her closer. Her eyelids were feeling heavier and heavier. The warmth of the fire in front of her and Aidan's warmth at her back, plus the heaviness of the many blankets and quilts piled on her was lulling her to sleep. She didn't want to sleep, though. She wanted to learn more about this amazing person and the magical world he lived in. Now that she was thinking about it, that was the same world that *she* lived in. She wanted to know everything.

"I don't understand how all these magical beings can be real and nobody knows about it," she said around another huge yawn. Every blink seemed to last longer.

"But people *do* know. That's where the stories come from."

"I suppose. Would you tell me one?" She didn't know where the request had come from and felt a little silly asking. "I mean, if you don't mind."

He laughed again and nuzzled her hair. She let out a contented sort of cooing sound. If she hadn't been so tired, she would have been mortified.

"I don't mind at all," Aidan said. "Let's see…"

He started to speak, his deep, smooth voice lulling her to sleep before he'd made it past, "Once upon a time…"

Chapter Six

"Just because you can't grant wishes, that doesn't mean you have nothing to offer."

Sylvia's words replayed in Aidan's mind over and over. Each time he remembered them, how forcefully she had spoken, his chest filled with warmth that grew stronger. No one had ever valued him for anything aside from his wishes. No one had ever treated him as a friend.

Now, Sylvia was asleep in his arms. How could she be so trusting of him already when they'd just met? He knew he could trust her because he could read her heart. She had no such powers to use with him. He supposed it could be instinct. Still, the fact that she trusted him enough to be so vulnerable with him was humbling. Such trust was nonexistent among the Fae.

She also had courage. It wasn't just shown in how she had leapt in to help him without hesitation. Several times during their conversation, old wounds had threatened to reopen within her. Hurts from an unknown source, but he suspected were tied in with an early love. Those emotional wounds could take the longest to heal, and trust was something that often returned last.

It seemed she had regained the ability to trust herself, and that was the most important thing of all. He knew he didn't have to worry about her in that regard. He *was* worried about whether he was putting her in danger by being with her, though. If the Krampus found him, he could destroy the cabin easily, especially if he lost his temper upon finding Aidan in a form that was useless to him. Even if Sylvia wasn't harmed in that scenario, she'd be left to the elements. Aidan had seen firsthand how dangerous that could be for humans. Now, he had experienced it.

He was human. It was so hard to believe. He had watched people from outside their windows, hidden with magic or darkness and snow, and wondered what it was like to be one of them. To have people to love and who loved him. To be among family.

Sylvia hadn't just been granted her wish in helping him. She had also granted Aidan's. He wanted to enjoy every moment of it and experience everything he could. Eventually, the Krampus would find him, especially if he had somehow gained the power of the Lord of the North Wind. Then, this peaceful dream would be over.

Aidan couldn't fathom how Lord Snow could have taken Lord North's power. The Lord of Endless Snow and the Lord of the North Wind were friends. As close as brothers—the Krampus and the Yule Cat, both servants of the Winter Queen, ruler of the Yuletide Kingdom. Aidan couldn't imagine a situation that would make one of them turn on the other. He knew that North, as the Lord of the North Wind was called among the Fae, had been exiled to the mortal realm, but that was supposed to be temporary. After what Aidan had seen yesterday, he had his doubts. The memory returned to his mind, as clearly as if he was living it again.

A trail of joy led him to the Yuletide Bakery. Lord Kringle, the only Fairy Lord of the Yuletide Kingdom who answered only to himself, had passed this way. The White Stag followed, knowing the pair were kindred spirits. Kringle was one of the few beings in existence whose heart was filled with wishes for others.

The sun hadn't quite risen on the day after Christmas. The White Stag approached the large plate glass window at the front of the bakery. The glass was fogged from the warmth within, a thick coating of frost on the outside. He could still see inside. The snow was falling thickly around him, hiding him from sight. North was inside with a human woman with dark hair and eyes clear as blue crystal. Their smiles and laughter drew the White Stag closer.

So much joy…

Joy and love radiated from the couple as North wrapped his arms around the woman's waist. She was holding a silver tray piled high with cookies that she had been placing in one of the display cases. She turned to North to playfully scold him, but he caught her lips in a kiss.

What must it be like to kiss another? To have arms to hold them close?

The White Stag's wish had begun to form in that moment. He had been curious before, but a yearning sparked in his heart. He wanted to know, to experience that particular joy for himself. If he ever were to be granted a wish of his own, he wanted to experience love. To find the person he was meant to be with.

The wind picked up, biting and harsh against his flank. He stepped back from the window to see Lord Snow emerge from a whirlwind of flakes. His dark suit stretched across his massive shoulders and chest, untouched by the storm. A white silk scarf hung around his neck and he clasped his hands in front of his body, his stance poised with deceptive ease.

"Good evening," Lord Snow said. "I need a word."

The White Stag turned to flee, leaping into the air, but a driving gust of wind knocked him back to the ground. He pranced in a circle, eyes wild with panic at being caged. His panic subsided as he measured his foe—the one he was sure was hunting him in that moment. The heart within Lord Snow raged with grief and confusion.

"I need you to help my friend," Lord Snow said.

He turned to the window and looked within, his lips

turning down in a frown as he stared at the happy couple. A creeping cold filled Lord Snow's heart. In that moment, he was the Krampus, the monster mortals feared. The White Stag knew what his wish would be. He wanted to destroy the love between North and the woman inside.

The Stag couldn't allow it. He turned to flee, leaping into the air once more. Again, the wind knocked him to the ground with bruising force. Lord Snow stepped closer.

"I don't want to hurt you," he said. "This is just business. The Yuletide Kingdom needs both Fairy Lords. I can't keep things going forever on my own. North needs to come home."

A longing swept through the Krampus. Aching loneliness and loss that again gave the White Stag pause. He couldn't let the Krampus destroy a love that shined as brightly as that between North and his mate. If the Stag couldn't flee, he would fight. He scraped a hoof against the cobblestone street in warning. The Krampus stared at his hoof and smirked.

"If that's how it's going to be, okay," he said. "We do this the hard way."

Brilliant light enveloped him, so bright it burned the White Stag's eyes. The Krampus's form grew and morphed, turning into an enormous, monstrous polar bear. His teeth were so huge, they didn't entirely fit in his mouth, his claws stretched unnaturally far from his paws, and his pelt was filled with sparkling motes of energy. The door to the bakery opened and Lord North stepped outside.

"Snow?" he said. "What the heck is going on out here?"

The Krampus turned to his friend, and in that moment of distraction, the Stag knew he must flee. He turned and ran as rapidly as he could toward the edge of town, far from humans who might be injured if the Krampus lost his temper. He leapt into the air, at last able to take flight, heading toward the forest outside of town.

The night sky was not the refuge it had always been as the Krampus gave chase in a hunt that lasted days. Another gust of wind caught the White Stag, sending him tumbling. Snow whipped into his eyes, blinding him. He could sense the Krampus nearby with his heart hardened with destructive purpose. The Stag lashed out with his antlers, connecting with a pelt as hard as ice. The arms of the bear's form reached for the Stag, but he kicked away. Just then, the wind picked up further, spinning both out of control.

Pain burned across his shoulder as the Krampus's claws raked across his hide. They tumbled apart, the snow and wind swallowing each of them up. Panic tore at the White Stag's mind. He pushed all of his power into his escape. If he couldn't experience love himself, he could at least protect it.

A wave of warmth enveloped him, almost calling to him. He followed it deeper into the woods, latching onto it *like a beacon. As his strength failed him, he crashed through the trees, their heavy branches tangling in his antlers and dragging him further toward the ground. The frozen earth stunned him as he struck it, even with the padding of snow from the surrounding storm. Exhaustion won out over his panic for a moment, and in that moment, he felt a strange peace. He knew that someone was coming to help him. He wasn't sure how, but he was certain of it.*

And then Sylvia had arrived.

Aidan looked down at the woman sleeping in his arms, the same peace he had felt radiating from her. The emotional wounds she carried should make her not trust him, but her heart told her she could do so. Just as his heart was speaking to him now, telling him... something he didn't understand quite yet, but that he would strive to figure out with her help. He knew she would keep helping him. It was her nature to help others, just as it was his.

He pulled the blankets closer around her, making sure she would stay warm, and focused on memorizing every detail of the experience. He didn't want to forget anything about this moment. Or about her.

Chapter Seven

Sylvia had been buried alive. At least, that's what it felt like, waking up under so many blankets. She must have fallen asleep in front of the fire, as she had planned. As she shifted beneath the weight of them, she realized she was in her underwear. The events of the evening before came crashing back into her mind, making her heart race. She craned her neck over her shoulder, but found that she was alone. Had it been a dream? But then, why was she in her underwear?

Tentatively, she said, "Aidan?"

"One sec," he called back from the bathroom.

Her eyes widened. It hadn't been a dream. The deer-man she had found in the woods was real and he was still here. And she was mostly naked. She shimmied out from under the covers, the cold air hitting her like diving into icy waters. She threw more logs on the glowing embers of the fire and stirred them up with the poker quickly, then bolted up the stairs, ignoring the goosebumps rocketing over her skin and the way her muscles tensed from the cold of the cabin.

In the loft, she grabbed a fresh outfit. She quickly tore off what she was wearing and put on fresh underwear, then a set of thermal underwear, thick sweats, and two pairs of socks. She ran her fingers through her hair, though she couldn't imagine what prompted her to do so, then turned around and screamed. Aidan was standing at the top of the stairs, a huge smile on his face.

"How long have you been standing there?" she demanded.

"Not long." He pointed at the staircase that hugged one of the walls. "That was fun. I'm figuring things out." He marched in place as he turned back to her, his smile somehow growing even broader.

Her eyebrows hitched up her forehead as the movement drew her attention to his muscled thighs dusted with just the right amount of hair and… other parts of his anatomy that she had no business looking at. She hadn't really gotten a good look the day before and shouldn't be looking now. She forced her gaze up, trying to hurry, but her eyes would not be rushed.

The strong arms that had wrapped around her all night were larger than she'd thought, but not too bulky. He had a narrow waist, perfect rows of abs, and a sculpted chest covered in a fine coat of dark hair that was absolutely mesmerizing. It trailed down his abdomen, bringing her focus right back to what she was trying to avoid staring at.

"It's not as hard as I thought it would be," he said.

"Hmm?" she said, then remembered that his eyes were 'up there.' She finally managed to meet his gaze, though she could feel that her own eyes were round as saucers.

"Walking on two legs," he said. "Human stuff. Although, I think I could use some clothes. My muscles are starting to get kind of shaky and I think my teeth are getting ready to chatter again."

"Oh gosh, I'm so sorry," she said. She ran to the closet and pulled out one of the plastic storage bins that she'd been meaning to go through. "I think I have some old clothes of my ex's around here."

"Your ex?"

"Yeah." She hesitated, but then said, "My ex-husband."

Thankfully, Aidan didn't ask more questions as she dug through the clothes in the bin. She pulled out some sweatshirts and sweatpants, hoping the fabric would stretch enough to fit him. David was tall, but not as filled out as Aidan. She found some thermal underwear and thick wool socks as well. With the whole bundle in her arms she staggered to the bed and dumped them on the mattress.

"Here you go," she said, gesturing toward them. "Oh, you need to start with the thermal underwear, then I'd do the socks, then the sweats."

Aidan nodded toward the pile, approaching the bed. "Thanks."

Sylvia wasn't sure what to do. She didn't feel right gawking at him—at least morally. Physically, watching his muscles move as he walked and picked up the clothing was pure poetry. She quickly turned around, settling on that as a compromise. He might need her if he had questions, so she shouldn't go too far away.

"These are great," he said. "Really warm. I can see why humans wear things like them. I don't think I need the thermal garments, though."

"You might regret that later," she said, glancing back over her shoulder. His sweatpants were already on. The muscles of his back rippled as he pulled the sweatshirt over his head. "The cabin gets really cold…"

He turned back to her and she started guiltily. She wanted to turn around again, but the smile he cast at her was so warm, she couldn't bring herself to look away from it.

"If I get cold, we can always crawl under the blankets again, right?" he asked. "You would probably be cold, too, if it came to that."

She felt her eyes widen as she nodded her head like an idiot. "Yeah. Good point." She bet certain other parts of his anatomy would make a very good point.

What had gotten into her? She pinched her eyes shut and shook her head, willing away any other tawdry thoughts that might pop into her mind.

"You okay?" he asked.

"Yes, sure." She opened her eyes again, nodding vigorously. "You?"

"I think I'm hungry." He rubbed his stomach. "Do you have any ideas about what I should eat?"

"I um… I have some Christmas cookies left over that we can snack on till I can cook something. I got them from this great place called the Yuletide Bakery."

His eyebrows lifted. "I know that place."

"Really?" That seemed like too much of a coincidence.

"Yeah." He sat on the bed and pulled on the thick socks. His eyebrows rose and he wiggled his feet, staring at them. "Oh wow. That is an experience."

"What is?"

"My toes were freezing before. These socks are so warm and soft. They feel like they're giving my feet hugs."

She burst out laughing, then pinched her lips shut.

"What?" he said.

"Nothing." She was having trouble not laughing more. He was just so earnest and sweet. He gave her a look, and she shrugged. "I've just never seen someone so happy about a pair of socks."

He stood and crossed the room to stand close to her. As he approached, her breath caught in her chest. She wasn't nervous, she was excited. It had been so long since she'd felt anything like that. He stopped so close that she could lean forward and kiss him if she wanted to. Not that she wanted to.

Of course I want to.

"Well, they *are* my first pair of socks," he said.

Right. Because he had been a deer recently. She kept forgetting.

"How are you so good at being human?" she blurted out.

His eyes widened and his lips parted as if her question surprised him. She was stammering incoherently, trying to form an apology when his soft smile took her breath away yet again. He laughed and shook his head.

"You spend enough time on the outside looking in, you pick up a few things," he said. "I've had a long time to wonder what it's like to be human, but I never had a chance to actually try it out till I met you."

"I'm glad you're enjoying it," she said, and meant it. If he was trapped in human form because of her and didn't want to be, she would feel awful. He didn't seem upset at all, though. He seemed... happy. Sylvia resolved to help him enjoy being human as much as she could. "Let's get you those cookies."

His smile brightened and she couldn't help smiling back. She went first down the stairs, angling her head over her shoulder as much as was safe to watch that he didn't trip. Even if he did, there wasn't much she could do for him except cushion his fall. Which wouldn't exactly be a hardship. She imagined him landing on top of her, their faces close, breath mingling...

I have got to get a hold of this.

Back on the main floor, she hurried to the fridge, grateful that the solar panels had remained clear enough of snow to keep working. She grabbed a couple of mugs and filled them with milk, then set the mugs and box of cookies on the little island that separated the kitchen from the great room. Aidan sat on one of the stools next to the granite countertop, watching everything she did with interest. She circled around to sit next to him, then opened the box.

"Dig in," she said.

"Thanks." He picked up a Chocolate Crinkle Cookie and took a bite. His eyes rolled shut and he groaned.

Sylvia barely managed to suppress a similar sound. Watching his jaw work, even his throat as he swallowed... She wanted to say her reaction to Aidan was just a matter of how long she'd been alone, but she knew it was more than that. He was the most gorgeous man she'd ever seen. Thank goodness he wasn't attracted to her. There was no way she'd be able to resist him. Yes indeed, she sure was glad that he had just been a deer recently and couldn't possibly be attracted to her. Very glad. Not at all disappointed.

Chapter Eight

Sylvia had the oddest expression on her face. It was shielded—or at least, as shielded as she could manage—but her heart was singing loud and clear, broadcasting her longing. Aidan wasn't sure what it was she wanted. If he could figure it out, he would give it to her. It was the least he could do for her after she'd made his own wish come true.

Being a human was amazing. He loved having arms. And hands! He reached out to pick up another cookie, smiling at how his fingers responded to his desires. And the cookies… The one he had eaten had melted in his mouth, a burst of flavor coating his tongue and flooding his senses as he ate it. No wonder humans were always talking about how much they loved chocolate.

"These are amazing," he said.

"Have another." She scooted the box closer, taking a Crinkle Cookie for herself.

He ate another, then another, taking his time and savoring the flavors. The box was filled with an assortment that were as pleasing to look at as to eat. Small round cookies, flat ones decorated like snowmen, orangish-brown cookies that smelled of cinnamon. He relished each one, trying all the different flavors. Sylvia had only eaten a couple. He looked over to see her staring at him, her eyes wide and lips slightly parted. A sharp spike of guilt surged through her and she looked away.

"Am I eating too many?" Aidan asked.

"No, not at all. You're just... really enjoying them." She glanced at him, then quickly picked up another cookie and held it close to her mouth. "You said you know of the Yuletide Bakery. How is that?"

"It's run by the Yule Cat."

Sylvia had just started on the cookie. Her eyes widened at his words and she made an odd noise that turned into coughing. Aidan sat up straighter, unsure of what to do. She waved him off, then picked up her mug and gulped down most of its contents. Finally, she set it down and cleared her throat.

"The Yule Cat?" she said.

"Yeah. Lord of the North Wind." Although, he wasn't too sure about that second part anymore. "He's living with a human woman that he fell in love with, but I think he's still doing most of the baking."

"A human woman? Really?" That longing flared up in her again for a moment, but it quickly disappeared beneath a beautiful playfulness. Sylvia narrowed her eyes, picking up another cookie and holding it up. "So, you're telling me that a Fairy Lord made this cookie?"

Aidan nodded.

She picked up another cookie. "And this one?"

He laughed, then started pointing at cookies as he said, "And this one. And that one, too. Why is it so hard to believe?"

"I don't know. You think of a Fairy Lord, you don't imagine them baking for humans." Her eyes widened and she stiffened on her stool. "Unless these are magic and meant to cast a spell on people."

Aidan laughed again, shaking his head. "Nothing like that. Except for the magic of chocolate."

He picked up another Crinkle Cookie and brought it to his nose, closing his eyes as he took a deep breath and enjoyed the scent of it. When he opened his eyes, Sylvia was staring at him again.

"What?" he asked.

"Nothing." She shook her head, her eyes widening as she looked away.

Every time she did that gesture, her heart sort of trembled and shuttered. He could sense a wound there. One that had been healing, but still left a mark. Reaching out, he covered her hand with his. Again, her eyes widened as she stared at their hands resting on the counter, but her heart unfurled, the longing he sensed from her flowing into him like a warm breeze.

"You can speak freely with me," Aidan said. "I like

hearing your thoughts."

She half-smiled, but it was a rueful look. Worse, she pulled her hand away, holding them both on her lap and shaking her head. He wanted to encourage her, but knew too well what it was like to feel pursued. Instead, he sat with her silently, giving her the time and space she needed to decide what she was ready to share. After a few minutes of silence, she glanced at him quickly, then around the room, that oddly muted smile still in place.

"It's weird," she said.

He waited a few moments before saying, "What is?"

"The way I feel with you." She shook her head and laughed. "Almost... safe."

He reached for her hands again, slowly lifting them from her lap to rest on his knees. Warmth flowed through his arms and chest, then down through his abdomen. His skin tingled where they touched, his heart was beating faster, especially when he realized she wasn't pulling away again.

"I have been hunted constantly for as long as I can remember," he said. "And I can remember a very, very long time. It's hard to feel safe after that."

She nodded. "I can imagine."

He smiled at her and said, "I feel safe with you, too."

Her eyes widened. "How? I mean, you just met me."

"I can feel people's hearts," he said. "Kind of like Cupid."

She gasped, then said, "Cupid is real?"

Aidan stared at her for a few moments, one eyebrow arched and a soft tilt to his lips.

"Cupid is real," she said, nodding.

"I felt your heart in the grove where you found me," he said. "Everyone who's hunted me, they did so because they wanted something for themselves. All you wanted was to help *me*."

"I wanted other things at first." She shook her head. "When I remembered the stories about you granting wishes."

"I was aware." He chuckled. "Even then, your heart was open to others. I sensed the goodness in you."

She rolled her eyes and let out a brief laugh. Aidan tightened his grip on her hands.

"You are a good person, Sylvia. At your core, you have the most wonderful heart of anyone I've ever met."

"Hanging out with fairies, I suppose that makes sense," she said. "From the stories I've read, they aren't very nice."

"Don't do that," he said.

That look came to her eyes again. What was it humans called it? 'Like a deer caught in headlights.' He would have chuckled at the irony of it if he wasn't so focused on helping her understand what he saw in her.

"You don't have to diminish yourself for others," he said. "Especially me."

She let out a breath through her nose and laughed awkwardly. After a moment, she said, "Thanks."

Again, she pulled her hands away from his. This time, the absence of her touch echoed in his heart. He had never sensed that hollowness in himself before. An emptiness that longed to be filled.

That longing...

Sylvia picked up another cookie and chuckled. "I can't believe the Yule Cat made these. Does that mean the hot guy who owns the bakery can turn into a cat?"

Aidan's skin prickled and his chest tightened. He felt himself frowning, but wasn't sure why.

"The hot guy?" Aidan asked, unsure of why he was fixating on that.

She shrugged. "Have you *seen* him?"

"Yeah." Aidan didn't want the odd sharpness he felt around the topic to make her withdraw again. At the same time, he needed to sort through his feelings. "I didn't know you were attracted to him," he said, as noncommittally as he could.

"No way." She snorted and shook her head. "I'm not attracted to him at all. The guy is objectively hot, but not my type."

The sharp ache in his chest immediately blunted. "What is your type?"

Again, her eyes widened as she stared at him. Her cheeks turned bright red, the flush spreading down her neck. She crammed a cookie into her mouth and looked away, but not before he'd seen everything he needed—not before he'd sensed that longing inside her blaze to life once more. A longing he understood so much better now that he had felt it himself.

Her heart was reaching out. Reaching toward *him*.

Aidan's chest filled with warmth, his heart fairly bursting with it. His mouth went dry and his hands twitched with the urge to reach for her again. The arms that were so new to him wanted nothing more than to wrap her in his embrace. Something in her called out to him and everything in him responded. His very essence reached for her, and he knew she felt the same. He just had to convince her it was safe for her to reach back.

Chapter Nine

How could she avoid answering Aidan's question without lying? Sylvia didn't want to lie to him, ever. But she also didn't want to admit that he was exactly her type. From his dark hair and strong jaw to his golden-brown eyes and sensual lips. Not to mention his absolutely sculpted body.

But it was more than that. It was his easy smile and his warm laughter. It was how he listened to her and encouraged her to open up. How he didn't make her feel lesser or silly, but valued and... worthy.

She wasn't ready to admit how much she liked him, even to herself. So she dodged the question instead of answering.

"North looks way too much like David," she said.

"David?"

"My dickweed ex-husband. He and I used to come here every year for Christmas. I got the cabin in the divorce, so I'm enjoying it."

Aidan's eyebrows furrowed and he angled his head to the side. "Dickweed?" he said. "Is that some kind of plant?

She laughed and shook her head. "No, it's a… It's kind of a name we call people we don't like. I probably shouldn't use it, but 'if the shoe fits…'"

The furrow between his eyebrows deepened. God, he had amazing eyes. And face. And everything.

She sighed. "You don't understand any of this, do you?"

He looked off to the side, eyes narrowed as if he was thinking really hard. Then his lips pulled into a grin as he looked back at her. Her stomach started doing happy flips, her skin tingling at the sight of that smile. Then her brain kicked in.

"Wait a minute," she said.

He burst out laughing, then said, "I'm sorry. It was just too hard to resist."

She scowled at him playfully, narrowing her eyes. "So, you're up to date on all our mortal slang?"

"Mortal slang." He made a face as if contemplating the phrase, but nodded. "I guess you could say that."

"More things you've picked up over the years?" she asked.

He laughed and nodded. "Yeah.

He looked down at his body, prompting her to do the same. It was in no way a hardship, as more of that electric awareness zinged through her, lighting her up more and more as she knew him better.

"Two legs is kind of an adjustment," he said. "But the

rest of it is pretty fun. There's a bunch of stuff I don't quite get, though."

"Is there anything I can help you with?" She swallowed hard, her mouth going dry. There were so many things she would like to help him with.

"Well, like this stuff."

He pulled up his sweatshirt, revealing those perfect rows of abs, tapered waist, and broad chest. With his free hand, he plucked at the dark hair that lightly coated his pectoral muscles. Heat flooded her. Did he have to turn into such a gorgeous human? She was practically drooling as she stared.

"It's completely useless for keeping me warm," he said. "Why is it even there?"

"It's um…" Her fingers curled with the urge to reach out and touch his chest. How could she explain without humiliating herself? She finally landed on, "It's decorative."

"Decorative." He made his thinky face again, but this time, she figured it was for real. "Like for attracting a mate?" One eyebrow hitched up, as if he couldn't believe the prospect.

"Mm-hmm," she said, her eyes glued to his chest.

"Is it working?" His lips pulled into a lopsided smile— not quite a smirk, but close enough that she had a feeling he knew how his body was affecting her. Her only response was to narrow her eyes and glare at him.

Aidan looked down at his body again and made a, "Hmph," sound. He plucked at one hair, then winced. "Ouch."

"Don't do that."

She leaned forward to put her hand over his to keep him from hurting himself. Unfortunately—or fortunately —he had already moved his hand away, and she ended up planting hers on his chest. Her fingers curved reflexively, burrowing through the coarse hairs as more heat flooded her. Her cheeks tingled, her skin rising in goosebumps.

His eyebrows hitched up his forehead and his mouth dropped open on a quick intake of breath. She tried to move her hand away, but he grabbed it and held it in place. Damn, he was fast. Angling his head to the side, he stared at her with an intensity that made her belly heat and her muscles coil.

"Now, this is interesting," he said.

She licked her suddenly dry lips. "What is?"

"How this feels," he said, his voice growing low and husky. "Your touch."

"How... How does it feel?"

He took a step closer, his grip still keeping her hand tight to his chest as he let his shirt fall over their hands.

"Good," he said, leaning closer. "Very good."

His warm breath fanned her face, his lips almost brushing hers when she snapped herself out of it and turned away. This wasn't a good idea. He wasn't even human. She had probably lost her mind and was hallucinating the whole thing anyway. But if that last was true, why not go with it and enjoy what her broken mind was offering her?

She had thought she was doing better over the last year. Her confidence was higher and she was even starting to chat with people when she went in to town for supplies or just a bit of being around other humans, even if it was just to sit in a bakery by herself, eating cookies and sipping coffee. A bakery apparently run by someone who wasn't human.

"What is it?" Aidan asked, his voice exceedingly gentle.

"I um..." She shook her head, trying to find an excuse. She had told herself she'd never lie to him, but broke her word as she said, "It's just too fast."

He chuckled and she felt the vibration of his laugh through her hand. His heart beat strong and fast beneath it.

"One thing I never understood about humans was how long it takes them to listen to their hearts," he said. "Your lives are so short, and yet you sometimes waste years waiting for 'the timing to be right'—whatever that means."

"It means things take a certain amount of time."

"The timing is right when you choose for it to be right," he said. "I know you've been hurt before. Betrayed. If you let that close your heart to love, then that is a choice you're making. One that I would never wish on anyone, especially you."

She stared at him, eyes round, feeling paralyzed, like... like a deer in headlights. The thought might have made her laugh if she hadn't sensed how important the next few moments would be for her life. She wanted so much to let herself lean into him, to give in to the desire she felt. But he was talking about a lot more than physical intimacy. With him, she knew it would be all or nothing. That's what he would want and what she would want to give him. Was she really ready for that? To open herself up to that risk?

"Don't think," he said. "Just feel. Tell me what you feel when you look at me."

"Hope." The word sprang out too quickly for her to stop it. She snapped her mouth shut before any other truths could escape from it. Aidan's eyes widened and he smiled.

"I can still feel your heart," he said, gently rubbing the hand he held to his chest, his warmth seeping into her. "Even in this form. It's reaching for me. I know it seems dangerous and scary. That's why they call it 'falling in love.' But my heart is open to yours. It's waiting. Let yourself fall." His voice became even gentler as he said, "I'll catch you."

The room seemed to spin around her as her head grew light. Her heart was pounding, her skin electrified with the awareness of his closeness, her hand beneath his shirt, his skin beneath her palm. This was what she wanted. His heart, even more than his gorgeous body. She wanted his kindness, his warmth, his… love. She wanted to love him. And she knew all she had to do to get her wish was let herself go. She stepped closer, grabbing the back of his neck with her free hand to pull him into a kiss.

Chapter Ten

Heat blasted through Aidan's body, stronger than anything he'd ever known. Sylvia was kissing him, her soft lips pressed against his, her body close. He released the hand he had been holding to his chest, but only to clasp her hips and pull her closer. The moment he did, she wrapped both arms around his neck, trapping him against herself. For once, he didn't mind.

The taste of sweet ginger and chocolate flooded his senses as they deepened the kiss. She ran her fingers through his hair, her nails lightly scraping along his scalp and sending waves of goosebumps over him. He slid his arms around her back, holding her even closer. This was so different from last night. That same fullness was in his heart, but this time, it filled his entire body, flooding him with need. He had never felt anything like it.

"Sylvia," he murmured, moving his kisses along her neck. "Tell me what to do."

"What do you mean?" she said, in a breathless voice.

"I want to be closer to you. But I've never…"

She stiffened against him, taking in a swift breath that

she held. For a moment, it felt as though his heart had stopped, fear lacing through him that she would pull away. That was the opposite of what he wanted, but he would deal with it if that was what she needed.

Slowly, she let out her breath, but then whispered, "Let me show you."

Relief made him almost giddy. He kissed her, willing all of his passion, all of his hope and longing and dreams for what their future could hold into that kiss. She kissed him back with just as much passion. When they were both breathless, he pulled back, but left their foreheads touching.

"I would really, really like to make love to you now," he said.

Her eyes widened again, but then she smiled. "I'd like that, too. We should probably get the fire going a bit better. I mean, the fire in the fireplace. Human bodies and all that."

"I'll build up the fire," he said. "And you can maybe help me out with some of those layers."

Her cheeks darkened further, but she nodded. He took her hand and rose, pulling her after him. The idea of not touching her was unwelcome, but he knew he needed both hands to tend the fire. He squeezed her hand before letting go, then turned to the fire and started piling on logs, working them into position till he had a blaze going.

Behind him, the soft sound of fabric sweeping over

Sylvia's skin brought more goosebumps to his. Seeing her mostly undressed last night hadn't had the same meaning. He couldn't wait to see her again. He wanted to explore everything—the warmth and joy they could bring to each other's hearts and bodies and minds. It was all he wanted, forever. To be with her.

His wish to experience what it was like to be human had started out as a curiosity. Now that Sylvia was in his life, it was a necessity. He had to be with her. Had to hold her and kiss her and make love with her. His heart seemed to swell as he realized that he truly never wanted to change back. Not if it meant leaving her.

The fire was blazing, putting out almost more heat than he could bear when he rose and turned back to her. She stood in the middle of the pillows, staring at him with wide eyes and a clenched mouth. She held a blanket in front of her—not wrapped around her to keep her warm. It was as though she was trying to hide from him.

The firelight caught in her hair and made it blaze like molten copper. Her soft, heart-shaped face had a dusting of freckles across her nose that made him want to kiss it. She stared at him with large brown eyes that he could gaze into forever.

"What?" she asked, nervously shifting her weight from one foot to the other, as if she was considering taking flight.

The sentiment was so familiar, it brought a brief flutter

of pain to his heart. He hated that something in her life had made her feel this way. Insufficient. And yet, he was sure it was part of what had made her so strong, part of who she was. He would never change anything about her.

He shook his head and kept his voice gentle as he said, "You. In all the time I've existed, you're the most beautiful woman I've ever seen."

Chapter Eleven

Sylvia couldn't have heard him right. Aidan had been around for millennia, probably. He'd seen more women than she could conceive of. Maybe they looked different to him when he was in his deer form. The incredible kisses they'd shared probably worked in her favor, too, along with what they were about to do. She realized she was staring at him again and looked away with an uneasy laugh.

"You don't have to do that," he said.

"Do what?"

"Hide from me. I will never, through my words or actions, cause you harm. Not if I can help it." He spoke so earnestly, it was impossible not to believe him. "May I see you? Please?"

When he asked like that, how could she say no? Her heart was beating in her throat, butterflies threatening to overflow her stomach, but she at least managed to nod. She took a deep breath, then lowered the blanket and let it drop to the ground.

Aidan was silent and still. She felt her cheeks heat and fought the desperate urge to cover herself with her hands if nothing else. Instead, she forced herself to stay put.

"Sylvia, look at me."

It took her a moment to will her eyes toward him, and her cheeks burned like she had a fever. She didn't want to see his judging gaze. When David had looked at her naked, she had always come up short. Too flat-chested, no butt, yet too many muscles from trying to stay strong enough to lift larger animals at the vet school—and with no fashion sense to cover up her flaws. David could go on and on about her faults, and often did. Now, she was staring at the most unbelievably gorgeous man she'd ever seen, and trying not to catalogue everything that was wrong with her. Everything that would eventually drive him away.

Aidan pulled his shirt over his head and tossed it aside, then quickly did the same with the rest of his clothing.

"Really look at me," he said.

Her breath came more quickly as she eagerly catalogued all of his strengths. His strong, muscled thighs and arms, his broad chest and shoulders, his narrow waist and hips. His skin was lightly tanned, complementing the dark hair that coated his legs and chest.

It all felt like a dream. There was no way this beautiful man was interested in her. No way that he would share this intimacy with her—his first intimacy.

"I do want you," he said, his body backing up his words. "And I'm not going anywhere."

Her gaze snapped to his and her lips pressed into a thin line. "Can you read my mind?" she asked.

"No. And even if I could, I wouldn't without your permission." He looked at her chest and said, "But I can see your heart. I can't *not* see it. Your fear. Your worry." He stepped forward, closing the distance between them, but not touching her. "I don't want anything to happen between us that you don't want, too. But I want us to be together. I look at you, and I see a part of myself that I didn't know I was missing. I see my other half."

"I don't know how you do it." Again, she spoke without meaning to. This time, there was no crushing self-doubt that accompanied it. No fear over how he'd react.

"Do what?" he asked.

"Make me believe. In you. In me. In us. In... love."

His gold-tinged eyes widened and his lips parted. Her heart pounded again, but for a very different reason. She reached for him, pulling herself up to kiss him. The butterflies still filled her belly, but when they overflowed, it sent warmth and awareness through her entire body, like they were fluttering through every cell, filling her with light and love.

Yes, it was happening fast. Yes, it didn't make any sense—for her to be falling in love with the White Stag in human form. But she didn't care. All she cared about was holding Aidan close, being in his arms and feeling his warm lips and his even warmer heart.

He lowered them to the pillows, his eyes glowing with a bright golden light. He might look like a man, but they were a beautiful reminder that he was still a magical being. She smiled then laughed, her heart filling with warmth. She didn't think she had ever laughed while making love before. Aidan was opening her up to all kinds of new experiences. With him at her side, she wasn't afraid of them.

She'd never felt more desired. It gave her a confidence she'd never had before. He was looking at her this way because he wanted her. Because he loved her. Of everything else happening, that was the most unbelievable thing. Yet she believed it. She believed in him. As they lost themselves in each other, she let herself bask in the joy of this moment, this union. She let herself feel loved.

Chapter Twelve

Light filtered into the cabin from the windows, joining with the golden glow of the fire. Aidan rolled over and reached for Sylvia, but she wasn't there. She must have run to the restroom. From the look of the fire, she had stoked it and added more logs before she left. Her sweats were also gone, which didn't surprise him. The cabin was chilly, even with the fire.

He had lost track of how many times they had made love or how many times he woke as they napped in between to watch her sleep, her back tight against his chest and her hair draped over his arm. He rolled onto his back, smiling up at the ceiling as he studied the Christmas lights. Sylvia had said they should take them down soon, but he was in no rush. The cheerful lights always made him happy. They reminded him of the pixies he spent time with in the woods—tiny magical beings that glowed in every color he'd ever seen on Christmas lights. They could be mischievous to those who crossed them, but Aidan had always considered them friendly companions, if not actual friends. Now, he had Sylvia.

Tonight was New Year's Eve—a powerful time of

transitioning. He would use what magic was left to him to crystalize the spell that had made him human and become fully mortal. He would make sure that he remained Aidan forever, or at least as long as his mortal form lasted. A lifetime with Sylvia was worth it. He'd had enough of immortality if it meant more of being alone. His heart was filled with warmth and hope and... something else. He reached up and rubbed his chest, trying to identify the new emotion on the edge of his awareness.

Purpose. Cold, relentless purpose.

"Sylvia!" Aidan bolted upright just as someone pounded on the front door so hard that the windowpanes rattled.

Sylvia ran out from the corner that led to the bathroom, eyes wide.

"What is it?" she asked, hurrying toward him while she kept glancing over her shoulder at the door. "Is it the Krampus?"

She reached Aidan just as he made it to his feet. The chill in the air tensed his muscles, and he could already feel his teeth start to chatter. Cold mist seeped in under the door, coating the floor near it in a thin layer of snow.

"It has to be," he said.

Sylvia ducked down and grabbed his sweats, then pressed them into his chest. Another knock shook the cabin, light appearing around the edges of the door under the strain. Aidan pulled on his clothing as quickly as he could while Sylvia stood at his side. Snow swirled up the door, the mist rising and wrapping around the doorknob. The locks clicked as they retracted and the door flung itself open.

The Krampus filled the doorway, ducking low to avoid bumping his head on the lintel and turning at an angle to fit his massive shoulders through the space. For a moment, Aidan thought he might be in his polar bear form, but it was just the man, enormous as he was. A blast of cold air entered along with him. Sylvia trembled, wrapping her arms around her middle. She scurried closer to the fire, probably trying to keep from freezing in the presence of the Lord of Endless Snow.

"There you are." The Krampus turned and closed the door behind him, then rose to his full height. He stomped into the great room, snow falling from his shoulders in wet clumps that splatted on the wooden floor. "I've been looking for you."

Before he could reach Aidan, Sylvia leapt between them, swinging the poker from the fireplace. The metal of its tip glowed red-hot, sizzling as it swept through another clump of snow that fell as the Krampus lurched back.

"What the hell?" he said. "Who leaves a poker in the fire?"

"Someone expecting the Lord of Endless Snow to come for the man she loves," Sylvia said.

The man she loves?

Aidan knew what he had sensed from her, what he had seen in her heart. He didn't know she was already prepared to face the deep emotional connection that had been forged between them. His own heart swelled with love, warmth flooding his chest strong enough to fight off Lord Snow's cold.

The Krampus shook his head and swung a massive arm, gesturing toward Aidan. "He's not a man."

"He is now." She looked over at Aidan and held his gaze. "Man enough for me."

"What is it with you mortal women?" The Krampus shook his head, then swirled his finger in the air. A mini snowstorm grew around it, then swept out to surround the poker. The metal cooled to its usual dark color in seconds. He plucked it from her hands as her eyes widened in shock, then set it in its place by the hearth. "If you don't mind, this is Fae business. Not your concern."

"I do mind, and anything involving Aidan is entirely my concern," Sylvia said.

The Krampus narrowed his eyes. "Who?"

"She means me," Aidan said. "I'm not the White Stag anymore. I'm just a man."

The Krampus laughed. "That's a good one. Did you feed that line to her before you hooked up?"

"What do you mean?" Sylvia looked back and forth between them, a sliver of doubt rising in her heart. "What line?"

"I've been nothing but honest with her," Aidan said. He turned to Sylvia and emphatically restated, "With *you*. I still have enough magic in me to read your heart, but I can't grant wishes."

"Not in this form," the Krampus said. "But you will, as soon as I get you changed back."

"No." Sylvia took a few steps forward. "No, you can't turn him back."

"Look, let's all just take a few deep breaths and talk this out like reasonable beings." The Krampus turned to Aidan and said, "We got off on the wrong foot. I was upset and not thinking clearly and my behavior was way over the line. For that, I apologize."

"You apologize?" Aidan said. "You nearly tore my head off."

"Like I said." Krampus made a gesture like he was forming a wall with one hand and used the other to mimic jumping over it as he said, "Over. The line. I just need one wish, and then we can both be on our way."

Aidan shook his head. "I won't. Even if I could, I wouldn't."

The Krampus clasped his hands in front of his body and stood straighter, making himself seem even bigger. "Well, then. We might have a problem."

"Krampus, please," Sylvia pleaded.

"Call me Lord Snow." The Krampus sort of shivered as if trying to shake something off. "Or just Snow. I hate that other name."

"I wondered." She gestured toward him and said, "You don't look like any of the pictures of you that I've seen."

What was she doing, striking up a conversation with him? Aidan could sense her own purpose. She was trying to protect him, to protect their love and the love that the Krampus—Lord Snow—threatened. If Aidan could figure out her plan, maybe he could help with it.

"Those pictures are offensive." Snow shrugged his shoulders as if loosening the pull of his jacket on his massive arms. "And hurtful," he added. "I haven't looked like that since I became the Lord of Endless Snow. That's who I am now. Snow."

"I get it," Sylvia said, nodding with wide eyes. "We will call you Snow."

"Good," he said.

"You'd probably be really upset if you had to turn back," Sylvia said.

"Of course I—" He narrowed his eyes and took a step forward. "Don't try to trick me."

"She's not trying to trick you," Aidan quickly said. "No one is. She's just trying to make a point. I don't want to change back. I want to stay like this forever."

Snow let out a snort. "Forever wouldn't be very long." He gestured toward Sylvia and said, "These mortals rarely last a century."

"I know." Aidan swallowed hard as he gazed at Sylvia.

His chest constricted at the idea of going on without her. "Whatever time I'm given, I want to spend it with her. If I had a wish, that's all I would ask for."

"Aidan…" Sylvia reached for him, clasping his hands and pulling him close. She rose on her tip toes to kiss him, her lips warm and soft.

"Ugh," Snow said, rolling his eyes. "Stop that."

Aidan ignored him, his focus solely on Sylvia as he said, "I love you."

Sylvia's smile was brighter than the Christmas lights. "I love you, too."

"It doesn't matter," Snow said. "This guy—"

"Aidan," Sylvia said, her voice like iron. "We're respecting what you want regarding your name. You need to do the same for us."

"Fine," Snow said, his voice tight. "*Aidan* is the White Stag. He has to return to that form or it will throw off the magical balance. It's already bad enough without a Lord of the North Wind. Losing the White Stag as well would throw the Court of the Yuletide Fae into chaos and make us a target for the other Courts."

"That wouldn't be good," Aidan said, pulling Sylvia against his side.

"No kidding," Snow said.

"But the Winter Queen can choose another Lord of the North Wind," Aidan said.

Snow shook his head and let out a long sigh through

his nose. Aidan didn't think he'd ever heard such a clear sound of exasperation.

"She already has," Snow said. "Jack Frost."

Aidan felt his eyebrows rise. "Jack Frost?"

"He's real, too?" Sylvia said. She shook her head. "What am I saying? Of course, he's real."

"He's real and he's also…" Aidan let his voice trail off, thinking of the few encounters he'd had with Jack Frost and the many, many tales of mischief, frustration, and woe surrounding the fairy.

"He's also a dick," Snow said.

Aidan couldn't argue.

"He's bad enough with his current powers," Aidan said. "If he becomes Lord of the North Wind…" His stomach churned at the thought.

"Which is why I need you back as the White Stag to buy me time to make a case with the Winter Queen to reinstate the Yule Cat as the Lord of the North Wind."

"Aidan…" Sylvia tightened her grip on Aidan's waist. He could sense her fear, a cold coiling in his chest. She turned back to Snow and said, "There has to be another way. A better way."

"I happen to agree."

All three of them started at the cheerful voice coming from somewhere behind Lord Snow. Snow was so huge, he could easily be hiding several people from view. Snow's eyes grew wide as he wheeled around and stepped back, revealing a tall man wearing a red jacket and dark red jeans over gleaming black boots. His fingers were interlaced over his stomach and Aidan could see his smile even through his thick white beard and mustache. His hair was just as snowy white, dusting the tops of his shoulders.

Within his chest, a golden light spread forth, suffusing his entire body with a soft glow that radiated out from him. It was powerful enough to chase the chill away from the room. Joy and love flooded Aidan, so powerful that his knees felt weak. He leaned on Sylvia as she took some of his weight, helping him to remain standing. As if that wasn't wondrous and terrifying enough, Lord Snow—the Krampus—backed away another step.

"I hope you don't mind," the man said. "I let myself in."

"Lord Kringle," Snow said, bowing low.

"No need to be formal." With a beaming smile, Lord Kringle said, "Call me Kris."

Chapter Thirteen

Sylvia let out a laugh as the Krampus—Lord Snow—finally straightened. She'd been doing okay with the idea of fairies and Yule Cats and Krampuses and magic stags, but this? No way. Aidan had said that this particular magical being was real, but it was easier to entertain as a possibility when there wasn't a guy standing in her great room who looked—who *felt*—like this.

"You have got to be kidding me," she said. "There's no way this is Santa."

She glanced up at Aidan to see that his eyes were wide and his mouth slack. Looking at Snow didn't help matters. He was glaring at her like she'd seen celebrity bodyguards do when regular people came too close. His eyes burned red—literally glowing red—and a muscle twitched on his massive jaw. She leaned a little closer to Aidan, which was easy, since he was half-flopping on her.

"People don't respect Father Christmas anymore," Snow said.

"Come now," Kringle said, then somehow managed to pull off a perfect 'ho, ho, ho' laugh without making it sound cheesy or forced.

"They make these weird, cartoony light-up balloons of you and put them in their lawns," Snow said. "It's creepy."

"Oh, I don't know." The famous twinkle sparkled in Kringle's eye. "Have you seen the ones of me riding a dinosaur?" He chuckled and shook his head. "I love those."

"Seriously?" Sylvia said. "*You're* Santa?"

The smile he cast at her somehow flooded her chest with warmth. Her eyes teared up and she had an almost uncontrollable urge to fling her arms around him and give him the biggest hug.

"You can call me Kringle, if you'd rather," Santa said. "But right now, we need to get moving. It's almost midnight, and we're going to need all the juice we can get if we're going to change Aidan back into the White Stag."

Sylvia's heart seemed to freeze in her chest. Her ears rang so loudly from the blood rushing through them that she was certain she had to have heard him wrong. She shook her head as if that would clear it, then wrapped her arms tighter around Aidan's waist.

"You can't," she said. "There's no way Santa would do this. No way he'd separate us."

"Indeed." He had the gall to smile at her, but then he tilted his head forward a bit, so that Snow couldn't see his face, and winked at them. "I'm going to ask you to do something that has been a challenge for you ever since that ex-husband of yours..." He raised his eyebrows. "Well, let's just say 'was exceedingly naughty.' I need you to trust me, Sylvia."

She wasn't sure that she could. She had only just managed to open her heart to Aidan. How could she trust this stranger to somehow manage to change Aidan back without separating them?

"You trust me," Aidan said. He looked down at Sylvia and said, "And I trust him. He said himself he agrees that there's a better way. If anyone can figure it out, it's Lord Kringle."

"Aidan…"

If she lost him, it would be the end of her heart. She would never love anyone again. She knew it in her bones, in her essence. This was her soulmate. She would do anything to be with him. But if there was a hidden cost…

"Is Jack Frost dangerous?" she asked.

"He can be." Aidan nodded. "Mostly when his tricks go sideways. I've never known it to bother him much when it does."

"Then we can't let him become more powerful." She turned to Santa and said, "Okay, what's the plan?"

"First, we need to move outside." He gestured to Snow and said, "If you wouldn't mind? Some proper attire for our friends."

"Of course," Snow said.

Sylvia's heart raced as she wondered what exactly they meant by that and what Snow intended to do. She didn't have to wait long to find out. The massive man lifted one foot, then stomped it down on the floor so hard, she was amazed that it didn't go right through the boards. Instead, a pattern of snowflakes appeared beneath his boot, quickly flowing across the polished oak hardwood toward her and Aidan.

She tried not to flinch as it reached them, but still yelped as the cold crept up their legs. Glancing at Aidan, she saw that he had closed his eyes, but she couldn't bring herself to. She didn't want to miss a moment of this, and as much as she trusted Aidan and was trying to trust Santa, she didn't trust Snow at all.

The snow wrapped around her legs quickly, spreading up over her entire body and encasing her in light and frigid cold. Her body shook with it, arms tightening around Aidan further without thought. The light grew brighter as her sweatpants transformed into snow-white fleece leggings that flared around a pair of matching glossy leather boots, lined with fur and sporting laces that went all the way from her toes to her knees. She felt warm socks encase her feet within them, the fabric softer than anything she'd ever felt before.

Her sweatshirt transformed, flowing down her body as a white dress coat with white wooden clasps in neat double rows up the middle. The neck of it expanded into fur-covered lapels that rested across her collarbones and snugged against her neck, trapping in all her body heat and making her cozy and warm. Matching white gloves spread over her hands, the material soft as kid leather. The snow swirled up through her hair, pleating it into two braids entwined with white ribbon that tied them off. She felt something soft wrap around her head and dared to reach up, finding a soft fur cap on her head. The snow whirled around her once more, then fell to the ground, vanishing as soon as it hit the floor.

"What... I mean... How... That was..." She couldn't find the words to encapsulate her thoughts, which were running crazy anyway. She looked at Aidan and became utterly speechless.

His clothing had also transformed into a similar outfit. The white pants hugged his muscular legs, his jacket stretched across his broad chest and tapered to show off his trim waist, then flared a bit at his hips. Her only complaint was that the length of his coat covered up his backside, but she was sure she could get over it. A soft cap sat on his head, the white fur contrasting brilliantly with his dark hair and the stubble that graced his strong jaw. They looked like they were ready to hit the red carpet or visit royalty in a northern country or something.

"Enough gawking," Snow said. "We're on a tight timeline."

"Wait, this isn't real fur, is it?" Sylvia said, reaching toward her hat as if to remove it.

"Of course not." Snow let out a disgusted grunt. "It's

all magic."

"Oh, okay then," she said.

Something about his indignation was endearing, even with the threat he represented to them. Maybe his heart wasn't as icy as she had originally thought.

"Nicely done," Kringle—Santa—said, beaming at them. He leaned closer to Snow and said, "She'll like this."

"Who will?" Sylvia asked.

For a brief moment, Santa's smile shuttered and his eyes grew unfocused. He opened his mouth a few times, but no words came out. How could a simple question make the man who traveled to every household on Christmas Eve appear so lost? Sylvia took a step toward him, uncertain of what she was about to do, but feeling compelled to comfort him. Snow stepped between them and took a deep breath, puffing up his chest to make himself even bigger than before. She was still wrapping her head around standing in a room with Santa, but had no trouble at all believing that Snow was a polar bear shifter.

"Outside," Snow said gruffly. "Get moving."

Aidan tucked her arm in his elbow and headed for the door. His hand on top of hers was a comfort, though she was still terrified. What was about to happen? The door opened on its own when they approached. Beyond, she could see that the snow had been swept away from her porch. A large area in front of the cabin looked to be covered in packed snow instead of the huge drifts she'd expected.

"Being the Lord of Endless Snow must have its perks," she muttered as they stepped onto the porch.

Snow loomed behind them and leaned down to say, "It does. Now keep moving."

She grimaced at him, but hurried down the steps with Aidan. Above them, the clouds had cleared, leaving an inky black night dotted with diamond-like stars and a bright moon shining above. The light of the full moon caught on the snow in the trees and on the ground, illuminating the entire area with soft white light and making it easy to see everything. The landscape was utterly magical, even without the Fae surrounding her. Her breath came out in puffs of fog, her heart pounding as she worried over what would come next.

Brilliant, tiny lights of all colors flickered into view among the branches, a rainbow of winter fireflies. They floated closer, like the most beautiful Christmas lights that had come to life, filling the clearing with magic. Despite the situation, Sylvia found herself gasping in wonder as they circled around her and Aidan.

"What are these?" she asked.

"Pixies," Aidan said. "They're beautiful, but they can be mischievous, too."

"Most of the Fae can," she agreed. "At least, according to the stories." She turned to Santa and said, "I hope that doesn't apply to you as well."

"Me? Oh no." Santa managed another of those ho-ho-ho laughs in the middle of his sentence. "But I'm a bit different from the others."

"How so?" she asked.

"Enough questions." Snow stepped forward. "Midnight is moments away. Tell me what to do to break the spell keeping Aidan in human form."

"You don't have to do anything," Santa said. "It's all on Aidan. All he has to do is let go."

Aidan's hand tightened around Sylvia's almost enough to hurt. His eyebrows knit together and he shook his head.

"No," he said. "Please, no."

"Wait a minute." Sylvia's heart was pounding, her skin felt electrified. There was no way she was going to sit by and let this happen. "You said there was a better way. You agreed with me."

"A better way than Lord Snow forcing Aidan back into the form of the White Stag." Santa nodded. "There is. He fulfilled your wish and made it so that you could help him, which you've done. And his wish is fulfilled in experiencing what it's like to be human…" There was a wistfulness in his tone as he finished, "if only for a little while."

"No," Sylvia said. "No, you can't take him from me."

"Sylvia." Aidan's voice was painfully gentle.

"No," she said. "If you turn back, the Krampus will use

you to grant his wish. He'll destroy a love. You sensed it. We can't let that happen. And if you turn back—" Her voice broke as tears filled her eyes. "What about us? What about our love? You'll be the White Stag, and I'll just be human."

Aidan cupped her cheek and she shook her head. He leaned in and kissed her, so bittersweet and tender. All his love flowed into her through the kiss, telling her everything they didn't have time to explore, everything he wished they could be and would never have a chance to discover. When he pulled back, a tear spilled from his eye.

"Snow is right," Aidan said. "The balance of power has been thrown off too far. The repercussions could be devastating to so many people, to so many worlds, Fae and mortal alike. There has to be a White Stag."

"Just as there has to be a Lord of the North Wind," Santa said, his booming voice breaking through their moment.

Sylvia looked over to see Santa nudge Snow's arm with his elbow. Snow looked down at him, his eyebrows raised and his mouth hanging open.

He shook his head and said, "No. Absolutely not."

Santa sort of shrugged, then turned to her and winked again. She didn't know what was going on, but she had a sense that it was important. Incredibly important. She struggled to find a way to help.

"Is that any way to talk to Lord Kringle?" she said.

Snow scowled at her, but then turned back to Santa and bowed. "With all due respect, I've been given orders—"

"That you have already disobeyed." Santa clucked his tongue. "That was a bit naughty of you."

Snow blinked a few times, then ran his hand over the close-cropped hair on his scalp. He walked a few steps away from Santa, shaking his head.

"All I wanted was for my family to be whole again," Snow said.

Santa nodded. In a gentle voice, he said, "That is a wish we share. But if you want to bring people together, you can't do so by driving them apart."

Snow let out a sigh that seemed to drop the temperature around them another dozen degrees. Even with her warm gear, Sylvia shivered. Her heart was racing as she wondered what exactly was going on. She didn't dare ask, seeing the turmoil in Snow's features. She had to... to trust Santa.

How has my life become this strange?

"If we're going to do this, we need to do it now," Santa said, his voice softer. "And if she has a problem with it, she's welcome to take it up with me."

Sylvia didn't know who they were talking about. She was the only 'she' in the clearing. Stepping closer to them, she kept a firm grip on Aidan's hand as she said, "If there's anything you can do to keep Aidan and me together, please do it. I don't care what it is, as long as it doesn't hurt anybody else."

"There isn't a way for no one to be hurt." Aidan stared at Snow as he said, "That's the real reason behind your wish. You want North back as your partner in the Yuletide Kingdom. You miss him and want things to go back to the way they were."

That's what this was about? Aidan had told her that Snow and North were like brothers, but that North had found love with a human woman. She had only been happy for North, not thinking of how it would affect Snow. When she was younger, she had always believed that bringing in someone to love made a family bigger, it didn't split them apart. But she knew from bitter experience that wasn't always the case. If North was no longer Lord of the North Wind, did that mean he had left Snow behind?

Snow's eyes began to glow red again. His chest heaved with quick breaths as white light enveloped him. The light grew, burning her eyes and changing his silhouette, then finally vanishing to leave behind an enormous polar bear. Mist rose from his pelt and snowflakes swirled around him as he let out a roar that shook the trees, dislodging huge clumps of snow that splatted to the ground.

"Now, Snow," Santa said, stepping between them.

Sylvia released Aidan's hand and ran forward. She ducked past Santa and plowed right into Snow's furry belly, wrapping her arms around him as far as she could. A tremor flowed through him as she tightened her embrace.

"I'm so sorry," she said. "I'm sorry that he left you to be with someone else. But if he really is like a brother to you, that doesn't mean you've lost him. That doesn't mean you can't figure out a way to still be close. To be family." She leaned back so that she could look up into Snow's startled, glowing eyes. "And I swear to you, I will do everything I can to help you find that new path. Even if you have to turn Aidan back into the White Stag, you don't have to destroy North's love to be part of his life. You don't have to use your wish for that."

Snow let out a sigh that rustled her hair. She felt his paws on her back and tensed, wondering if he was about to tear her apart for daring to speak to him the way she was, to hug him. Honestly, she couldn't believe that she'd done it herself. All she had known was the pain that she finally understood. The pain that connected them. The urge to do something to ease his suffering had blinded her to anything else. Now, looking into the eyes of the giant, magical polar bear that was the Krampus, she wondered if that impulse would cost her everything.

He let out another sigh, his breath becoming more even. His skin rippled beneath her arms as a softer light covered him. The soft fur brushing against her retreated into his form as he shrank down to his still enormous—but on a human scale—size. His arms remained around her.

"Dammit," he muttered under his breath. "Go on. Go stand by your man, for as long as you can call him that."

Her heart started to pound again. This was it, then. He was going to turn Aidan back. But as she turned to go to Aidan, she realized that Snow held on for just a moment longer than she expected. He was hugging her back, not just leaving his arms where they'd been. She glanced up at him, and swore she saw a slight smile as he finally let her go.

Sylvia hurried to Aidan's side. He was staring at her with the same wonder that he'd shown to Santa when he first arrived.

"What?" she said.

"I can't believe you did that." Aidan smiled at her, tucking her arm into his elbow once more and resting his hand on hers. "I am... so honored that you've chosen to share your incredible heart with me."

"For as long as it lasts," she murmured and instantly regretted it when Aidan's smile faltered.

"Let's do this." Snow nodded at Santa, coming to stand by his side. "With the power of the new year, the full moon, and both of us working together, we should be able to manage it."

"Sounds like you have a new plan." Santa chuckled and winked at Snow.

Snow shook his head, then clapped his hands together. A circle of light burst into view at the edges of the clearing, with Aidan and Sylvia at its center. Aidan gripped her hands tightly, staring into her eyes as the light crept closer.

In a strong voice, Snow began to speak. "As the clock strikes midnight with the changing of the year, two souls stand before me, human and deer."

"Aidan..." Sylvia stepped closer to Aidan as the light formed a silhouette of golden antlers that rose from his head. He was turning back. She blinked away her tears and forced herself to smile. "You have opened my heart to love again. And all the love I have, I give to you. For as much time as we have. I love you. Forever."

"I love you, too," he said. "Forever."

Aidan's face elongated back to the snout of his deer form as the light seeped deeper into his body. His skin paled as it returned to his white pelt. His hands fell away from hers as they turned to hooves, his legs and arms straightening into those of a stag's. For a moment, despair washed through her as she remembered how happy it had made him to be able to hold her in his arms. He would never be able to do that to someone again. Never hold anyone close.

How could this be the better way? The better plan? The light warmed her, spreading over her skin and soaking into her muscles and bones. She wasn't sure what it was doing to her, but she didn't care. She only wished there was a way for them to be together. She closed her eyes and imagined each moment when Aidan had held her in his arms, replaying each heated kiss, each tender moment. A wave of dizziness assailed her and she fell forward onto her hands and… feet? Her head was oddly heavy.

She heard Santa say, "Finish it, son," before Snow spoke again.

"Aidan, I no longer call you foe. White Stag, I give to you the White Doe."

Her eyes flew open to see Aidan staring at her with his wide golden eyes, his antlers glowing gold and his pelt gleaming in the moonlight. He stamped his front leg and shook his head, then let out a bellow that made her heart race with excitement. She wanted to run into the forest, to leap into the air and fly up to the stars above them. Anticipation of their run heated her blood as she stamped her arm… her foot… her… hoof?

What did Lord Snow say before? The White Doe?

She curved her neck to look at her body, her head heavy with a strange weight. Her body was covered in a coat of white, four long, slender legs stretched beneath her to the ground, and a tail flicked on her rump. She was a deer! She turned back to Aidan and made the most bizarre noise she'd ever heard. It was the closest thing to a laugh she could manage. If this meant they could be together, so be it. She would miss being human, but it was worth it to be with him.

Aidan stepped forward and nuzzled the side of her head with his. She felt her antlers bump against his, though they felt smaller. That was probably for the best as she became used to her new form. She tried to take a step and stumbled, but Aidan was there to help her keep to her feet —all four of them.

They both turned toward Snow and Santa, the one looking grumbly and the other beaming with a smile. This must have been Santa's plan all along. Sylvia wished that he had asked her first. She would have said yes, but it would have been nice to have an idea of what to expect. An odd thought popped into her head that she and Aidan could join Santa's reindeer at Christmastime and she let out another of the odd bugling laughs.

Santa joined her, then nudged Snow again. "And the last part. The new year is upon us. A time of growth and hope. A time of change."

Snow sighed, then nodded. He turned toward them and lifted both arms. Once again, the circle flared with light. This time, a whirlwind of snow rose with it. She had to close her eyes against the driving flakes. Aidan pressed his flank against hers, shielding her as best he could. At least she didn't feel the cold anymore. Still, her heart thudded, her new instincts screaming at her to run.

I trust them. I choose to trust them. I choose to open my heart to love, even with its risks.

The wind whipped against them, infusing her with an energy unlike anything she had ever felt before. Her muscles sang with it, her mind opened to possibilities she had never entertained. Flight would be nothing. Stepping between worlds an afterthought. The universe shifted and made sense in ways her mortal mind could never have comprehended.

My mortal mind... is gone...

In that moment, she knew she had become something else. Even before Snow finished, with, "Now you are my kith and kin—Lord and Lady of the North Wind."

Chapter Fourteen

The moment the wind had touched his pelt, Aidan knew it carried great power. He never would have dreamed it carried the power of the Lord of the North Wind, nor that Snow was planning on dividing that power between Sylvia and himself. It made sense, though. Even with the magic of the turning of the New Year, he wouldn't have been strong enough to turn Aidan back if Aidan had fought him. He certainly wouldn't have been able to turn Sylvia into the White Doe.

He had felt Lord Snow and Lord Kringle's powers drawing on his own, along with the powerful magic of that moment and place, but had no idea what their plan was. Aidan looked over at Sylvia, his heart filled with worry. She hadn't agreed to this. They should have asked her. Being together as humans was so different than being together as deer. Would she even want this? He hated that he couldn't just ask her, but in these forms, they couldn't speak.

I said I wanted them to do whatever it took to keep us together, and I meant it.

He felt his eyes widen as he stepped closer to her. *I can*

hear your thoughts! Can you hear mine?

I can. She nodded, the small antlers on her head glinting gold in the moonlight.

He wished she could see his smile, but that was another thing that would be hard to do in these forms. Instead, he nuzzled the side of her head again.

"The plan is not complete," Snow said, trudging toward them, his voice a low rumble. "Whatever you do, do not run. That would be very annoying."

Sylvia's muscles twitched beneath her pelt. The instinct to flee was hardwired into these forms, especially when confronted with such a powerful predator. She took a step back, but her legs went every which way. Aidan tried to keep her from falling again, but he didn't have arms to catch her and this was so much worse than before. She ended up splayed in the snow.

She let out a heavy sigh. *I thought deer were supposed to be naturally graceful.*

Aidan filled his mind with reassuring laughter. *You're a magical deer, not a natural one. But think of the perks.*

Such as?

Flight? Immortality?

It had only just hit him in that moment. Yes, they had lost a lot by taking these forms, but she was immortal now, as he was. They would have eternity together to explore the worlds. He couldn't wait to teach her everything he knew about the Faerie realms and show her all of their wonders.

I would share your excitement, but Snow is still heading our way, she thought.

He turned just as Snow arrived. Aidan held very, very still, though his own instincts screamed for him to run. Sylvia wouldn't be able to keep up. He couldn't leave her behind.

Snow shook his head, then reached down and plucked Sylvia from the snow, setting her on her feet. He kept his hands on her sides till she was steady.

"Just give me a minute before you try to walk or anything," he said.

Now that they were calmer, Aidan could better sense his heart. There was an emptiness there that had scared him before. Now that he knew its source, he was sure that he and Sylvia could help him. What made Aidan's muscles calm and his heart slow to a steadier beat was the one thing he hadn't seen before in Snow's heart—hope.

"I'll take that wish now," Lord Snow said.

Aidan blinked, but then nodded and lowered his head in a bow. Snow sucked in a quick breath, as if surprised. Beside him, Sylvia bent her front knees as if also trying to bow, but her legs wobbled and she started to fall again. Snow caught her easily and stood her back up.

"What did I say about not trying to move?" He let out a frustrated grunt, shaking his head, but his expression softened when she nuzzled his cheek with her nose.

Aidan didn't know what Snow's wish would be. He was surprised he still wanted one, after everything that had happened. But Aidan had asked Sylvia to trust Snow and Kringle. Aidan would do the same. He stood still, waiting for Snow to grip his antlers and make his wish. Instead, Snow spoke again.

"You know, when the Winter Queen found me, I had one friend in all the worlds. North. He was in his Yule Cat form all the time then. We each only had the one form. Nobody wanted to be near me, the way I looked before." He shook his head and sighed. "It was so hard to help people. But the Queen knew we could help. We could do more, if we had the right tools, the right powers, the right forms."

Aidan's heart seemed to pause, then it pounded in his chest as hope flooded him. What was Snow about to do?

"As Lord and Lady of the North Wind, you're going to need to be able to give guidance to your subjects," Snow said. "You need to be able to represent the Yuletide Kingdom in our affairs with the other Courts. You can't do it like this and you can't do it if you're constantly being hunted. I can't make people stop chasing you..." A huge grin stretched his face, his eyes crinkling up at the edges. "But I can make them really, really sorry when they catch you."

He reached up and placed one hand on Aidan's antlers and the other on Sylvia's. "My wish is for the both of you to become shifters, like North and me, but more. To have the ability to take on any form that you want or need for a given situation. Maybe you'll be deer most of the time. I'm guessing a lot of your time will be spent in human form. But I am very curious to see what else you'll get up to, especially when the next jackass comes around looking for a wish that shouldn't be granted."

Aidan's heart swelled in his chest. His eyes glazed over, blurring his vision as the greatest gratitude he had ever felt filled his body. He didn't have to look at Sylvia to know she felt the same. Their link let him feel it, her own joy was flooding through him. This was a wish he could wholeheartedly grant. Sylvia would be safe from hunters. They both would be. And they could be together. He could hold her again.

He let his joy grow within him, his power rising as the wish unfolded, mirrored in Sylvia's new powers. Their antlers glowed beneath Snow's hands, the golden light spreading over their bodies and filling the clearing as bright as a summer day. He felt his muscles shifting once more, his coat retreating. As their antlers shrank back into them, Snow's hands were drawn along with them, leaving his large palms on the sides of their heads.

Aidan looked down to see that he was back in his human form, wearing the outfit Snow had made for him. He turned to see Sylvia in her human form and snow gear as well. Her eyes were wide and flooding with tears as she smiled up at Snow. To Aidan's amazement, Snow returned her smile, warmth and affection flowing out from him.

"Thank you," she said, then threw her arms around his middle again.

"Lord Snow…" Aidan began.

"Ahh, come on." Snow shook his head, then wrapped his big arms around them both, lifting them from the ground. He squeezed them hard enough that Aidan could barely breathe, but Sylvia's reassuring laugh made him join in.

"Now, that worked out quite well, I think," Kringle said from behind them.

Snow turned and set them on the ground. The moment their feet touched the earth, Sylvia reached out and took Aidan's hand in hers, smiling up at him.

"This was your plan all along," Aidan said to Lord Kringle. "To have Snow use his wish to make us shifters after giving us the power of the North Wind so that Sylvia could become like me."

Kringle shrugged, his smile making the corners of his eyes crinkle.

"That plan had a lot of moving parts," Sylvia said. "A lot of risk."

"Not at all," Kringle said, gazing at Snow fondly. "I know Lord Snow quite well. I know his heart, as I know all of yours. As I know everyone's."

A cloud passed over his own heart briefly, some

sadness that had touched him deeply flitting through his mind. Sylvia's grip tightened on Aidan's hand, and he knew she had sensed it, too. They both took a step forward, wanting to help if they could, but Santa raised a hand and shook his head.

"Now, now," he said. "You have much to do and even more to learn. Sylvia must master her deer form, and you must both learn what it means to be Lord and Lady of the North Wind. The Winter Queen... Well, she likes things just so, isn't that right, Lord Snow?"

"Yes, it is," Snow said, nodding. "We need to train you before we present you to the Queen. That will take time, but if we mess up, she'll exile us all and replace us with jerks like Jack Frost."

"And she doesn't like to be kept waiting," Santa said. He made a point of schooling his expression in thought. "Aidan can help with the deer form, but the powers of the North Wind... Perhaps you'll need the help of an expert? Someone who has already filled the role?"

Aidan smiled as he turned to Snow. "It'll be a great opportunity for you to bond with North as he is now. Just the Yule Cat."

"And we'll be there with you to support you every step of the way," Sylvia added.

Snow nodded, then rested his large hands on their shoulders. "Then it's time for your first lesson as the Lord and Lady of the Yuletide Court."

"What's that?" Sylvia asked.

Smiling, he said, "Portals."

Chapter Fifteen

Sylvia sat at one of the tables in The Yuletide Bakery. It wasn't her usual spot at the two-seater in the corner, out of everyone's way. She was right in the center, at the biggest table they had, and every chair was filled. Snow took up two seats as he shook his head and laughed at yet another hilarious story North Cotter, no longer Lord of the North Wind, was sharing with them all. Those two had really been up to some mischief in the millennia of their existence.

Melanie, the human woman North had fallen in love with, kept running back and forth from the kitchen to the bakery, bringing them more cookies and pastries, while North kept their cups filled with coffee or cocoa or tea. Sylvia had offered to help, but they definitely already had a routine going, and with the bakery closed for the New Year's Day holiday, they had the place to themselves. Melanie had also shared that Santa had given her the gift of immortality, technically making her one of the Fae, just as Sylvia was.

She still couldn't believe it. She was the White Doe, whatever that meant. Would she be able to grant wishes?

Would she be forced to? The powers that Snow had given them were beyond what she could conceive of at the moment. Then again, the powers of the North Wind were nothing to mess around with, either.

A few times, the napkins at the table had begun to stir as she or Aidan became too carried away with their stories. North had been quick to jump in and coach them through the moments, but there had still been an incident or two when cups were overturned and napkins blew away. She had so much to learn, but then, she had forever to learn it.

Aidan smiled over at her, squeezing her hand that he held under the table, their fingers interlaced. His love flowed through her, reminding her that she wouldn't be alone in this. She would never be alone again.

I'm not the only reason you won't be alone, he thought. He nodded toward the table, bringing her attention back to the people sitting around it.

"Hey, we're out of cookies." Snow held up a massive plate that only held crumbs.

"I'll go get more," Melanie said, rising. A glowing golden pixie flitted around her head, following as she headed toward the kitchen. Just another magical thing that everyone treated as everyday in the bakery.

"I'll help so we can put a few more batches in the ovens." North took the plate and nudged Snow with his shoulder. "This one is a bottomless pit."

"Ehh." Snow 'nudged' him back, sending North

staggering a few paces. Both men grinned.

When they were alone, Sylvia reached out with her free hand and grasped Snow's hand that was resting on the table.

"I don't feel like I've properly thanked you," she said.

Snow shrugged. "You did. But, hey, I made out on the deal. I have the White Stag. I have a Lord and Lady of the North Wind to present to the Winter Queen—when you're ready. And best of all, I don't have to work with that jackass, Frost."

Sylvia shook her head, sensing that he was deflecting the greater part of the emotions roiling through him. She had gained the same ability to read hearts that Aidan had when she'd been made his counterpart as the White Doe. Snow was concerned about his choices. He worried about how the Winter Queen might react to him not obeying her command. He had taken a huge risk for them.

Sylvia squeezed his hand, and said, "You gave me all these powers and immortality and a chance to be with the love of my life." She turned to smile at Aidan, his love warming her. Addressing Snow again, she said, "But there's something else I haven't thanked you for yet."

"What's that?" Snow asked, one eyebrow arched as genuine curiosity flowed from him.

"You brought me into your family," she said. "A family like I've always dreamed of having. And any sort of family isn't something I've had for a long time."

He tightened his grip on her hand and nodded tersely. "No one should be without a family. Least of all someone with a heart as warm as yours."

His eyes widened and he looked away, embarrassment edging out the curiosity from just before. Sylvia rose up from her seat and wrapped her arms around Snow's neck, giving him a huge hug. He stiffened at first, then chuckled, patting her back as he returned her hug.

The door to the kitchen opened, and she heard North say, "Are we missing out on hugs?"

Sylvia stood straighter, but left one arm around Snow's shoulders. She smiled at Aidan, then glanced down to point out that Snow had left one arm around her waist as well.

"This guy gives the best hugs in all the worlds, you know," North said, setting another huge plate of cookies in front of them before pulling out Melanie's chair. "At least, when he means it."

"There's a reason bear hugs are so famous," Snow said and chuckled.

They all joined in, laughter ringing through the space. Sylvia's heart was filled with such warmth, she thought she might burst. The wind picked up, stirring her hair, but she was able to calm it herself this time. Aidan nodded, his face beaming with pride as he rose and stood by her side, wrapping an arm around her shoulders as she clasped his waist with her free arm.

Thanks to a New Year's wish and so many people being willing to trust each other, this was her future. A place where she belonged with friends, family, and the most magical gift of all. True love.

Epilogue

Five Weeks Later

Snow set out down the sidewalk, heading toward his closest home, not far from the Yuletide Bakery. He needed to contact Malachi, the steward who was acting in Snow's place while he was in the mortal realm, and check on the newest members of his Court. There were many things to keep moving in the Yuletide Kingdom. Snow looked forward to when Aidan and Sylvia would be ready to assist him with them. They were almost there.

Snow had to believe he had made the right choice. Otherwise, what he had done was certain to get him banished form the Yuletide Kingdom. The idea of working with Frost, giving that jackass more power... Snow would never regret making Aidan and Sylvia the Lord and Lady of the North Wind. Snow just had to figure out what his next move was.

How could he spin this so that the Winter Queen wouldn't banish all of them and take back the powers she had given them? At least she couldn't take the powers granted by Snow's wish for Aidan and Sylvia. He was comforted in knowing they would be safe.

"Well, well, well," an obnoxious voice said. "Look what the cat dragged down to his rebellious level."

Snow's skin prickled with the urge to take on his polar bear form, turn around, and in one fluid movement knock the speaker's head from his shoulders. He took a deep breath and let it out slow, forcing himself to calm. Glancing over his shoulder, he saw Jack Frost sitting on a mailbox, one knee raised and the other dangling over its side.

"What do you want, Frost?" Snow asked.

"What do I want?" He pressed his fingertips against his chest, his ice-blue eyes widening in mock surprise. "Wow, it's so kind of you to ask. Let's see, what *do* I want?"

"I have stuff to do." Snow shook his head and continued down the street.

"Stuff like defying the Queen?"

Snow stopped, fists clenching at his sides. Frost slid from the mailbox, then turned and kicked it over.

"That's a felony," Snow said.

"Like I care about mortal laws or mortal..." he waved his fingers in the air dismissively "anything."

The more he talked, the more certain Snow became that he had done the right thing. He walked back to the mailbox and righted it, picking up the letters that had spilled from it and tucking them into the box.

"How very civic-minded of you," Frost said. "If only

you had half as much respect for the rule of the Winter Queen."

"Keep talking," Snow said. "I'm pretty sure I can shove you into that mailbox, too."

Frost snorted. "You could always mail me to Kringle. Maybe he has an opening since you just gave away what is rightfully mine. And to that dumb deer-guy and his previously mortal whatever-she-is?"

"Watch it," Snow said. "They'll be a thousand-fold better at being Lord and Lady of the North Wind than you would be."

"That wasn't for you to decide," Frost snapped.

Rage twisted his features into a dark maelstrom, his black eyebrows arcing on his forehead, his eyes glowing livid blue as the sound of crackling ice spread from where he stood. A blast of frost shot out from his body, enveloping Snow in a thick coat of cold. Snow smirked, then stomped a foot, the frost falling harmlessly to the ground.

"Neat trick," Snow said. "Kinda tickled. I'm the Lord of Endless Snow, remember?"

Frost stepped forward, then blurred, appearing right in Snow's face. Well, a foot down from it. Snow didn't flinch. Frost stared at him balefully for a few moments before his features reverted to their usual appearance. He smiled.

"I'm a pain in the ass on a good day, right?" Frost said.

Snow shrugged, but nodded.

"And that's when I'm being my usual playful, whimsical self," Frost said. His features darkened slightly as he continued. "Just imagine what I can be like when I'm *pissed off.*" He shook himself and smiled again, then reached up and straightened Snow's jacket. "You won't have to imagine for long."

In a puff of cold mist, he disappeared.

Snow stood on the sidewalk for a few moments. It wasn't that he was worried about Frost. That blowhard wouldn't be able to touch Snow. But he could cause trouble for the people Snow cared about, both in the Yuletide Kingdom and in the mortal realm.

Snow needed to get Aidan and Sylvia firmly set in their places as Lord and Lady of the North Wind. He needed the Winter Queen to recognize them to keep them safe from Frost and others that would come running at the first sign of weakness. Their training had gone well with North's help. They couldn't delay it any more. It was time to go home.

—

Thank you so much for reading *The White Stag!* This trilogy has become one of my own comfort reads, and this book is especially tender for me. I hope it brought you joy and laughter and can't wait to share with you what happens next!

The magic comes full circle in the final book of the trilogy, *The Krampus*. I have so much in store for Lord Snow before he reaches his own "happily ever after." Read on to see how the Krampus fares when he introduces the new Lord and Lady of the North Wind to the Winter Queen!

COURT OF THE YULETIDE FAE

THE KRAMPUS

USA TODAY BESTSELLING AUTHOR
CASSANDRA CHANDLER

The Krampus

Court of the Yuletide Fae
Book Three

Cassandra Chandler

Chapter One

Five weeks, two days, eleven hours, and thirty-five minutes. That was how long Lord Snow had been in the mortal realm training the new Lord and Lady of the North Wind for their duties. He was ready to go home.

While the mortal realm wasn't quite the pit that most of the Fae thought, Snow still didn't want to hang around any longer than he had to. They called him 'the Krampus,' by the Gods' sake, and made up horrible stories about him. *Him*—the Lord of Endless Snow. Why would he want to stick around a place like that?

Across the main room of the Yuletide Bakery, his best friend, North snuck up behind his mate, Melanie, and wrapped his arms around her waist to pull her against his chest in a hug. She laughed and swatted at him, trying to arrange a plate of cookies in their bakery. Snow's newest friends, Aidan and Sylvia—also known as the White Stag and… the Fae Lady soon to be known as the White Doe— observed, also laughing. Aidan darted forward and snatched a handful of the cookies, earning him a playful swat of his own from Melanie and a look of reproach.

Snow's heart ached oddly and he rubbed the spot. It felt hollow, like something was missing in his chest. The mortal realm often had this effect on him. He didn't like it. The longer they stayed, the stronger the feeling became. He was certain it would also make it harder for Aidan and Sylvia to leave.

"It's time," Snow said, his voice calm and low, yet carrying across the space.

The others froze in place, their smiles falling. Aidan and Sylvia looked to each other and nodded, but Melanie rushed forward.

"It's too soon," she said. "They need more training."

Snow shook his head. "They're more than ready. The longer we wait, the more angry the Winter Queen will become at our absence."

"All the more reason to—"

"Melanie," Sylvia said. "It's okay. Really, it's okay." She looked to Snow with a smile that suffused the hollowness in his chest. At least it also warmed the space. "If Snow says we're ready, we're ready."

North pulled Aidan into a bro hug and clapped the man on the back. "Remember everything I taught you. You'll be a fine Lord of the North Wind."

"I learned from the best," Aidan said.

Melanie's eyes filled with tears, but she forced herself to smile as she hugged Sylvia as well. "You'll come to visit me, right?"

"As often as I can." Sylvia kissed Melanie's dark hair before pulling back.

All of them had become so close during Aidan and Sylvia's training. Snow hated to separate them from their friends, but it was inevitable. If things went well, they would be able to come and go from the mortal realm whenever they liked. If things didn't go well...

This will work. It has to work.

Snow had several contingency plans, each more desperate than the last. He was certain he wouldn't have to use any of them. He stood straighter, exuding confidence to help inspire those who looked up to him. Aidan caught his eye and nodded, then offered his arm to Sylvia. The pair approached Snow with perfect posture, shoulders back and heads held high like the Fairy Lord and Lady that they had become. Snow smiled down at them, then pulled them into a hug. He was so proud of all they had learned.

The Winter Queen would accept them. He was sure of it.

The castle seemed bigger than Snow remembered. And much, much colder. Spending weeks in the mortal realm had made him too accustomed to warmth. He led Aidan and Sylvia toward the throne room, pausing briefly to glance at their attire and make sure the magical clothes he had fashioned for them were acceptable.

Sylvia's red hair was a flame against the white gown she wore. The fabric sparkled with diamonds that gleamed in the light cast from the crystal walls of the castle. A mesh of diamonds in platinum chains held her hair in a chignon and a white silk cape lined with gray-specked fur was fastened around her shoulders.

Aidan wore a similar cape, along with a princely jacket that suited his new station. Or at least the station that Snow was hoping he would soon officially be bestowed. His dark hair was a sharp contrast to the white clothing Snow had created for him.

"You're going to do great," Snow said quietly as they entered the room. "Just remember everything I taught you."

The Winter Queen sat on her crystal throne in the middle of an enormous dais. The entire room had been grown from magical crystal that glowed from within, granting a soft light to the space. Usually, two ornate thrones sat at her sides, one for Lord Snow and the other for Lord North. Today, there were none. Snow led Aidan and Sylvia to the center of the room, then approached the Queen's throne and bowed deeply.

After a silence that stretched on for several minutes, the Winter Queen said, "Lord Snow, you have been gone far longer than expected. I had begun to wonder if you, too, had abandoned me."

"Never, my Queen," Snow said, rising to meet her stern gaze. "I regret that it took me too long to succumb to your wisdom. I see now that North is lost to us."

His stomach churned with nerves. Did she know that North was still the Yule Cat? And that Snow had defied her decrees in so many other ways? He was certain that she would be happy with his choices eventually, but not so sure she could forgive his willingness to go against what she had proclaimed.

"I have done as you said and brought back the Lord of the North Wind." He swallowed hard, hoping fervently that she would accept Aidan and Sylvia. If the Queen rejected them, he would protect them. Any punishment would fall on his shoulders alone. He'd make sure of it.

"Yet I do not see Jack Frost," she said, looking pointedly over the heads of Aidan and Sylvia.

"True, but I bring another." He gestured toward Aidan. "I present to you the new Lord and Lady of the North Wind."

Aidan bowed low and Sylvia curtseyed, both of them holding the postures of deference, their eyes cast down to the floor.

"You present to me the new Lord and Lady of the North Wind?" the Winter Queen said. "Their manners are better than the last 'new Lady' you brought before me, but that hardly makes up for defying me. I know that North remains the Yule Cat. And now you have taken the power I entrusted to you and placed it within these people who are unknown to me."

"Majesty, I beg your forgiveness," Snow said, bowing even lower than before. "I could not bring myself to take away the essence that North was born with. He has been the Yule Cat for as long as I have been... the Krampus." He hated claiming the name, but knew the importance of this moment. "When you found us, you saw potential and gifted us with powers to serve you better, to serve the Yuletide Kingdom. I believe that North can yet be of service to us, but this pair will be an even better Lord and Lady of the North Wind."

"And why would you think that?" she asked in an imperious voice.

Snow stood, then nodded to Aidan and Sylvia, stepping away. Aidan took Sylvia's hand and nodded to her as well, no doubt encouraging her. She was trembling slightly from nerves. The cold no longer affected her after gaining the powers Snow had granted to her—some of which she was more proficient at than others. Shifting... she was still getting used to.

Silver light covered their bodies, suffusing their forms until they were merely silhouettes. Their shapes began changing, antlers sprouting from their heads, faces becoming muzzles, and bodies falling forward onto four legs as they assumed their deer forms. The light withdrew, leaving them white as snow, their coats gleaming with inner radiance. Their antlers were gold and put off their own light, as did their golden irises.

The Winter Queen's eyes widened as she rose from her throne, her hands clasped tightly in front of her. She took a step forward, then another and another. When she reached the steps, she hurried down them, approaching the White Stag and the White Doe with what Snow hoped was wonder in her eyes. She reached out to touch them, and Snow held his breath. Though Aidan and Sylvia were skittish in this form, neither flinched as the Winter Queen rested her hands on their muzzles.

"Oh, Krampus," the Queen said, a wistful note in her voice that he had never heard before. "You have done well."

She continued to touch both Sylvia and Aidan's faces, even going so far as to stroke their foreheads lightly. Snow couldn't believe the wonder in her expressive face as she looked at them. His heart gave a little tug as he realized he had never seen her truly happy. Not as he'd seen North and Melanie being, nor Aidan and Sylvia. For the briefest moment, Snow wondered what that would feel like for himself. He quickly buried the thought.

"You will be wondrous additions to my court," the Queen said, resting one of her hands on each of the deers' cheeks.

Her expression clouded, her eyebrows pinching together and her smile fading as she stepped back, pulling her hands away as if startled. Aidan followed, as did Sylvia. Krampus was about to intervene, uncertain of what was going on, but all they did was gently bump their noses against her arms. The Queen's lips tightened and she pulled her fisted hands up to her heart, holding them there like a shield.

Aidan dropped to his knees in a cumbersome bow for his current stag form. He bowed his head so low that his nose touched the ground. Sylvia looked over at him, then made a disgruntled squeak. Her legs shook as she gingerly maneuvered herself into a position they had never practiced in this form.

Sylvia stared at the knees of her forelegs—which did not bend at all the way her elbows did when those limbs were arms—then let out a sigh and started to lower herself. Snow held his breath to see if she could manage it. At first, it looked as though she would make it, but then she started to lose her balance. Aidan began to rise, but it was the Queen who reached Sylvia first.

The tall woman launched herself forward, wrapping her arms around Sylvia's chest and steadying her. Together, the women lowered themselves to the ground. Sylvia's ears flicked with interest as she looked up into the Queen's wide green eyes. The doe bowed her head in the Queen's embrace.

"You may be in the form that is of greatest ease to you, child," the Queen said.

Silver light swept over Sylvia as she reverted to her human form. She was still on all fours on the floor. Snow wanted to cover his eyes and shake his head, but he also couldn't look away from the scene unfolding before him. The Queen kept her hold on Sylvia, grasping her elbows and helping her rise amid the voluminous folds of her gown.

The Queen glanced at Snow as they rose, her cheeks actually flushing pink for the first time—in his presence at least. This was so much better than he had even hoped. The Queen was not only accepting Aidan and Sylvia, but seemed delighted by them. He was well on his way to bringing his family back together again. He just had to get the Queen to forgive North for choosing Melanie over his duty to her.

The Queen turned to Aidan and said, "You as well, Lord North."

Snow's cheeks pinched as he felt the biggest smile he'd ever had stretch his face. She had accepted Aidan. Snow was sure she would accept Sylvia, too. Aidan glowed bright silver as he rose up on his back legs, resuming his human form. He bowed again, and the Queen angled her head toward him in response.

She pulled Sylvia up the steps of the dais with her. As they approached the throne, two more chairs grew from the crystal floor—smaller, of course, but just as ornate and beautiful. Snow felt his mouth drop open as the Queen swirled her finger and a cushion appeared on the chair at her left. She set Sylvia on it, then turned to Aidan and gestured him toward the other seat. With a quick glance to Snow, Aidan hurried after them. He didn't sit until the Queen did.

Snow's heart was pounding in his throat. She had definitely accepted them, but there was a coldness in her bearing as she looked at him. His misgiving grew when she turned to him with a distinct frown.

"You have done well in bringing me Lord North and Lady... Silver," the Queen said. "But that does not excuse your defiance. I had expected Jack Frost to be among my court."

Snow opened his mouth to say something, but snapped it shut. Sylvia was squirming in her seat, obviously also wanting to jump in, but they had gone over this time and time again. The Queen had a temper that burned icy hot. It was best not to get in the way of it.

He dropped to one knee, bowing his head deeply. "Majesty, I beg your forgiveness," he said.

Silence grew in the room. Snow's heart was a constant drumbeat in his ears. If she exiled him, as she had North, then Aidan and Sylvia would be on their own navigating their new duties. He didn't want that for them. Snow knew that his subjects could keep things running. He had trained them well. But this was his home. He had done all of this because the Queen and her court and all their subjects were his family. He didn't want to lose that.

"Forgiveness is something that takes time," she said, her voice barely above a whisper. "And sometimes distance as well."

Was she banishing him? He wasn't sure. Her demeanor was so unlike what he was used to. Again, the silence stretched on.

"Lord Snow," she said.

He closed his eyes and let out a huge breath, the tension knotting his back easing somewhat. She still called him 'Lord Snow.' He wasn't being banished.

"Return to the mortal realm," she said. "I will summon you to return when I am ready."

When would that be? How long did she need him to stay away? She hadn't said he couldn't contact anyone in the Yuletide Kingdom, so he would be able to check in with his seneschals, but still… His mind filled with a thousand questions, scenarios, and endless lists of tasks required to keep things running well. It had only been himself alone for so long while North was in exile—an exile Snow had hoped to ease, not share.

"Majesty, if I may?" Sylvia said in a gentle voice.

Snow's heart sank. He didn't want her to get in the middle of this. Things were going too well for them. He didn't dare look up, but he heard the swish of fabric as Sylvia approached him. She wrapped her arms around his shoulders, her hug bringing her lips close to his ear.

"We'll be okay, you can trust us," she whispered. "Just give her the time she needs." Sylvia rose and returned to her spot at the Queen's side.

"You are kind," the Queen said. "As can I be as well."

"Of course, majesty," Snow said.

He stood, but didn't dare look up at her. He did give Aidan a quick nod. The White Stag's eyes were wide, his jaw tense. Why wouldn't he be nervous, watching his ally and mentor leave him in a situation where Snow was supposed to be to guide him through?

His heart was heavy as he walked from the throne room. Once more, he had disappointed his Queen. Worse, Aidan and Sylvia were being left to navigate this tricky situation on their own. Snow had at least prepared his seneschals for such an eventuality, but he had thought it an unlikely scenario for the new Lord and Lady.

His steps were slow as he ascended the steps that would lead him outside of the castle. This wasn't the start Aidan and Sylvia deserved. Most of all, he hated the feeling that he had failed them.

Chapter Two

The Yuletide Bakery always had something special going on. Christmas was the biggest holiday of the year, of course, with the bakery being Christmas-themed year round, but the owner, North Cotter, dressed up the store for every holiday Spring had heard of and several that she hadn't. He baked special holiday-themed cookies as well as serving everyone's perennial favorites. Valentine's Day was no exception.

Bright red hearts that seemed to sparkle from within dangled from the ceiling or hung against the weathered brick walls. The ever-present tree glittered with silver, gold, and red ornaments that continued the theme. Little silver sculptures of lovers kissing or embracing— tastefully, of course—sat along the tops of the display cases. Inside the cases, all kinds of chocolate treats, cookies, and petit fours delighted the eye before delighting the tastebuds. This was truly one of her happiest places.

Spring was sitting at one of the tall tables near the main display cases and the register in a sort of nook nestled between the tree and a rough-hewn stone fireplace that crackled with a lovely fire. The nook was partially under a staircase that wrapped around two walls heading for the second story. It wasn't her favorite place to sit, but it was warm and cozy, and she could see and hear all the most interesting happenings while staying out of everyone's way.

The bakery was hopping. People came in to buy boxes of heart-shaped cookies for Valentine's Day office parties or more specialized pastries as gifts or self-indulgences. The baristas were doing brisk business as well, what with all the snow piling on. Ever since Christmas, it seemed like there was a steady stream of flakes coming down. Spring loved the wintery weather and all the cozy sweaters, stylish coats, and cute matching hats, gloves, and scarves involved, but she was starting to really look forward to… well, spring.

Everything in its own time.

She didn't want to rush through one of her favorite holidays, even if she was spending this one on her own. She settled into her spot as she took a sip of her frappé coffee. The sweetened condensed milk was perfectly balanced with the bitter coffee. Knowing she'd be tucked away near the fire, she had opted for the cold beverage to help keep her from overheating in the snug space.

She had brought her own travel mug, and sipped from the built-in straw as she looked out over the bakery. Several tables had families sitting around them. Her smile softened as she watched a mother with a toddler sitting on her knee, her arms tight around the child's middle as she gave him a hug. He lifted a heart-shaped sugar cookie to feed it to her and they both laughed as it took him several tries to get his aim right for her mouth.

A familiar pain lanced through Spring's chest along with the warmth of the moment. Not physical pain—but the pain of loss. She would never have children of her own. Fate had other plans for her. At least, that's what Spring chose to believe when doctor after doctor told her the same thing. Maybe she couldn't have her own family, but she could use her PR company to help support non-profits that supported families in need. Her team did regular pro-bono work with several local foster care and adoption agencies, and she donated a hefty amount of their profits to social services organizations that helped children.

She put her hand over her heart and took a deep breath in through her nose, then blew it out slowly through her mouth, visualizing a golden light soothing the hurt and filling her heart with warmth. Someday, she'd meet a man who understood her circumstances and how she felt about it and would support her in her own dreams of fostering.

Luck hadn't been on her side with that so far, either. The few guys she'd been serious with who had said they were okay with her goals and her situation eventually bailed. That was fine with her, though. No serious relationships meant more time to build up her company and devote to her charity work. Plus, it gave her more opportunities to enjoy herself with the men who caught her eye.

As if summoned by her thought, a huge man strode past her table, circling around behind the out-of-the-way display case that was nearest the staircase Spring was tucked beneath. He must be pushing seven feet tall and looked like he spent most of his day at the gym bulking up. His gait was filled with confidence, his bearing clearly broadcasting that he was the absolute alpha in the room. Of course, he hadn't met Spring yet. She smirked at the idea of how that introduction might go, tingling warmth spreading over her arms as she imagined different scenarios.

He walked right to North, who was working behind the display case, and the two men stood chatting quietly. With his chiseled jaw, and constantly windswept hair, North was as easy on the eyes as his baked goods were on the tongue. Spring was sure many of the female clientele for the bakery came in just to see him, though they were in for a disappointment. He had acquired a shadow recently in the form of a lovely brunette with big blue eyes, pale skin, and a smile that made it impossible to hate her, even if she'd landed one of the most eligible bachelors in town.

North was nice to look at, but Spring had never pined for him. He was too much like the guys she usually dated, and honestly, she was so bored with 'the usual.' Maybe that was why her heart seemed to stutter when the new man flexed his back, his muscles rippling beneath his dark blue three-piece suit. It probably cost as much as a small car. The silky material of his jacket accentuated his broad shoulders and hugged his massive biceps. His slacks showcased his long legs and muscular thighs.

Yeah, Spring was pretty smitten. It had been a long time since she'd been so attracted to a man. Actually, the more she thought about it, she'd never been this attracted to someone before. She took another sip of her frappé, watching the pair as they stood near enough for her to hear every word of their conversation. Although, the more she listened, the less it made sense.

"Look, it's been less than a week," the huge man said.

"I know." North shook his head. "All I'm saying is that I think you should be asking Malachi to step in for them more. Help them out with the political stuff."

"And have them be seen as weak by the other courts when they're making their first impressions?" the man said. "No way."

North shook his head. "It won't be seen as weakness, Snow."

Snow? That huge, gorgeous, incredibly well-dressed guy was named *Snow*?

"Just because Melanie blew it—" Snow said.

"Hey!" The brunette was actually with them, though

she was so small, Spring hadn't been able to see her at first, the men blocking her from view. Now, Spring had a name for her, too.

"Come on, man," North said, pulling Melanie against his side as she glared at Snow.

Snow took a deep breath, expanding his chest to an incredible size, then let it out slowly. The silken fabric of his jacket pulled across the muscles of his back, the seams straining to hold together. Spring could relate. She pulled her lower lip between her teeth, imagining what it would be like to slide her hands along those shoulders. Maybe while they slow-danced to some soft jazz music.

"Okay." Snow's rumbly voice grew tighter as he spoke. "Just because Melanie didn't know what she was doing and made an epically bad first impression…" He trailed off, noticing how North and Melanie stared at him.

North shrugged to Melanie. "That's probably as good an apology as we're going to get."

Melanie frowned, but she was the one to speak next. "We were just thinking that if Malachi was able to give them a little more guidance, maybe they could work together and find a way to help spring return."

Snow shook his head. "Everyone keeps forgetting that I'm the Lord of Endless Snow. *Snow.* Not spring. You know what spring has going for it?"

North and Melanie looked at each other and shrugged.

"Not snow, that's what," Snow said.

Spring busted out with a laugh. She couldn't help it. Snow glanced over his shoulder at her, his lips a thin, disapproving line. Oh goodness, he was even better to look at from the front. Black hair close-cropped against his scalp, though a bit longer on the top, strong features, dark eyes that seemed to bore into her. Her skin rose in goosebumps as he quickly assessed her, then glanced back again, as if the first look hadn't been quite enough. She smirked at him, lifting her phone and intimating that she had been scrolling through messages when she laughed. He was so huge, it was easy to see him in her periphery when he turned his attention back to his friends.

"I have to go help out in the kitchen," Melanie said. "But give it some thought."

She squeezed Snow's arm, then stood on her tip toes and stared at him expectantly. He sighed and shifted his weight from one foot to the other, then bent down so that she could plant a quick kiss on his cheek. North didn't seem the least bit jealous, so Spring didn't see why she should be. Besides, she couldn't keep from smiling at the sweet gesture, or the way Snow's posture had relaxed a little when he straightened. Both men watched Melanie hurry through the kitchen door.

"I know you mean well and you want the best for us all," North said. "But ignoring this won't help anyone. It's time. We need to make a move to try to—"

"Try to what?" Snow said. "Start a rebellion?"

"Hell no." North actually took a step back, shaking his head emphatically. "Try to help the Winter Queen," he said. "Bringing back spring will mean she's healed. It'll mean the whole kingdom is healed."

Kingdom? Winter Queen? This was starting to sound like a fairy tale. Maybe they were in a play together. Except, the seriousness on both men's faces struck her as absolutely real.

"I need to help out the others in the kitchen," North said. He also reached out and gripped Snow's arm, then leaned in as if to plant one on him. Though he was obviously joking, Snow recoiled and flailed his arms, making North retreat.

"What, no sugar for me?" North said, feigning confusion.

"Get out of here," Snow said, an exasperated note to his voice.

North kept laughing all the way through the kitchen door while Snow stood with his hands on his hips, shaking his head. The view was spectacular, but Spring was done being a spectator. She slid from her stool and approached him from behind so he wouldn't see her till she was ready.

"Everybody's so in love with spring," Snow murmured. "I don't get it. It's just a season. Has a lot of flowers. So what?"

"Wow, were you born that cynical, or has life just been too hard on you?"

Spring made sure that she was standing in the perfect pose to catch his attention when he turned. Arms crossed over her chest in a way that would 'enhance her assets,' one hip stuck out at a cocky, yet alluring angle. She plastered her best 'I know a secret you don't know' smirk on her face and waited to assess his reaction. This one wouldn't be an easy conquest.

"Excuse me?" he said, looming over her.

The shirt beneath his jacket and vest was such a dark blue, it was nearly black. His midnight blue tie caught the light and sparkled almost like there were diamonds or stars woven into the fabric.

"Do you think you intimidate me just because you're huge?" She shook her head, stepping closer. "The bigger they are, the harder they fall." Her smirk deepened as she leaned close, daring to run a fingertip over the lapel of his suit. "Besides, I'm a size queen."

"What does that even…" He shook his head, but she noticed him intently studying her again. He didn't seem to know what to make of her. Finally he took in a deep breath and said, "It's bad manners to listen in on other people's conversations."

Running to the rules for a rescue? She could work with that. She lifted his tie, delighting in the silken texture and mesmerized by the starlike pattern that seemed to dance and weave among the fibers. Looking up at him, she gave it a bit of a tug, then let the fabric slip through her fingers.

"Well, if you think I've been naughty, you're welcome to spank me," she said.

His eyebrows shot up and his mouth dropped open. It wasn't quite the reaction she had expected or hoped for, but it was definitely entertaining. The way she figured it, either he would take her up on her offer, and they would have a grand time together, or he'd be intrigued enough to ask her out maybe.

Of course, there was the chance he'd be offended and storm off. That would be a helpful reaction, too. If he couldn't laugh at himself or let loose and have a little fun, there was no way she would want to start something with him. Deep down, she had a feeling he was a softy, though. And the idea of unraveling that tightly wound exterior was an irresistible challenge.

"But you're the one being rude and badmouthing spring," she said.

"What the hell do you care what I think of it?" he said.

"Well, for one, it's a glorious season, full of hope and promise."

He crossed his arms over his truly massive chest. "And allergens."

"And bunnies."

"Aha," he said, pointing a finger at her as he towered over her. "Winter has bunnies, too."

"But those are cold bunnies." She stepped closer, and pushed her mouth into just enough of a pout to draw his attention to her lips. "Don't you want the bunnies to be warm?"

"I don't..." He blinked a few times, his voice trailing off as he stared at her mouth. "Wait, what?"

He was even cuter when he was flustered. His gaze once more darted over her, lingering in some... interesting areas. His eyebrows pulled more tightly together over his eyes.

Oh, this guy would be really fun. That much passion crammed into such an amazing package. She wanted to be the one to loosen the hinges and watch it fly everywhere.

"I don't care if spring ever comes." He said each word forcefully, again stepping closer. The lapels of his very expensive suit brushed against her chest.

She bit the inside of her cheek to keep from laughing. In a low voice that had him leaning closer to hear her, she said, "Then you are never taking me to dinner."

"Why would I want to?" he said, his voice exasperated.

She arched an eyebrow at him and cocked her head to the side, pouting her lips. A muscle in his jaw started to twitch as she let the silence stretch on.

"And why can't I?" he finally demanded.

She ran her fingertips under the lapels of his suit, smoothing them, then brushed her hand down along his tie with just enough pressure to tantalize him.

"Well, that's the other reason I care what you think of this particular season," she said. She lifted his tie, then used it to pull him closer as she rose on her tip-toes. With her lips a breath away from his ear, she whispered, "Because my name is Spring."

Chapter Three

What was wrong with this mortal? The things she said didn't make any sense, but the way she talked drew Snow in. Her hair was gold as warm sunlight, spilling over her shoulders in soft waves. Her large blue eyes sparkled with mirth even when she wasn't laughing, and her smirk made him feel like he was missing out on something important. Something he needed to know. Worst of all, she wouldn't stop touching him.

She said her name was Spring, and a thrum of magic let him know she spoke the truth. For a moment, he wondered if perhaps she was from the Court of the Springtime Fae, but none of them would carry that name. He doubted the embodiment of spring itself would have manifested just to drop by and talk to him, even with all the happenings in the Yuletide Kingdom.

No, this was a mortal. A strange, compelling, aggravating mortal.

"This is when you tell me your name," Spring said. "It's only polite."

"Names carry power. They aren't to be tossed around

lightly."

"I can't just call you Snow."

"Aha, I knew you were listening."

Her lips pulled into an odd frown, almost like an upside-down smirk. "What I heard didn't make any sense. And it doesn't really count as eavesdropping when people are standing right next to you having a conversation as if you aren't there."

"We didn't know you were there."

"Did you expect me to get up and leave?" she asked, dropping his tie and placing one fisted hand on her hip. "Flail my arms and say, 'Guys, I can hear you' maybe?"

"I expected you not to come up and talk to me like... Like..."

"Like what?"

She stepped closer, whispers of her perfume swirling around him with the light scent of flowers. The sweet fragrance clouded his mind. Everything about this woman was clouding his mind, and he didn't have time for it. When she reached for his tie again, he stood straighter and pulled the fabric from her fingers, tucking it back beneath his vest and smoothing it down.

"Like you know me," Snow said. "You don't." The words sent an odd pang through him, fluttering within that hollowness in his chest.

"True," she said. "But I'd like to."

Something in him sparked, a quick bolt of energy

charging along his nerves and sending tingles of awareness over his flesh. The way she looked at him, the warmth in her eyes and smile… It was dangerous. Mostly because he wanted more. He wanted to explore what that sultry smile meant and unravel the secrets hidden in that mysterious smirk.

The smirk was the worst. And the single arched eyebrow. She was staring at him as if she knew secrets that not even he was privy to. He didn't like it.

"Why do you always have that smile on your face?" he said.

Her eyebrows both lifted at that. "Wow, that's a refreshing change. Usually guys are always telling women to smile, but you prefer a scowl." She cocked her head to the side, her smirk softening a bit. "Spoiler alert. I'm going to smile if I want to. But maybe I'll throw you a scowl from time to time. If you earn it."

"Lucky me."

She brought her beverage up to her mouth while holding his focus, lips slowly parting before wrapping around the straw. Somehow, the sight sent more of those electric tingles zinging through his body. His hands opened and curled into fists, and he had the strangest urge to grab her and pull her closer.

"What is that thing that you're drinking?" he asked, scowling.

"This?" Spring took another sip of her drink, holding

their eye contact and smirking as she did. "It's a frappé. Want some?"

She held the drink out to him, but he shook his head.

"What the heck is a frappé?"

"Coffee and condensed milk over ice." She lifted the cup and stared at it, assessing. "It's cold and bitter at first, but really sweet once you get used to it."

As she said the last, she lowered her drink and winked at him. He found himself leaning forward, his body inching closer to her. She was a distraction, and he did not have time to be distracted. Too many people were counting on him. He pulled himself back, shaking his head.

"You seem really..." His voice trailed off. What did she seem like?

Provocative. Beautiful. Aggressive.

"*Aggressive*," he said, a bit louder than he intended.

That's what it was that intrigued him. Well, among a host of other things. Another wave of appreciative heat flowed through him. He respected when people went after what they wanted with everything they had. But he didn't know what she wanted or who she was or what her hidden motives were. Everyone had hidden motives and agendas. With the Yuletide Kingdom going through so many transitions, he didn't dare let himself slip.

"I know what I want and I'm not afraid to go after it." She lowered her voice as she went on so that once more he had to bend closer to hear her. "And between you and me,

I usually get it."

He straightened again, shaking his head. She was too good at drawing him in. He stepped away, straightening his tie.

"If you'll excuse me," he said. "I have business to attend to."

"I bet you do."

That damn smirk of hers. What did she know that he didn't? What was she hiding?

He didn't have time to unravel her mysteries. She was mortal. That was all he needed to know about her. Mortals had no business with the Fae. He turned and walked away, hurrying through the bakery toward the front door. He swore he could feel her eyes on him the entire time.

As soon as he was outside, he took a deep breath of the freezing winter air. It flooded his lungs, invigorating him. This was his season, his energy, his power. This, he understood. He was the Lord of Endless Snow. And he did have business he needed to tend to.

He turned toward his closest office, his long strides carrying him quickly over the sidewalk. Three steps from the bakery's front door, his foot hit a patch of glassy ice and flew out from under him. He flipped up into the air and landed flat on his back, the wind knocked out of him.

That should not have happened. He should have sensed the ice on the ground, just as he could feel the energy of the snow all around him. This was his season, except...

Except he shared it with others. Others who held sway over the elements of cold, just as he controlled the snow.

"Frost," he rumbled, banging his head against the sidewalk beneath him.

Jack Frost had warned Snow that Frost would be tormenting him. This was just the sort of trickery for which the other Fae was infamous. Actually, it would probably get much worse. Snow didn't have time for this. He needed to find Frost and confront him. Wring his little neck until he understood that the Lord of Endless Snow was not to be messed with.

As he was about to rise, a hint of clear sky broke through the thick clouds above, the robin's egg blue a striking contrast. Snow held still, seeking out the energy that had managed to break through the cloud cover he'd been generating for days. He closed his eyes for a moment, centering himself, but whatever had caused the break in the clouds was gone. When he opened his eyes, Spring was standing above him, her eyebrows drawn together in concern.

"Are you okay?" she asked. "I saw you fall through the bakery's window."

"I'm fine," Snow grumbled.

She arched an eyebrow and gestured toward him with her beverage. "Then why are you still lying on the ground?"

He sighed. "I'm contemplating the life choices that

have led me to this moment."

At least he understood the tiny smirk that brought to her mouth. What he didn't understand was the odd flutter in his chest that stirred in response to it.

"I bet you could use a little Spring pick-me-up now," she said, offering her free hand.

He waved it away, rolling to his side and leaping to his feet. "I don't need spring," he bit out each word.

"Wow, you are a cranky bear," she said, scowling.

"What?" Snow said, nearly gasping.

Movement across the street caught his eye. Leaning against one of the buildings, a tall, lanky man watched them with piercing ice-blue eyes. His dark hair stood out in an unkempt mess and equally dark eyebrows lowered as he cast a smirk that was much less pleasant toward them.

"Frost," Snow growled. He was going to put a stop to this once and for all.

Snow stalked forward, but someone grabbed the back of his jacket. He spun around to face the new threat, but he slipped on the icy ground again. He was vaguely aware of someone grabbing his jacket, but kept spinning, arms flailing as he fell to the ground. This time, a light weight landed on top of him. Seconds later, a bus careened past. It hit a pothole near the curb, filled with thick, cold slush that erupted from under its tire, dousing Snow. He looked down to see Spring lying across his chest, her hair a wet mess and eyes wide.

"What the…" Snow quickly rose, pulling her up with him. He turned back to the alley, but Frost was gone. Snow had missed his chance. Growling, he turned to Spring and bellowed, "What did you do that for?"

"Excuse me? I was trying to stop you from being hit by a bus," she yelled back.

"What do I care about a bus?"

Her eyes widened and her mouth opened and closed a few times in the first response he clearly understood from her. Exasperation.

"Who doesn't care about being hit by a bus?" Her voice rose as she spoke, ending as a high squeak.

Before Snow could respond, Melanie ran out from the bakery.

"Oh my gosh, are you guys okay?" She wrapped her arm around Spring's waist and immediately continued. "What am I saying? Of course you're not okay. You're freezing. Come inside. You'll turn into an icicle if you try to walk home like this."

"Thank you," Spring said, still scowling at Snow.

Something about the change in her demeanor made that aching hollowness flare up in Snow's chest again. There was no playful scowl, no teasing glances. The warmth had changed to an icy cold, and for once, he didn't like it.

"North and I live above the bakery," Melanie said. "You can get dried off and warmed up."

"That sounds nice and very considerate," Spring said,

angling her head to glare at Snow. "Kind of like stopping someone from being hit by a bus."

"I would have been fine," Snow snapped.

Spring let out a little disgusted grunt and shook her head. "I was wrong about you," she said. She turned away, letting Melanie lead her into the bakery.

"Wrong how?" Snow called after them.

The door swung shut.

He stood in the slush for a few moments, replaying the last few moments and trying to figure out exactly when everything had careened completely out of control. Out of *his* control, anyway. Frost was probably having the time of his life. But Spring had gotten caught up in their issues, and that was unacceptable. She had stopped Snow from confronting Frost and...

And she had pulled Snow back when he'd been about to step in front of a bus. Sure, he could have summoned a bank of snow to sweep him away from danger with only a thought. The driver might have had a scare, but would have felt better when the wipers cleared the windshield and all they saw was snow.

Spring didn't know about Snow's powers. She had seen what she thought was a mortal man on the verge of ending his mortal existence in a potentially very painful way. Not to mention the emotional turmoil it would have caused to the driver and passengers. The turmoil it would have caused her to witness.

In her mind, she had saved him, and he was sure it had been instinct. As she'd said, she knew what she wanted, and she went for it. She wanted him to be safe. She wanted to get to know him. At least, she *had* wanted to. Now, she thought she was wrong about him. But what did that even mean?

Her words rang through his mind, echoing in that hollow place in his chest. The clouds began to drop thick flakes of snow, coating his shoulders and sticking to the slush that had soaked through his jacket. His skin prickled, his scalp itched where his horns had once been. He clenched his hands into fists and yelled, "Wrong how?"

His control was slipping. His muscles bunched with the urge to change—to his new form. The form the Winter Queen had given him. But beneath it, he felt the old. He felt the Krampus lying in wait. Always waiting for him to make a mistake. To lose everything that he'd been given. Everything that he'd worked for and held dear.

This mortal woman was a threat to his existence. A threat to his new nature, possibly his sanity. And yet, he couldn't turn away from the building. Instead, he stalked to the door and tore it open, the hinges creaking in protest and the bell above the door jangling in distress. Snow ignored the stares of the people inside and headed straight up the staircase to North and Melanie's apartment above. Headed straight for Spring.

Chapter Four

"Are you all right? What happened?" North met Melanie and Spring at the door of the bakery, his eyes wide as he looked Spring over. She cringed to think of what a mess she must be.

Her coat was soaked and her hair was a filthy mess. She could see gray clods of slush stuck to their ends. She was going to need a deep conditioning treatment after this. But instead of complaining, she forced herself to smile, pulling her best professional persona to the surface and stuffing the seething anger deep beneath.

"I'm fine," she said, but even she could hear the strain in her voice.

"We're going to go upstairs so she can clean up," Melanie said. "Can you handle the cookies for a while till I get back?"

"Forget the cookies." North glanced out the front windows, grimacing. His usually-smiling lips were pulled in a deep frown and his eyebrows lowered ominously. "How could Snow let this happen to you?"

"Leave it," Spring said.

She'd seen enough fights to know when one was brewing—and that North didn't stand a chance against Snow. Even after everything, the thought sent a little thrill shooting up and down her spine. If something had happened between herself and Snow, she definitely would have felt safe staying out late with him. Though, it would have been more fun to stay in…

"You sure you're okay?" North said, turning his attention fully back to her.

Spring's smile was a bit more sincere as she looked over to Melanie and said, "We girls have got this, right?"

Melanie's eyes widened, and she smiled back, nodding eagerly. "Yeah, we do."

"Don't let those amazing cookies burn." Spring nodded toward the kitchen.

"If you're sure." North slowly backed away, watching them as if he expected them to change their minds.

"Come on," Spring said, heading up the staircase as Melanie eagerly followed.

A door on the second level right above the kitchen led into one of the most gorgeous apartments Spring had ever seen. Melanie paused to pull off her shoes in the entryway, and Spring followed her example, taking the opportunity to study the intricate tile flooring just past the door. Each tile was a mosaic of blues and whites, with a swirling pattern that reminded her of a windy day.

"The bathroom is just in here," Melanie said, leading

her through a living room with plush carpets that Spring's feet sank into.

Soft, romantic jazz filtered through the air from speakers Spring couldn't see, and a fire sprang up in the fireplace as they crossed the room, the fake logs glowing cheerily in seconds. Spring was tempted to just plop herself down on the gray faux fur rug in front of it, but she shuddered at the thought of what the mess in her hair would turn into if it dried in place. A couple of chairs and a matching large, poofy couch sat a ways back from the fireplace, a soft fleece blanket draped over its back that was equally tempting.

Spring hadn't worn her warmest clothes for this outing. She had on a dark red woolen skirt that ended just below her knees with a brighter red button-up sweater—her favorite Valentine's Day outfit for when she was going out-and-about as opposed to how she dressed up for a fancy evening with a date. Thankfully, she'd opted for dark tights. White would have stained terribly. The black boots she'd left at the door had protected her from the brunt of the slush that hit her legs. Her favorite red peacoat had taken most of the damage. She had no idea how she would ever get it clean again.

Melanie led her into a cozy bathroom with a tub and a shower. Spring wasn't looking forward to trying to stick her head under that to rinse her hair, but she was not comfortable with the idea of taking a shower at a stranger's house. At least the shower head was detachable.

"There are plenty of towels in here," Melanie said, pointing to a cabinet in the wall. "This is the guest bathroom, so everything hanging out is fresh and clean. Please feel free to use anything you want. I don't think my clothes will fit you, but I can bring you some of North's while we wash your outfit. I'll leave them outside the door here."

"I think most of it just got on my coat," Spring said.

"Yeah." Melanie pulled a face. "It's such a beautiful coat. I think I can get most of that out, though."

"It's okay, I don't want to trouble you."

Melanie smiled, her blue eyes sparkling. "It's no trouble at all. Snow is family and I appreciate what you did for him."

"At least someone did," Spring mumbled under her breath.

"He really is a nice guy underneath." Melanie half-shrugged. "He just hasn't quite figured out how to show it."

Spring snorted. "Trust me, I know the type and have had my fill of it."

Melanie's smile faded and it was almost as if the lights dimmed in the room. She was such a sweet person.

"Hey, I'm sorry," Spring said. "I'm just grumpy because I'm covered in slush."

"Then let me help you with that."

She was so earnest. Spring didn't want to disappoint her. She nodded, then carefully slid her coat down her arms, trying not to let anything splat on the floor as she did. Most of the slush had already fallen off—probably in the entryway to the bakery or on the stairs.

"I'm so sorry, I must have made such a mess when I came back inside the bakery."

"Don't worry about it." Melanie was already scrutinizing the coat. She beamed up at Spring and said, "I'll make Snow clean it up."

Both women laughed, then Melanie headed for the door.

"If you need anything, just call me," Melanie said. "But maybe be a little loud. The laundry room is on the other side of the apartment."

"I'm sure I'll be fine."

Melanie gave her one last smile before exiting, closing the door behind her. Alone at last, Spring took a few moments to center herself—but only a few. Without her coat, the cold was starting to set in. She quickly took off her earrings and the rings and bracelets she wore, then set them on the bathroom counter, doing her best not to look at her reflection. The few glimpses she caught reminded her of a wet Pomeranian. Not flattering. She had just turned to the tub, thinking through the logistics involved in washing this crap out of her hair, when the door opened behind her.

"I thought you were leaving the clothes outsi—" Her voice cut off and her eyes widened as she saw Snow standing in the doorway. The small space made him seem even bigger, especially when he turned and shut the door.

Spring's mouth went dry. Even with how rude he had been, she couldn't deny the attraction she felt. Though the room temperature seemed to rise a hundred degrees, she still shivered. She wrapped her arms around her middle and forced herself to scowl, narrowing her eyes.

"Most people knock," she said. "I could have been naked in here."

"You'd really take a shower in someone's house that you don't know?" he asked.

"Maybe." She hadn't been planning to, but she didn't like that he had figured that out about her. "What are you doing here, anyway?"

"I wanted to apologize," he said. "You thought you were helping me—"

"I *thought* I was helping you? I stopped you from being hit by a bus."

He took a deep breath, then let it out slowly. He held her gaze for a few moments, then looked her over and shook his head. Reaching up to his neck, he undid his tie and pulled it from his shirt, then opened the top few buttons. Spring felt her eyes widen again, but didn't care this time. He hung the tie on a hook behind the door, then unbuttoned his jacket and hung it up as well. A little choking noise came out of her. Somehow, he looked even bigger the more clothes he removed. And he wasn't done.

He removed his vest and hung it with the jacket and tie, then turned to her and unbuttoned the sleeves of his dark shirt. Heat exploded in her, her skin rising in goosebumps that were intensified by the cold dampness still in her hair. She could glimpse the edges of his collarbones in the gap at his neck, and the gleaming skin of the biggest pectoral muscles she'd ever seen. He rolled up one sleeve past his elbow, then started on the other.

"Come on, you're a mess," he said. "Let's get you cleaned up."

"Excuse me?" Spring was so stunned, she just stood there as he slid past her and started up the water. It was his rudeness, his gall, and not at all that she was mesmerized by the tight pull of his pants across his backside as he bent over to check the temperature and arrange the shampoo and conditioner the way he wanted.

He turned back to her and said, "Take off your sweater."

Her heart pounded in her chest, her mouth dropping open, but only stuttering sounds emerging from it. She lifted her hands to the top button, but she wasn't sure if she wanted to do as he said or clutch the fabric to her chest.

Okay, she knew she wanted to do as he said.

"You don't want your sweater getting messed up and

wet," he said. "I know you have a chemise on under there, but I'll look away if you want."

There was something oddly comforting in the way he was speaking. His tone, his demeanor, they were so different than what she'd seen before. Aside from a slight darkening in his cheeks, there was no sign of interest in her. She'd never had a man find her so… resistible before. Again, she thought of the challenge he presented, but did she really still want to go there?

Her eyes roved over his shoulders and chest, then down his legs and back to his strong features. She absolutely still wanted to go there. But did he?

"It'll be a lot easier for me to wash your hair while you support yourself over the tub," he said. "I've done this a thousand times. You don't have anything to worry about from me."

That's what worried her. That she *didn't* have to worry about him making a move. Wait, what did he say?

"You've done this before?" Spring asked.

He shrugged. "I have girls."

The brief warm smile that accompanied the statement was so wholesome that Spring's chest filled with warmth. He was a dad? Oh crap, did that mean he had a wife or a partner? That would explain a lot. And here Spring was, lusting after him and making plans that she had no business making.

Spring turned away to try to hide her disappointment.

She fumbled with the buttons of her sweater, but managed to get it off, then set it on the counter near her jewelry. Somehow, knowing that nothing was going to happen between them made her feel more vulnerable under his gaze. She was wearing a bra beneath her chemise, but she still crossed her arms over her chest when she turned back to him.

He wasn't even looking at her. He had the shower nozzle started and was pointing it toward the wall. As she approached, he gestured toward the far end of the tub, where he'd placed a stack of towels to cushion her knees as she knelt over the rim. He had even placed a folded towel over the edge of the tub to pad it there. It really did seem like he had done this before.

"I can manage on my own," she said, suddenly dreading the thought of his hands in her hair, the closeness of his body. When there had been a chance of further intimacy, this had only seemed like an appetizer. Now, it seemed totally inappropriate.

"I'm sure you can," he said, surprising her. "But it'll be a lot easier if I help."

"Are you sure your wife will be okay with that?"

He stared at her, his mouth hanging slack. Maybe she'd misread him even more than she thought.

"Husband?" she offered.

A huge smile spread across his face. Snow busted out laughing, throwing his head back. The rich sound sent a frisson down her spine, despite her efforts to stop finding him attractive. When he finished, he shook his head and wiped a tear from his eye.

"You think I'm married?" he said. "Gods, that's funny."

"Why?" She waved her hand in his direction. "I mean you have... stuff to offer."

Wait, did he say, 'Gods,' as in plural?

His smile fell and he snapped his mouth shut, his eyebrows lowering menacingly. That muscle in his jaw twitched again. What had she done to offend him so deeply?

"Nobody's going to be jealous," he said, a bitter note to his voice. "Now, come on. Let's get this done."

Chapter Five

Spring was staring at him like a deer about to bolt. Snow had plenty of experience with that. He stepped aside, giving her space so she didn't feel threatened, and waited for her to come to him. It gave him time to get his own emotions under control.

That dig about him having a wife... It had cut deeper than he would have expected. Who the hell would want to be with him? The monster of childhood legend?

Spring didn't know he was the Krampus, though. Maybe when she looked at him, she saw... What? A viable candidate for... affection? A potential partner in life?

Those were dangerous thoughts for him to have. That echoing hollow in his chest stirred again. He wanted to rub it, to soothe the ache, but didn't dare move for fear of scaring her off. As it was, she stared at him, then the shower head in his hand, then back to him again. He tried to keep his expression as neutral as possible.

Finally, she stepped forward, then lowered herself to the towels he'd provided. She braced herself with her hands on the base of the tub, then turned to face the wall away from him so that the water wouldn't get in her eyes.

Or so that she wouldn't have to look at him. He had plenty of experience with that, too. Not so much since the Winter Queen had given him his new forms, but still. Things like that were hard to forget.

He lowered himself to one knee behind Spring, keeping his other leg bent so he could rise easily if needed, and tried to let as little of their bodies touch as he could. The water was a good temperature, but he was still careful to watch her response as he started to rinse her hair. The golden strands were caked with road dirt from the slush.

He hated that she'd put herself through this for no reason. He would have been fine, though she hadn't known that. For the first time, he realized the danger she had placed herself in—for him. No one had ever done anything like that before. The feeling of hollowness in his chest retreated a little, warmth filling the space instead.

He didn't have to help bathe his children often, but sometimes, there were kids who would act out with their caretakers in the Yuletide Kingdom, and Snow would have to step in to make sure neither they nor any other members of his court were injured. Most of the children had seen him in his polar bear form when he came to take them as tribute to the Winter Queen. They weren't as likely to lash out at Snow as his other subjects. And though he could use his magic to clean them, they needed to learn to care for themselves and let others care for them. Plus, nobody he had met liked the chilling experience of being cleaned with snow-based magic.

Washing Spring's hair was not at all like helping his kids. Physically, the motions were similar, but she was bigger than they were for a start. It was hard not to bump against her as he held the shower head close to her hair. Running his fingers over the strands to coax out the dirt was different, too. The warmth in his chest spread, his skin prickling with the awareness of her proximity.

He often used stories to distract the more ornery kids he tended back in the Yuletide Kingdom. This time, maybe he could distract himself. He just had to be careful not to let anything slip that would make Spring suspect he was anything other than a mortal man.

"I had this kid named Malachi," he began. "When he came to us, he was a mess. I don't know what he'd gotten himself into, and I honestly don't want to know. But he had layers of grime, and he refused to let anyone bathe him. I don't think he'd ever had a bath in his life. He was too young to leave on his own safely, and he was such a spitfire. Gertrude, one of the women assigned to care for him, came to me and asked me to help her."

Snow set aside the shower head where it wouldn't spray Spring and picked up the shampoo, working it into a rich lather as he spoke, making himself focus on the memory and not the soft texture of her hair sliding between his fingers.

"The smell was just... incredible," Snow said. "We had the tub all ready with plenty of warm water, fresh, clean clothes laid out for him, plus toys and towels. This little four-year-old boy stood there, arms crossed over his filthy clothes, glaring at me like he was ready to take me down while Gertrude was just shaking her head in the background." Snow chuckled as he lost himself deeper in the memory, rinsing the suds from Spring's hair till the water was clear, then started working conditioner through the golden strands.

"What happened?" Spring prompted.

"Well... He did."

She twisted around a bit so that she could look him in the face, her eyebrows high on her forehead. Snow laughed at her expression as much as the memory.

"Malachi was the first child I helped under my... current boss," Snow said. "I had no idea what I was doing. Figured I could pick him up and dump him into the tub, clothes and all." He chuckled louder as he rinsed out the conditioner in her hair. "That kid clawed his way up my arms like a housecat. Made it all the way onto my shoulders and jumped off. I was kind of off balance to start, so I fell into the tub headfirst."

Spring started to laugh. The sound brought a deeper smile to Snow's face. He turned off the water and squeezed the excess moisture from her hair, then reached for a towel as they both rose to their feet.

"The joke was on him, though," Snow said, placing the towel on her head and starting to gently dry it.

"Why?"

"When I hit the water, I splashed so much out of the tub that Malachi was drenched from standing there next to it. We sort of stared at each other for a minute, and then we both busted out laughing. He was still holding his sides when I sloshed my way out of the room to let Gertrude take over."

"And that's the same Malachi I heard you talking to North about?"

Snow thought back over their conversation. Had they said anything they shouldn't have within earshot of a mortal? Snow wasn't used to giving mortals any consideration beyond what he needed to keep his operations in the mortal realm running. At the same time, he couldn't bring himself to outright lie to her.

"It is," Snow said. "He's grown now, into a fine man. Helps me run everything."

"Ah." Spring nodded, an odd glittering in her eyes. "So, you work in a place that takes care of kids? Like an orphanage?"

"It's closer to foster care. They stay with us forever and learn to contribute to our realm."

Crap, did mortals talk like that? If Spring had thought it an odd turn of phrase, she didn't act like it. She was still staring up at him, her eyes a little glassy.

"You give them a home," she said.

"Exactly."

How was it that this mortal understood his mission when North had totally lost sight of it? As the Yule Cat and the Krampus, the pair of them had been responsible for bringing new people into the Yuletide Kingdom for almost more years than Snow could remember. They selected children who were neglected or abused, who weren't getting the love and care that all children deserved.

So what if the Yuletide Kingdom had been locked in winter for as long as they had been working together. Their ruler was called the Winter Queen for a reason. But now, North had it in his head that their realm wasn't good enough, just because the weather never changed. Snow looked into Spring's eyes and more of that warmth bloomed in his chest. Was North right? Did the Yuletide Kingdom need to bring back spring and all that came with it to infuse the realm with love once more?

Snow knew the seasons used to come and go with as much regularity as in any other Faerie Kingdom. He didn't know why winter had come and suddenly never ended, but it was right around the time that the Winter Queen had brought him and North into her Court and made them Fairy Lords. Around the time that Lord Kringle had been banished to the farthest reaches of her realm.

When the Winter Queen had found Snow, he had been trapped in the mishappen form of the Krampus, with curving horns sticking out from his head and goat legs. He had still tried to help people, as naive as that had been. One look at him, and they'd all run in terror. He wondered what Spring would think of his original form. The thought of her running from him brought a sharp, stabbing pain to his chest.

She stared up at him, her large blue eyes wide and shimmering with moisture. Had some water reached them when he was wrapped up in his story? He needed to be more careful. She was mortal, after all. He lightened his touch further as he worked to dry her hair.

Her lips parted slightly, working noiselessly for a few moments before she said, "I think... I think I've got it."

Her voice was rough and she coughed to clear it. Then she reached up and placed her hands on his, halting their motion.

The skin of her hands was impossibly soft, their warmth soaking into him so quickly, it was almost as if he'd been scalded. At the same time, electric awareness coursed through him, his chest lit up with an energy powerful enough he was shocked he wasn't glowing from it. She pulled his hands away from her head, clutching them tightly.

Did she feel the same pull that he did? The same strange energy connecting them? He wanted to ask, but... What if she didn't? And even if she did, would she feel the same if she knew that he was the Krampus?

Before he could pull away himself, she released his hands and stepped back, staring downward as she swallowed hard. The distance she placed between them felt like a wedge driven into his heart. She tugged the towel off her soaked hair and held it in front of her.

"If you don't mind, I'd like a moment to myself to finish up," she said. She cast a quick glance at him, but her eyes narrowed almost as if it pained her to look at him. She quickly looked away.

"Yeah, sure." He stiffened, pulling the door open and striding from the room without looking back. He yanked it shut behind him.

Why was this different? Why did her rejection hurt so much worse than all the other times people had turned him away? He headed for the staircase, eager to leave. When he reached the foyer, he realized he had left his jacket in the bathroom with Spring. And with it, his phone, his wallet, his keys…

He could get around without them and even gain access to his offices, but doing so would risk people witnessing his magic. And his phone… Who could get by without their phone in the mortal realm anymore? Growling low, he turned toward the living room, pacing back and forth in the small space. Small for him, anyway.

He heard movement behind him. His heart did a funny little flip in his chest, his stomach fluttering as he turned around, expecting Spring. Melanie stood there, holding

Spring's red coat. She let out a yelp and jumped back.

"Snow? What are you doing here?"

What *was* he doing here? He'd come to apologize. And he had sort of done that. He had stayed to help Spring. To spend time with her. The way she'd spoken to him before had riled him up in a way no one else ever had. Then again, no one had ever tried. She had *flirted* with him. With *him*.

"I don't even know," he said.

Melanie looked back and forth between him and the closed door to the bathroom. A smile slowly crept across her face.

"Wait, did you come up here to apologize?" she said.

"What? No." He shook his head, then said, "I mean, yeah. Maybe."

Melanie pinched her lips between her teeth, something he'd noticed that she did when she didn't want to say something or show how excited she was. If she thought something was brewing between Spring and Snow, she was going to be disappointed, and Snow couldn't allow that.

"Don't make that face," he said.

"What face?" She pointed at her chin. "This face?"

The smile she was barely suppressing flooded over her features. More warmth fluttered in Snow's chest. Not the kind that soaked into his bones, such as Spring had started to bring out of him, but a gentler warmth.

"What are you doing up here?" Snow asked. "The bakery is busier than I've ever seen it."

"The new cookie recipes North and I came up with are really popular, aren't they?" Melanie said, crossing the room to stand in front of him. "I always wanted to be a baker. Working here, living here, everything that's happened, it's better than a dream come true."

"I'm glad." Despite the weight in his own heart, he couldn't help but be happy for her. He looked down at the red coat that Melanie held, forgotten in her hands. A dark gray stain covered half the fabric. "What the heck are you doing to that coat?"

"I'm cleaning it," Melanie said, her smile dimming a bit. "Trying to, anyway. I've never been good at this kind of stuff."

He looked over her head at the bathroom door to make sure it was still shut, then said, "Give it here."

Melanie looked over her shoulder, then turned back to him and smiled, nodding eagerly. She handed him the coat, her eyes wide with wonder as she waited for him to work his magic—literally. Snow shook his head, but he couldn't help but smile at her.

He held the coat up by its shoulders with both hands. A light, floral scent emanated from it. Of course, Spring would smell like flowers. He chuckled as he worked his magic into the fibers, the remaining liquid stiffening as it froze. The fabric crackled as he gave it a shake, gray snow falling to the ground from the areas that had been saturated with slush. He shook it again and again, till the snow he was pushing through the fibers came out white. As she critically checked the now-clean coat, Melanie's smile broadened—until she saw the pile of snow on the floor beneath it.

"Oh crap," she said. "I'll go get a towel."

"No need." He stomped his foot in the center of the mess. Snowflakes swirled out from beneath his boot, sweeping up everything that had dropped onto the floor and carrying it a few feet into the air in a whirlwind before vanishing.

"That is so cool," she said, her eyes wide.

"The coolest." He winked at her as he folded Spring's coat over his arm. "I'll take it from here."

"But don't you want me to deal with her when—"

He reached out and grasped Melanie's arm gently, giving it a squeeze. Slowly, he repeated. "I'll take it from here. You can head back down and help out North in the bakery."

"Okay." Her lips pinched together as she tried to hold in her smile again and utterly failed. Rising on her tip-toes, she planted a quick kiss on his cheek, then hurried from the room, casting a last glance at him over her shoulder as her smile finally emerged, completely free.

Snow shook his head as he heard the door to the apartment shut behind her. North was definitely going to tease him about this. Snow had no doubt that the pair would be speculating about what was going on upstairs. Snow was speculating about that himself.

Spring had seemed interested in him. Aggressively so. But, when he'd left her just now, she was different. Quieter. More subdued. Maybe his help hadn't been as welcome as he'd thought it might be. Maybe she didn't like his story or didn't like kids. That would be a total dealbreaker. Snow's life revolved around the people he brought into the Yuletide kingdom—the children who grew to be members of his household. Anyone who wanted to be with him would have to understand that.

Was that what he wanted? To be with her? Somehow, a glimmer of hope was burgeoning within him that maybe she felt that way about him, but... Maybe she wasn't interested. If she knew who he really was, she wouldn't want to be with him at all. She would run away, as had so many others.

This was stupid. He had other things to do. Important things. People to take care of. He draped her coat over the back of one of the stuffed chairs, but couldn't bring himself to leave. His jacket and vest were still in the bathroom. That's why he was lingering. Not because he wanted to see her once more before she walked out of his life forever.

A low growl built in the back of his throat. He didn't want her to walk out of his life. He kept his hand resting on the chair, feeling the rough wool of her coat. What was it about this woman that was drawing him in?

The door to the bathroom opened and Spring emerged. Snow's heartbeat picked up and his mouth went dry. His fingers curled into the fabric of her coat and his breath quickened. She had dried her hair as much as she could, but it hung in tight strands around her face, darkened from the water that remained in it. She stared at him with those same wide eyes as before. Almost fearful, but not quite. Why was he suddenly making her nervous now?

He hated the idea of her being afraid of him. A crushing pressure seized his heart at the thought, as if it were in a vise. Where was the smirk that drove him crazy? Where were the innuendos that set him spinning? He wanted to bring those out of her again.

This was a challenge he wouldn't back down from. He wasn't the Krampus anymore. He was the Lord of Endless Snow. This woman had been happy to interact with him just moments ago. He would make that happen again. Somehow…

Chapter Six

He is way too dangerous.

Spring wrapped her arms around her middle, wishing she'd worn a thicker sweater, even if it didn't match the holiday. This was turning into the worst Valentine's Day ever. Moisture clung to the fibers of the garment, chilling her almost as badly as her damp hair. She knew she shouldn't go out like this, but it would be worse to stay here—with him.

Snow stood across the room, his dark shirt unbuttoned enough to give her a mouth-watering view of the best chest she'd ever seen. Smooth, gold-tinged skin stretched across massive pecs. One fist was propped on his hip while the other gripped the back of a chair, giving her an excellent view of the shape of his enormous back. With his sleeves rolled up past his elbows, she could see the corded muscles of his forearms.

She'd felt those strong arms around her. Not in the passionate way she'd originally intended. No, he had held her with such tenderness and care that her heart was still flopping in her chest like a fish out of water. He had told her that wonderful story. Shared that he was already living her dream—helping as many children as possible in the best way he could.

He stared at her with such intensity she would have sworn his eyes had a faint red glow to their dark depths, like the embers of an endless fire. But she had no idea if it was because he was as attracted to her as she was to him or that she was still driving him crazy—the annoying kind of crazy, not the sexy kind she had hoped for. Certainly not... Not the forever kind. Not the first flutters of love.

She realized that one hand had gone up to her heart, covering it as if that could keep it in her chest. As if that could stop its longing for him and keep her safe. Physical stuff could happen fast, and she was fine with that. But this? She was falling too hard and too fast. She shook her head sharply, breaking her gaze away from his. She had to get out of here.

"Thanks for washing my hair," she said.

He chuckled, the low sound rumbling across the room to her like distant thunder. Her eyes snapped back to him despite herself. He ran his hand over his dark, close-cropped hair.

"Maybe someday you'll be able to return the favor," he said.

Her lip twitched into an almost-smile, drawing his gaze. Why was he staring at her mouth with that intense look, his eyes narrowing and his shoulders squared? She needed him to go back to being perplexed and annoyed. This predatory scrutiny made her feel as if she needed to run. The trouble was, she was pretty sure if she did, it would be straight into his arms.

A shiver racked her and she hugged herself tighter. Her coat was right next to him. Too close to him. She could take her chances with the cold. Except, when the tremor passed through her, he hissed in a breath. He shook his head as he stood straighter, then stalked across the room toward her. Her eyes widened with each step he took, her breath quickening and tingles spreading through her body.

What was he going to do? Was he going to kiss her? To lift her from her feet so she could wrap her legs around his waist and return his kiss with equal passion? Heat flowed through her at the thought. No one had ever made her feel like this, and he hadn't even touched her.

When he reached her, he didn't stop moving. He swept her up off her feet, but not as she'd imagined. Instead, he lifted her into his arms. She gasped at the momentary sensation of weightlessness as he practically threw her into the air. Gravity reasserted itself, settling her against his chest. She felt so perfect against him. It was as if she was meant to be there.

"Wh—what are you doing?" she asked as he turned back toward the couch.

"Getting you warmed up."

She was already warmed up—practically on fire

wanting him. He strode to the couch. That would work, too. It was a big couch. Well, for her. He was so huge, she wondered how he would fit. It would be better if he set her on the faux fur rug in front of the fire. Instead, he strode up to the back of the couch... and dropped her over it.

She bounced on the cushions a few times, staring up at him in shock. He picked up the blanket draped over the couch and unfolded it, snapping it in the air once above to spread it fully, then let it fall over her. This was really not going the way she'd expected. Snow reached one long arm over the back of the couch and bent down behind it. What was he doing now?

Gravity seemed to stop working for a moment again as he lifted her, couch and all, and started walking toward the fireplace. Her mind reeled with a mix of frustration and excitement. How strong was this guy? As he set the very large couch down only a few feet from the fire's protective screen, she caught a glimpse of his face. There was no sign of strain whatsoever.

"Okay," he said, staring down at her with his fists on his hips. "Better?"

"What?" she gasped.

He gestured toward the fire, then toward her. "The fire. The blanket. You were cold."

She had been so focused on what he was doing, she hadn't had a chance to really think of the 'why' behind it. Now that she knew... It was really sweet, in a super sexy, how-the-heck-did-he-do-that kind of way. This guy was a heady mix of contradictions, and he was hitting all the right buttons with her.

She shook herself inwardly. Nobody pushed her buttons. Not the emotional ones, anyway. Not anymore. She had learned her lesson too many times. She needed to go back to just seeing him as a fun diversion. A Valentine's Day challenge to have a little fun with, and then they could both move on. She arched an eyebrow at him and pulled the blanket closer around her neck.

"I don't know," she said. "I'm still pretty cold. Maybe you could help me warm up." She cast her best sultry smile at him.

He nodded, then started walking past the back of the couch. "I'll get more blankets."

"Wait." Spring let out a frustrated gasp. She grabbed his arm as soon as he was within reach. "That's not what I meant."

He stared down at her hand on him, dark eyebrows drawn over his forehead. His eyes traveled slowly up her arm and over her shoulder, leaving a wake of goosebumps as it did. She could swear she felt his gaze like a caress. It lingered on her lips and a muscle in his clenched jaw started to twitch. Her breath picked up again, her heart pounding in her chest. Their eyes locked, and the longing deep within his eyes seared her to her soul.

She could barely breathe. Her fingers tightened around

his arm, her back arching as if her entire body was straining toward him. He felt like gravity, and she wanted to fall into him, even though she was terrified. Because when she stared into his eyes, she felt a mirror of that longing within herself.

He wasn't just a conquest—no matter how hard she tried to fool herself into thinking so. Somehow, she knew... he was her *forever.*

Snow gently placed his hand over hers, his strong fingers wrapping around it and detaching her grip. He held on, though, his head bowed.

"I'm not that kind of guy," he said.

"What kind of guy?" she echoed. "The kind with a gruff exterior, but who's caring and kind beneath? The kind who's cold and bitter at first, but when you get down to it, actually sweet? Did you even see the beverage I was drinking in the bakery?"

He chuckled, but wouldn't look at her. He squeezed her hand one more time, then said, "I'll get you those blankets."

"Snow—"

She stopped speaking as the lights cut out abruptly. The fireplace went dark as well, and a biting cold swept through the room. She clung to Snow's hand, not even able to see any light from the windows. What was going on?

Once again, gravity felt like it couldn't decide what was up and what was down, but this time, it was an entirely unpleasant experience. Her stomach lurched as she fell up off the couch, her wet hair was rising around her face, then falling along with the rest of her.

She landed against a warm chest, shivering violently as her breath came out in clouds. At first, it was all she could see, but then Snow emerged, as if he'd been wrapped in a darkness that was retreating from his form. It seemed to merge with the inky blackness surrounding them.

"What's g-going on?" she asked, though chattering teeth.

"I'm not sure." Snow pulled her closer against his chest, wrapping his arms around her and giving her what warmth he could. It wasn't enough.

"I'm f-freezing," she said, the cold burning her even through her clothes. "H-how are you st-still w-warm?"

He bent over her, as if trying to shield her from the cold with his body. Her hair crackled as she burrowed against Snow's chest. The lingering dampness in it had already frozen.

"H-how l-long t-till I g-get f-frostbite?" It wouldn't be long, with her icy hair against her ears.

"Frost," he hissed under his breath.

"W-what?"

"Frost!" he yelled, searching the darkness around them.

"Better do something quick." A man's voice came from somewhere—from everywhere—in the void, sing-songy and mocking.

"Dammit." Snow looked down at her. The reddish glow in his eyes was back, distorted and bright through the crystals of frost coating her eyelashes. "I'm sorry."

He took a deep breath and stood straighter. She whimpered as his warmth retreated, but then a blast of cold radiated out from his chest making her shudder. The cold wrapped around her, touching every part of her skin. Instead of burning, it tingled, sending goosebumps over her flesh. She looked down to see a swirl of snowflakes whirling around her body, penetrating her clothes and flooding them with light.

The snowflakes swept up past her face, racing over her scalp and down her hair, drying it and pulling it up on the sides with what felt like combs. The rest tumbled down her back and around her neck, warming her. She felt something rest across her forehead and a light weight on her ears as if she had put on a heavier set of earrings. The cold that had been biting her vanished, her eyes clearing as the frost disappeared from her eyelashes.

The snow brightened around her body as her thin red sweater and woolen skirt expanded to a rich velvet dress of burnished gold, inset with satin as bright as rays of morning sunlight in complex patterns of ivy and flowers. Though the dress showed off a lovely amount of her décolletage, the cold raced away as a platinum necklace formed around her neck, the metal channel set with diamonds and suspending a bright golden-yellow citrine as big as an egg that nestled over her heart. She felt more jewelry form on her fingers, but didn't dare let go of Snow to look at it.

Snow's grip on her waist tightened, his breath hitching as he pulled her closer. Beneath the skirts of the dress, her tights turned into something that felt like the softest, warmest fleece she'd ever encountered, brushing against her skin in a tantalizing wave of warmth.

Snow let out a low, rumbling growl, bending closer. Heat bloomed in her stomach, quickly spreading to the rest of her and chasing away the last of the aching cold. She wrapped her arms around his neck, pulling herself up till their lips were a hair's breadth apart. Just before they touched, that annoying voice intruded on the moment.

"*That's* the kind of guy he is," it said.

Chapter Seven

Snow held Spring tightly in his arms. He never wanted to let her go. He wanted... He wanted all kinds of things. Things he had never considered before. His skin was on fire where they touched, and his lips were tingling with the urge to kiss her. From the heat in her eyes, the warmth he could sense flooding her body, he was sure she wanted the same. But first, he had to deal with Jack Frost.

Snow straightened, keeping Spring secure against his side. He didn't dare release her, with them being stuck in a pocket of Faerie that Frost had created around them. If Frost tried to spirit her away... Snow's shoulder's bunched, his bear form pushing against him, urging him to change so that he could more effectively protect her, could kill Frost faster. But if she saw Snow change...

The thought doused his ardor, sending something over his skin he almost never felt—a chill. She knew he wasn't a regular mortal now. Maybe she could accept that he was a Fairy Lord and even that he was a magic-wielding shapeshifter. But what would she think if she knew of his original form? Would she still let him touch her? Hold her? Would she still look at him with heavy-lidded eyes as if she wanted to kiss him as much as he wanted to kiss her?

Frost had done this. He had forced Snow to blow his cover and reveal himself—breaking the most sacred law of all Fae. Snow would have been expected to let her die, but he couldn't. Just the thought almost broke his control, snow ghosting up from his skin as if asking if it was time to transform.

"Frost, I am going to snap you in half," Snow growled.

"Why would you want to do that?" Frost said, his voice cloyingly sweet. "After I've been so kind and given you two your own private paradise."

In a blink, the darkness around them vanished, leaving them in a small cabin. Snow looked around, taking in the huge fireplace with its natural stone, the smooth-polished oak floors, the stairs hugging one wall leading up to a loft, and the kitchen island separating that part of the great room from the living area. He knew this place. He also knew the smarmy dickweed who was leaning against the wall near the fireplace.

Jack Frost stood with his arms crossed over his chest, his dark eyebrows lowered over ice blue eyes and his black hair a carefully crafted 'mess.' His lips were pulled into a condescending smirk that Snow wanted to punch off his face.

"You teleported us," Snow said. "This is Sylvia's

cabin."

"Sylvia's cabin?" Frost leaned forward, a guileless expression crossing his face that Snow didn't believe for a second. "You mean the place where you betrayed your Queen and used the power that was rightfully mine to turn some deer guy and his girlfriend into the Lord and Lady of the North Wind? That cabin?"

"Frost," Snow growled in warning.

Frost pushed himself away from the wall, strolling closer to the fire. He snapped his fingers in front of it, and a raging blaze appeared from out of nowhere.

"We wouldn't want dear Spring to get chilly," Frost said. "Mortals are so sensitive to the cold and all."

"You are way over the line." Snow took a step closer.

Frost laughed, his form turning to cold vapor that hung in the air for a moment, then dropped to the ground. A chill breeze swept through the cabin as he flew across the room. He reformed in the hallway that led to the outer door of the cabin.

"You know, I think you should have opened up a bit more with your student," Frost said. "He could have given you tips on some much more entertaining ways to help a mortal woman stay warm, as he and Sylvia did their first night together. Right here in front of this fire."

Snow stiffened, his legs refusing to obey him as the implications of Frost's words sank in. Spring didn't have the same problem.

"Oh my God, you perv," she shouted. "Did you watch them?"

"Of course not." Frost rolled his eyes and snorted. "How bored do you think I am, that I would peep on a couple in the intense throes of passion?" His voice became mockingly dramatic toward the end of his sentence.

"Well, you're bored enough to mess with us," Spring said. "And that chill you sent my way was no joke."

"It wasn't meant as one," he snapped. "Your lover boy here was entrusted with a sacred power after his bestie decided to go off the rails and desert his post. North Cotter? He's the Yule Cat." She laughed, but Frost just went on. "Not going to believe that when you're hearing it straight from Jack Frost?" He whirled his finger in a circle, making a tiny cyclone of ice crystals that vanished along with her smile.

"The Winter Queen ordered Snow to give that power to me. But instead, he gave it to his little deer pal, Aidan, and his mortal girlfriend, Sylvia."

"Wait, Aidan and Sylvia from the bakery?" Spring said, glancing over at Snow. "I've chatted with them before."

"They're the White Stag and the White Doe." Snow's voice was low and somber. She knew so much already, it seemed better to tell her everything.

"Oh, wow," she said, her eyes widening. "I've really stumbled into something, haven't I?"

"Their power was meant to be mine," Frost cut back in.

"But just because Mr. Control Freak here couldn't let go of his best friend, the Yule Cat, he decided to give it to someone else."

"Wow, I can't imagine why." Spring's voice dripped with sarcasm. "I mean, you seem like such a nice and stable person. Absolutely, the best choice for so much power."

Snow snorted, his chuckle turning into a genuine laugh at the outraged expression on Frost's face. Frost barely spared Spring a glance.

"It must eat you up inside, knowing you can't get to your precious protégés, 'the Lord and Lady of the North Wind.'" Frost pushed an impressive amount of contempt into his voice.

"Aidan and Sylvia will do fine," Snow said. "And I'll be able to help them in person eventually."

"Eventually." Frost scoffed. "Unless the Queen decides this little time-out in the mortal realm you're in should be permanent."

Snow tried to hide how much the thought of that worried him. He wasn't sure how successful he was, but Frost was off on a different tangent, it seemed.

"That little trick of yours, turning a mortal into a Fae to get around our rules, only works once, even for a little suck-up like you," Frost said. "Especially since you don't have any spare power to give anyone now. Unless, of course, you decide to make Spring here the Lady of

Endless Snow."

A wave of unease swept down Snow's spine. The cruel look on Frost's face just made it worse. He made a tutting sound, his eyebrows furrowed as if he was thinking hard on something.

"But wait, if you gave her your power, that would mean you wouldn't be the Lord of Endless Snow anymore," Frost said. "You'd just be plain old *Krampus*."

Snow's skin erupted in tingling prickles, as if he'd rolled in stinging nettles. His bear pushed at his flesh, begging to be let loose to rip Frost to shreds. But if Snow did that, he was certain to frighten Spring. He couldn't handle the thought of her looking at him as if he was a monster. But if she knew what the Krampus was... then it was already too late.

"Krampus?" Spring asked, her head angled as if she was trying to remember something. "Why does that sound familiar?"

Frost's smug smile sent more dread tearing through Snow. He lurched forward, arms snapping together to grab Frost and squeeze him till he stopped talking. Frost dropped his corporeal form again, and Snow was left coated in a thin layer of frost. The annoying Fae reformed above the mantle this time, lounging along its length.

"I have to run," he said. "But to answer your question, he is the Krampus." Frost nodded toward Snow. "You probably didn't recognize him in his new form, so let me help you out with that before I go."

"Frost," Snow roared.

The other Fae smiled, his face was twisted in a cruel mockery of mirth. A thick layer of frost formed over his body, the tiny crystals morphing into a visage Snow hoped he would never see again. That long, sharp nose and matching chin were too familiar, even in this terrible ice-sculpture, as were the long, curving horns that rose straight from the top of his head. His lower body morphed into the cloven-hooved goatlike legs that Snow had hobbled on for so long. A sinewy tail made of ice with a tufted end flicked once, and then the entire thing crumbled in on itself, the ephemeral frost it was made of vanishing in a puff of steam before the fire.

Snow couldn't move. He couldn't breathe. All he could do was relive the moments when he had been trapped in that form and remember people running from him, screaming. Using darkness to mask his appearance as he tried to help others, and always—*always*—being found out for who he was and met with revulsion. Mist rose from his skin, swirling around him as his polar bear form burst forth in a blinding flash of radiance.

His heart was pounding, his mind filled with rage. The windows shook as he roared, the force of it extinguishing the fire and coating the walls before him in a thick coat of snow. He would destroy the walls holding him in this small space, then find Frost and rip him to shreds. He lifted one white-furred arm, ready to smash through a window, when he felt a small hand on his elbow. Breathing heavily, he paused and turned to see who dared try to keep him from his prey.

Spring stood next to him, eyebrows drawn together in worry. Her lips were parted, and a look of such compassion was on her face that it extinguished his anger instantly. She dared to move closer as he held himself still and pressed her other hand on his chest above his heart.

"Don't let Frost manipulate you," she said. "Show me the kind of man you truly are. Stay with me."

He let his bear form drop from him like a cloak, snow circling him in a whirlwind, then expanding out to restore the room to the way it had been. He added more of his own magic to it, summoning a glowing fire in the hearth, then expanded the sphere to create a bubble around the cabin that would shield them from any prying eyes—even those of the Fae. When he was done, he stared into Spring's eyes, his chest still heaving, his heart filled with more uncertainty than he'd ever known.

How could she want him now? He braced himself for her rejection. Instead she stared at him with that assessing look of hers. The moments dragged on in silence.

"I remember the stories now," she said. "The ones I heard about the Krampus."

He clenched his jaw, lips pressed in a thin line. There had been many places she could have started this conversation. How he had made her gown, his powers as Lord of Endless Snow, Jack Frost and their history. But she had gone straight to the topic that could hurt him most.

"The children you're fostering…" she said. "You take them, don't you? Those are the 'naughty' children from the tales."

It felt as though she'd punched him in his chest. He had thought his being the Krampus would be the most painful topic they could discuss, but she was going after his relationship with his kids? He drew himself up taller, hands curling into fists.

"I take the unwanted," he said. "The broken and forgotten. I give them purpose. Teach them to channel their anger and pain. I bring them to the Yuletide Kingdom and present them to the Winter Queen to give them a home. To give them a chance to be part of something instead of always being on the outside. Always alone."

She was quiet for a long time. Was she watching him squirm? Could she see that there was still a glimmer of hope within him? Always that stupid hope—back when he'd been the Krampus, and even now, looking at this beautiful woman and realizing just how much he already cared what she thought of him. He should never have let this happen.

"Frost is wrong," she said. "I don't think you're a control freak. No, I think what you do is all about fear."

"Fear?" Snow said, a laugh bursting from him despite

their situation. He pounded a fist on his chest, then stepped closer so that he was hovering over her. A little frisson of awareness shot up his spine at how close they were, but he shoved it away. "I am the terrifying Krampus. What do I have to fear?"

She didn't back down or even cringe. In fact, she leaned closer to him. The frisson turned to heat that entered through his chest. The fire in her eyes could melt all the snow in the universe.

"It isn't about control," she reiterated. "It's about caring. You care so much for your loved ones, you're terrified something will happen to them and you'll lose them. That's why you want everyone in their place, everyone doing the tasks you think will keep them safest. That's why you couldn't let North go and why it's bothering you so much that you're unable to get to Aidan and Sylvia."

The heat in his chest instantly chilled at her words, dread taking its place as his imagination filled in the details of what she suggested. The Winter Queen could be so cold, even to those in her court. Look at how she had exiled North so abruptly—and then made it permanent. Just because he wasn't the Lord of the North Wind anymore didn't mean he wasn't interested in visiting their home, the people that he had helped raise from the time they were young.

Snow couldn't imagine being cut off from his people so

completely—his children. He couldn't even think of his own pseudo-exile becoming permanent without changing back to his polar bear form and destroying the cabin. Sure, he'd trained his people well enough that they could keep things running without him, but he didn't want them to. The only thing keeping him from going completely crazy was that his holdings in the mortal realm gave him a conduit to his operations in the Kingdom of the Yuletide Fae.

He hated being cut off from his people. He hated that North wasn't standing at his side anymore. He hated that he couldn't support and guide Aidan and Sylvia as they got their bearings. Most of all, he hated that this mortal had laid this all out so plainly in front of him that he couldn't ignore it anymore.

"Stop talking," Snow growled.

Spring snorted, then stepped even closer to him, their chests almost brushing as she craned her neck back to fiercely hold his attention.

"You're afraid they'll mess up and need you and you won't be able to get to them in time," she said.

"Stop talking." His stomach twisted at the thought. What would make this infuriating mortal stop flinging these painful truths at him?

"You're not trying to control everyone, you're trying to keep them all safe."

He grabbed her arms and practically lifted her from her

feet as he crushed his mouth to hers in a searing kiss. It hadn't been thought out, it had been instinct that made him reach for her. Self-preservation. But once his lips touched hers, something new burst forth in his chest. A need, a desire, so fierce that it consumed him.

His reason fled, his own self-control vanished, and all he knew was Spring. Her warmth. Her arms twisting free from his grasp only to wrap around his neck and pull him closer, deepening their kiss, demanding more. He would give her everything he had. Everything he was.

Chapter Eight

Spring had been certain that Snow was filled with passion under his carefully controlled veneer. She had not been wrong. He kissed her as if he were drowning and she was air. As if she was his... everything. She was starting to feel the same toward him, even with all that she'd learned, all that she was still trying to reconcile in her mind.

He was powerful. He was magical. He could transform and had been transformed. It would take time for those aspects of his nature to feel truly real. But what already felt real, what she knew in her heart, was that he was a good man. The best she'd ever met. And he was her match, no matter how he'd started out or what the future held.

She deepened the kiss, heat spreading through her, demanding more. More of his hands on her, more contact. The stupid—gorgeous—dress made it hard for them to get closer, with its full skirts. How was she supposed to get it off? He had made it with magic. Did it even have a zipper or a clasp?

She kissed her way along his epic jawline, distracted by the pine and crisp snow scent of him. How could someone smell like freshly fallen snow? Her skin raced with goosebumps, confused by the invigorating scent and the warmth he was wrapping her in. Tabling that for later, she finally reached his ear. His hands clutched her back as he hissed in a breath, pressing her harder against him.

She nuzzled his neck and said, "Can you maybe help me with this dress?"

"What do you need?" he rasped, his voice even deeper than usual.

She chuckled. "I need to take it off."

His hands twitched against her back, his grip on her tightening. For a moment, she feared he was going to just tear the gorgeous dress off of her. And what about the clothing she'd been wearing before? That was her favorite Valentine's Day outfit.

"Can you change it back?" she asked.

"You don't like it?" He pulled back a bit, and the doubt in his eyes tugged at her heart.

She reached up and stroked his cheek. "I love it. But I don't know how to manage it. You can dress me up again later. Right now, I'm more interested in getting undressed."

A low growl rumbled out from his chest. The fire behind him roared higher, heat flooding the room. It was a good thing, because a moment later, snowflakes enveloped her, sweeping across her clothing and turning everything back to the way it had been before. Her hair was still dry, thankfully.

Somehow, being in her familiar clothes made everything that had happened seem more real. She was still herself, not some princess swept into a fairytale. But Snow... He was definitely her prince.

He bent to reclaim her lips, kissing her as if that momentary pause had starved him. She couldn't say she didn't feel the same. When he paused and pulled back to stare into her eyes, her lips quirked up into her habitual smirk. Her smile faded at the intensity in his gaze, the vulnerability. Did he still doubt that she wanted him?

"I want this," she said, her own voice husky with need and desire. "I want you. Never doubt that. Snow or Krampus, I don't care. I want *you*."

A tremor sort of shook him, his mouth dropping open and his eyes widening. He snapped his mouth shut, and a bright red glow sparked deep in his eyes. This time, she was sure of it. It was almost too bright to look at, but she held his gaze as she reached for his shirt. Again, he grasped her hands. This time, he held them in front of his chest for a moment, right above his heart. Slowly, he bent down and kissed her, all the passion from earlier lurking beneath the tenderness of the kiss, waiting to be released.

Patience was something she had always prided herself on, but she had none with him. All she had was hunger. She pressed her lips to his, kissing him with more passion than she'd felt for anyone. She could kiss him forever.

Her heart seemed to stutter for a moment as she realized that was exactly what she wanted with him. Forever. She was certain he wanted the same. She would do everything in her power to prove it to him.

Chapter Nine

Kissing Spring was the most intense experience of his incredibly long life. Snow stared down at her, his fingers tangled in her hair, and wondered how he could ever return to a life without her.

He couldn't. It was that simple. This was his eternity staring back at him. His woman.

He might not have firsthand experience, but he had read hundreds of romances over the years of his long existence, letting himself explore this aspect of love through others' stories. So far, everything he'd learned was really paying off. He would give Spring everything he had, bind her to him forever. With a mix of passion and precision, he worked a different kind of magic on her—on both of them—showing her the emotions that he didn't have words for yet.

After, he held her tight, reveling in her closeness. She was his. He would never, ever let her go. She sighed, her body relaxing in his embrace. The smile she cast up at him warmed him even more than what they had just done.

"Does time move differently in this pocket of Faerie,

like in the stories?" she asked. "Because I could stay like this for eternity."

"We aren't in Faerie." Snow chuckled, then bent to press a kiss to the nape of her neck. "This is Aidan and Sylvia's cabin, a little ways outside town."

"Aw." Spring's lower lip plumped in a pout. "I really want to see what Faerie is like. But I'm impressed we were able to do all that in the mortal realm, because that was pure magic."

Snow laughed again, finally pulling away from her, but only so he could roll her toward the fire and wrap himself around her. She pressed her face against his chest, one arm draped over his stomach.

"It was magic for me, too," he said.

"Can you tell me about it at least? Your home?"

His heart gave a tug that she was asking about his realm. There was warmth in her question along with an understandable curiosity.

"The sky is always midnight dark, but filled with a glowing green aurora."

"Like the aurora borealis?" she asked.

"But brighter," he said. "And it fills the entire sky. There's always a thick layer of snow on everything, and it catches the light and glows brightly enough to see by."

"I heard you and North talking about how there's never spring."

"Yeah." He held her tighter.

"But there used to be?"

"We aren't sure what happened. Even though we're ruled by the Winter Queen, there used to be seasons. One day, they just stopped. Shortly after, she came to North and me and offered us a deal."

"What kind of deal?"

"Power. The ability to change forms. Places of honor in her court as her Fairy Lords."

"Wow." Spring was quiet for a while, no doubt thinking about all he'd said.

That none of this had freaked her out was a testament to her strength of mind and will. He had never met anyone like her before, in any of the realms, Faerie or otherwise.

"You're taking this all really well, you know," he said.

"You were a lot to manage." She grinned at him and waggled her eyebrows.

A laugh burst out of him, deep and loud and long. He didn't think he'd ever laughed like that before in his life. He hugged her closer as it subsided, and she tightened her own grasp of him as well.

"You know that's not what I meant," he said.

She shrugged, an odd, far-off look entering her eyes. The crackling of the wood in the fireplace was the only sound for several minutes. He wanted to know what was going through her mind, but wouldn't press her. She would share with him when she was ready. Something in her look made him feel she was delving into a topic of great importance.

"It's all about priorities." She lifted her arm and started tracing the lines of his stomach, outlining each abdominal. "Who doesn't want to believe in fairies and magic? What I've experienced with you has been incredible—especially the most recent activities."

He chuckled lightly. He definitely agreed. The closeness they had shared had been the most amazing experience of his life. A greater magic than anything he'd encountered.

"It could have been terrifying, too," she said.

He sucked in a breath without meaning to and held it. The idea of her being afraid of him… Well, it terrified *him*. The Krampus. He hadn't realized just how much power this woman had over him until now. But he trusted her. He knew she had a good heart. One of the best he'd ever encountered. She proved it as she went on.

"But when I looked past all that, at what you're using your power for, it stops being about dreams and becomes about reality." She raised herself on one elbow, bringing her hand to his cheek. "You help children. Children with no one in their lives who notices or cares enough to reach out to them. You give them a home and you love them. I could hear it in your voice when you shared that story about Malachi. I see it in your face every time you talk about them."

His eyes burned and the light from the fire glimmered

oddly as they filled with moisture. He grasped her hand and pressed it against his cheek, closing his eyes briefly before pressing her hand to his lips for a kiss. He didn't trust his voice to speak, so he nodded, hoping his face was conveying all the love he felt for her in that moment.

"I want to learn more about your operations," she said. "You can't just whisk children off to some Faerie realm, even if it's to help them. And your home, while it sounds beautiful, it also seems... cold. Stark. Children need love more than anything, and I'm so glad you're giving them that. But they also need sunlight and trees and grass."

"I don't know how to give them those things," he said. "The Winter Queen is the one who wields that power. She's also the one who insists we bring her a child each year at Christmas."

"Hmm..." Spring's eyebrows drew together, her eyes were getting that far-off look again that he now realized meant she was thinking.

Snow waited as long as he could stand it, then prompted, "What?"

"That's weird timing, don't you think? I mean, why Christmas? Why not the Winter Solstice or really any other day of the year?"

"I never really thought about it. Maybe it's because that day centers around children already?"

"I don't know." She was quiet for a moment, then said, "I never dreamed I'd ask this question seriously, but with all these Christmas fairies being real, is Santa real, too?"

Snow chuckled and nuzzled the top of her head. "Yeah. But we call him Lord Kringle."

"Wow. I need to process that. Give me a minute."

He ran his hands down her back, enjoying the soft texture of her skin. When he looked at her again, she still had that concentrated focus in her eyes.

"Lord Kringle..." she said. "So, he's a Fairy Lord, too? Like you and the Yule Cat."

"It's me and the White Stag, now."

A pang of loss thrummed through his heart, but not as intense as it had been. North was happy living in the mortal realm and simply being the Yule Cat. And from everything Malachi had shared, Aidan and Sylvia were doing a great job taking on the roles of Lord and Lady of the North Wind.

"Okay, but what about Santa?" Spring said. "Is he part of the Winter Queen's court as well?"

"No. She kind of has a tendency to banish people if they upset her."

"She banished *Santa*? Harsh."

"He at least gets to remain in the Yuletide Kingdom. He has a spot of land in the far reaches where he has his workshop and helpers."

Her lips pressed together as she tried to suppress a smile and failed. "Oh my God, I can't believe that's real. You have to take me there."

His own smile faltered. "As much as I hate to disappoint you, the Winter Queen decreed no one is allowed to visit him. I'm already on the Winter Queen's shit list. If I did that, my 'time-out' in the mortal realm would surely become permanent."

"That's awful." Spring rose up on her elbows again. "How could Santa have made her mad enough to get himself exiled? I mean, he's *Santa*."

"It was before my time. He was exiled right when North and I were brought into her court. I've actually never seen them in the same room together."

Snow hadn't given this much thought before, but now that Spring had pointed it out, it was hard not to think about. The Winter Queen had banished Kringle from her court, but not her kingdom. Was she supporting him in continuing his practice of bringing joy and cheer to children on Christmas? Staying in the kingdom would give him access to his people, as well as the tools and magic he needed to get his work done.

Knowing the Queen, Snow could absolutely believe she would want to keep that going. He also knew her temper. He was surprised she hadn't reassigned those duties to someone else. Something was going on there. He would have to look into it—very carefully—when she summoned him back to the Yuletide Kingdom.

Chapter Ten

Spring couldn't stop thinking about the Winter Queen and Santa. Well, she especially couldn't stop thinking about Santa. Why was it so hard to believe he was real when she'd fallen in love with the Krampus? And she *had* fallen for him. It was happening fast, but she couldn't deny the intensity of what she felt. It wasn't infatuation or wanting to be part of his magical world. She wanted *him*. She hugged him harder, pressing her face against his chest.

There had to be a reason for the Winter Queen's actions. As mercurial as fairies were said to be in all the legends, Spring had to believe that. Otherwise, how could she help keep Snow from meeting a similar fate? It would crush him to be cut off from his people—his kids. She would do everything in her power to prevent that.

"Why did the Winter Queen banish North?" Spring asked.

"He chose to be with Melanie. He loves being in the mortal realm."

"So? Haven't you guys ever heard of a timeshare?"

Snow chuckled, the rumbling sound vibrating beneath

her and warming her heart. Jack Frost had pulled her from Melanie and North's apartment. If that was all it took to go from one realm to another, what would have been the problem with North living in both worlds? Would Snow be able to? Would he even want to?

She didn't like the idea of leaving her life behind. She had worked hard to build up her business, and there were so many people who counted on her in the mortal realm. Though she didn't directly provide homes for kids, there were still a lot of organizations that benefited from her donations and pro bono efforts. She knew she was probably getting ahead of herself, but she at least wanted to know what her options were going forward.

"Is it hard to travel back and forth from the mortal realm and the Yuletide Kingdom?" she asked.

"Not at all. The first thing I taught Aidan and Sylvia was how to create a portal to take them anywhere they wanted."

"Like Frost did to us?"

"No, what he did was different. A portal is like a doorway between worlds that you can step through. He created a temporary pocket of Faerie around us."

"But he was able to move us. I mean, he dropped us in this cabin when he was done messing with us."

Snow snorted. "Frost will never be done messing with us."

"Then why did he leave us in this awesome cabin?"

Snow's chest grew as he sucked in a huge breath, his entire body tensing. She sat up to see what was bothering him. His eyes were wide and gleamed red. He launched himself from the floor and sprinted down the hall toward the door. A blast of cold air hit her as he opened it. Spring grabbed a blanket and wrapped it around herself as she followed him.

Snow stood in front of the door, silhouetted against a midnight sky filled with glowing green aurora. He had said this cabin was just outside of town. They were nowhere near far enough north to be seeing the aurora borealis. But that meant...

"That bastard," he murmured. "That unbelievable bastard. He left us in the Yuletide Kingdom."

"He recreated the whole cabin?"

"It was the only way he could get me to use my powers. I made a shield around it. The Winter Queen is sure to have detected it."

"But then—"

"She'll exile me."

"No." Spring took a few steps forward, though the chill from the door was already making her teeth chatter. "We're not going to let that happen. What can we do?"

Snow closed the door and marched down the hall, leaving a trail of snowflakes that swept across the floor as if they had a life of their own. They caught up with him, a whirlwind of snow surrounding his body and coating it in a gorgeous white uniform. The jacket had two rows of gold buttons that ran along a diagonal over his massive chest and the high collar that circled his neck was trimmed in bright red that matched the glow of his eyes. His white pants hugged his muscular legs and ended just above his gleaming black boots.

She had never seen anyone so gorgeous. Her heart raced as he strode confidently toward her, her very own fairytale prince. If she wasn't so cold, she would toss away her blanket and throw herself at him. That and the grim determination on his face held her back. He swept a hand toward her as he approached, and snowflakes flew across the floorboard, swirling up her body into the same golden dress as before. The moment the jewelry was in place, her chill vanished, along with the snow.

"His trail isn't too cold for me to track him," Snow said. "You'll be safe here till I get back."

"You're going after him? Now?"

"Without him, there's no way I can convince the Winter Queen that returning against her wishes wasn't my doing. I have to find Jack Frost."

Spring hated the thought of being trapped in a Faerie realm by herself. What if something happened to him? She tried to shake away the fear, but it must have come across in her expression.

"Don't worry." He pulled her close, leaning in to plant a searing kiss on her lips. When he finally released her, she was breathless and the room was spinning. "Nothing will ever keep me from you."

She didn't trust her voice to speak, but she nodded and forced a smile. He bent down to kiss her forehead and her heart fluttered at the sweetness of it. Then he turned and was gone, the door closing behind him and leaving her alone. She stood there for several moments, praying to anyone who was listening that Snow would be safe.

She should have been more specific.

"I thought he would never leave," a smarmy voice said right behind her.

She wheeled around to see Jack Frost standing so close, the skirts of her dress brushed against him as she turned. She backed away, and he followed, till her back was pressed against the island that separated the kitchen from the rest of the great room and she had nowhere left to escape to. Frost put one hand on the counter, leaning in close as he looked her up and down.

"You look amazing," he said. "But then, Lord Snow does have a knack for fashion. Appearances are really important to him, after being stuck as the Krampus for so long." He mock-shivered, then smiled.

"How did you get in here?"

"I built the place with my magic. Did you really think I didn't put in a back door?"

She lifted her chin and said, "What do you want?"

"Me?" He pressed his fingers to his chest, eyebrows

raised in an exaggerated expression of curiosity and innocence. "I just want you and Snow to have your very own 'Happily Ever After.'"

She snorted. She couldn't help it.

Frost tutted and shook his head. "That's not very ladylike. You'll need better manners when you meet the Winter Queen. She's big on all that formal stuff." He waved his hand dismissively. "You'll learn."

"I don't believe you."

"About the Winter Queen? No, no. She really is a stickler for that kind of thing. Just ask North's girlfriend, Melanie. She got them both banished for 'speaking impudently.'" He leaned closer and said, "Honestly, I think it was a bad call. Modern mortal women aren't afraid to state their opinions. Good for you. Just be aware that there are consequences for that when dealing with Fae royalty."

"What..." She made an exasperated sound. Every instinct was telling her that this guy didn't have a sincere bone in his body, but what he said made a lot of sense when she lined it up with all that Snow had taught her. "What's your angle? Because there's no way that you're sharing all this out of the goodness of your heart."

"Didn't you know?" Frost said, that smarmy smirk on his face that she wanted to just smack right off of him. He leaned closer and whispered, "I'm working with Santa." He rolled his eyes and spoke more conversationally. "Lord Kringle, as some call him. I'm like one of his little helpers

—temporarily."

"Why the heck would Santa want Snow and me to be a couple?" Spring asked. That didn't make any sense.

"Come on. Old Saint Nick? Bringer of joy and merriment to children of all ages? He wants everyone to be happy. Especially his family, and that includes every member of the Yuletide Court."

She folded her arms over her chest and glared at him. "A court that you would have been a Lord in, if it wasn't for Snow."

Frost made a dismissive snort and rolled his eyes again. "Like I'd want to be a Fairy Lord. At the beck and call of the Winter Queen? Have her bossing me around all the time?" He waved his hand as if shooing something away. "Not my scene."

"Then why have you been harassing us?" Spring said, exasperation lacing her voice.

"Harassing you?" He laughed. "You have it all wrong. I've been matchmaking."

"What?" Her mind spun. What was he talking about?

"I knew that Snow would never spend time with a mortal unless he thought he had something to make up for. He's such an honorable guy." Frost somehow managed to make even his compliments sound condescendingly derogatory.

"That little accident that brought you two together?" he went on. "Him slipping on the ice, right as you were looking out the window to see him fall? And then the bus coming, and yet another patch of ice making you land on top of him as you tried to pull him back?"

Frost made a tutting sound. "I hate to tell you, princess, but that meet cute was all me. I arranged it, just like I made sure you were aware of his true nature, both as a Fairy Lord and as the Krampus. Figured it'd be best to get all that drama out in the open and over with as soon as possible so you two could get on with... bonding." He waggled his eyebrows suggestively.

Spring's cheeks prickled, her eyes wide with disbelief. She hated feeling like she had been manipulated into this, even if it had resulted in her and Snow being together. And if she felt this enraged, how would it affect Snow? His feelings for her?

"Do you know what you've done?" Spring snapped.

Frost's lips pulled into a downturned line at her tone, but he waved his hand in a circle as if to encourage her to speak. "Enlighten me."

"You've ruined any chance we had at real happiness. There will always be that sliver of doubt now. Is it really love? Or is it just another spell?"

"My magic doesn't work that way," Frost said. "I'm not Cupid. I just... created certain situations that might lead to entertaining results and sat back to enjoy the fun. I had no idea it would end up this good—that was all Kringle. But, after all is said and done, you're perfect for each other, I assure you."

"I know that," she bit out each word. "He is everything I ever dreamed of and more. He's the one who's going to wonder for the rest of time if he really loves me or if this is just another fairy asshole trying to control him."

"I can explain it to him if you'd like," Frost said with a beatific smile.

She jerked forward, jabbing her finger into his chest so that *he* was the one who backed away. "You will stay the hell away from my man, or I swear to whatever gods are real I will build the biggest barbecue pit in history and roast you over it on a spit until all that's left of you is steam."

Deep laughter washed over her. She turned to see Snow standing behind her in the doorway, his arms loose at his sides and a huge smile on his face. He shook his head as he quieted.

"Woman," he said. "After hearing you say that, I will never, ever doubt that you are my perfect match."

Chapter Eleven

"What are you doing back so soon?" Frost asked, his brow furrowing.

Snow chuckled, glad to see the asshole genuinely perplexed. "You think I couldn't detect a fake trail? I knew you had doubled back within two minutes. I didn't know you were stupid enough to harass my woman, though." He walked up next to Spring and wrapped an arm around her, tucking her against his side.

"Harass?" Frost took a step farther away from them. "No. Spring and I were just getting to know each other better."

"Yes," Spring said, her voice oozing saccharine sweetness. "And Frost here knows me well enough now to be aware that I will rip out his spleen if he doesn't tell the Winter Queen that he is the one who transported us here—without our knowledge or permission."

Snow let out a rumbling growl of approval. He knew that Spring was strong. He hadn't known how fierce she was until he returned and heard her lighting into Frost. Sure, she didn't have a chance of really doing anything to him. Frost was a powerful Fae in his own right. But Snow had a feeling that wouldn't matter to Spring. She would stand up to anyone that she thought meant him harm.

His chest filled with warmth at the thought. No one had ever stood up for him before. Not like this. He reached down and trailed a finger along her jaw, lifting her face to his, then bent down and kissed her. He pushed all his love and passion into that tender kiss, willing her to understand the words he hadn't had a chance to say yet.

"You're welcome," Frost said, cutting into their moment.

They both turned to him, scowling.

"I don't remember thanking you," Spring said.

"And I forgive you for your terrible manners." Frost bowed lightly.

"Fairies don't normally thank each other," Snow said, addressing Spring. "It can be seen as acknowledging a debt. There's always an angle." He focused on Frost and said, "We owe you nothing, Frost."

Frost tutted, shaking his head. "So ungrateful."

"What is it that you want?" Spring said. "Power? A favor?"

"I don't want power." Frost rolled his eyes. "I want freedom. Power is only a means to an end."

"What do you want freedom from?" Snow asked. "Are you looking to change courts? Because they're all pretty much the same."

"Exactly," Frost snapped. For a moment, a look of

anger crossed his features. It was the most genuine expression Snow had ever seen from the Fae. It didn't last long

"You got me." Frost smiled and lifted both arms as if surrendering. "I don't want to be claimed by any court."

"Every Fae is claimed," Snow said.

"And what kind of shitty system is that?" Frost paced back and forth in the small space between the kitchen island and the couch. "Claimed as subjects by the most powerful Fae around, but what they really mean is that we're resources at their beck and call. Little chess pieces to be moved around the board and used however they please." He paused near Spring, arms crossed over his chest. In a calmer voice, he said, "It's really not all that bad. Welcome to the family," and smirked.

"Wow, you've really sold me on it," Spring said. "But if you want me to be excited about Team Yuletide Fae, maybe do us a solid and confess to the Winter Queen that you're the reason Snow is here against her wishes so that he doesn't get permanently exiled."

"Mmm, can't do that," Frost said.

Spring let out a frustrated grunt. "Why not?"

"Couples grow stronger when they go through adversity together," Frost said. "Besides, you're not the only pair I'm trying to help."

"What?" Spring's voice rose, an exasperated edge to it.

Snow expected nothing else from Frost. He was

actually surprised the Fae had been so forthcoming. But who was the other couple he was trying to help? North and Melanie, maybe? Was he trying to get the Winter Queen to lift her banishment of North so that he could visit his home? Snow had to admit to himself that he would love that. At the moment, he was most concerned with avoiding the same fate.

"The Winter Queen will banish me when she finds me here," Snow said. "I'm surprised she hasn't shown up already."

"Well, you did that whole shielding thing." Frost leaned a bit closer. "Very impressive, I must admit. It did, however use a bunch of your magic, so as soon as the shield drops, she'll sense your mark all over this spot."

"Then he can just keep the shield up," Spring said. "Can you do that?"

"It'll be a strain on my power, but I think so." Snow nodded.

"See?" Frost said. "You're already problem solving together. You two are going to stand the test of time. I'm sure of it."

"Your faith in us warms my heart." Spring packed an impressive amount of sarcasm in her tone. Frost only laughed.

"I still don't understand why you're doing this," Snow said. "How is this going to free you from the Court of the Yuletide Fae? Whose favor are you trying to earn?"

"Come on," Frost said. "You said yourself that we're going to be claimed by someone, no matter what we do. Whoever has the most power gets to boss everyone else around. I just need someone who understands that I want to be left to my own devices. I have my own projects, you know."

The thought was not comforting. What kind of projects would Jack Frost be up to?

"I am starting to think I have a bit of a knack for this matchmaking thing, though," Frost said. "I might be able to give Cupid a run for his money."

"Wait, Cupid is real?" Spring asked. Snow and Frost both turned to her, each arching an eyebrow. She nodded. "Right. I have a lot to learn, apparently."

"And soon you'll have all the time in eternity to learn it," Frost said.

Spring's eyes narrowed. "What do you mean by that?"

Snow already knew. They hadn't had a chance to broach the subject yet, but Snow had begun to think of ways to bring Spring into the Yuletide Kingdom and what that would mean for them both. He was immortal. He couldn't stand the thought of forever without her.

"He means that for us to be together, you'd have to become like me," Snow said.

"Like *us*," Frost corrected. "You need to become a fairy."

Frost linked his thumbs together and spread his hands,

waggling his fingers like wings in an approximation of a butterfly. Snow just rolled his eyes at Frost, then turned to Spring and ran his hands along her arms. His chest felt tight, nerves churning his stomach. This was not how or when he wanted to have this conversation, but there was no way around it.

"I know this is all happening fast, but if you truly want to be with me—" he began.

"I do," Spring said. "Of course, I do."

Frost leaned behind her so that Snow could see his face but she couldn't. He mouthed, 'of course,' silently.

"Do you mind?" Snow said.

"Me?" Frost pressed his fingers to his chest. "Not at all. Continue."

Snow let out an exasperated breath and shook his head. He would deal with Frost in a minute.

Snow turned back to Spring and said, "I want to be with you, too. Not just for your mortal lifetime. Forever."

She smiled, her eyes lighting up as she nodded. "That sounds wonderful."

"Even if you have to deal with assholes like him?" Snow nodded his head toward Frost.

"I think I can handle it," she said.

"I can hear you, you know," Frost said.

Spring ignored him. "Is that something you can do?"

Snow had been expecting this question from her, and dreading it. He was powerful, but he couldn't grant immortality to others, effectively making them Fae. Very few had that ability. If the Winter Queen didn't accept Spring, he would have to petition someone else. The political ramifications of asking a ruler of another Court of the Fae were too horrible for him to contemplate, but that only left him with Lord Kringle. Kringle had been the one to make Melanie immortal. Maybe he could do it again for Spring. But Snow asking him would not sit well with the Winter Queen. Snow and Spring might have to join North and Melanie in exile.

"It isn't," Snow said. "But we can find someone who can."

Spring narrowed her eyes as she scrutinized him. "What aren't you telling me?"

"Just…" He tried to find a way to explain that wouldn't burden her, yet wouldn't keep her from the truth. "It's going to be very tricky to navigate. But I'm sure we can figure it out."

She smiled at him and wrapped her arms around his waist. "I am, too."

"See?" Frost said. "Look at you. Facing obstacles together."

"Are you still here?" Spring said, glaring at him.

"I am." Frost cocked his head to the side, lips pressed in a thoughtful line. "But it's about time I left." He took a few steps back and pressed his hand to his chest. "For what it's worth, I believe in you two. You will absolutely get through this and be stronger for it."

"Wait, get through what?" Snow said, taking a step closer.

Frost smiled, then snapped his fingers. In a puff of vapor, he vanished.

So did the cabin—and with it, the sphere of obscuring power Snow had linked to it.

Snow's eyes grew wide as he saw nothing but a forest clearing around them. The aurora overhead reflected off the snow coating the ground and the branches of the trees, giving them plenty of light to see by. Behind him, he felt a crackle of raw power so intense, he knew what that light would reveal. He turned in a slow circle, till he was facing the Winter Queen.

Chapter Twelve

Where the heck had the cabin gone? One minute, Spring was snuggled up next to Snow, standing in front of a warm fire, the next, they were in the middle of a clearing in a forest of evergreens and denuded trees. Everything was cast in a gold-green glow from the aurora above, the trees' branches nothing more than dark shadows to her vision. Snow stiffened beside her and sucked in a breath. He held it as they both spun around to see what was behind them. Or rather, who.

A tall woman stood a few paces away, her hands clasped elegantly in front of herself. Her blonde hair was pulled back in a tight chignon that was held in place partly by a crown of platinum spikes, like a starburst around her head. Diamonds glittered in the light both from above and that she seemed to radiate herself. Her skin was as white as the snow she stood upon, and her dress a pale blue silk, like moonlight wrapped around her. Her high cheekbones and pointed chin and nose might have made her more beautiful, except for the harsh frown of her red lips and the pinched skin around her emerald-green eyes. This had to be the Winter Queen.

Spring swallowed hard. The air was thick with tension. Snow had yet to release that breath he had taken. He stared at the woman with wide eyes, his mouth hanging open.

"My Lord Snow," the Winter Queen said.

Spring tried not to be irked by the claim in her greeting. She might have made it, if Snow hadn't immediately dropped to one knee, his head bowed.

"Majesty," Snow said.

Spring didn't know what to do. She sort of curtseyed briefly, but mostly wanted to draw as little attention to herself as possible. That didn't work out, either.

"Another mortal woman?" the Winter Queen said. "Why have you brought her here?"

"He didn't bring me," Spring quickly said. "Jack Frost did. He brought both of us and—"

"Spring." Snow reached out and grasped her hand. She looked down at him and he shook his head. The skin at the corners of his eyes was pinched with worry.

"Jack Frost has been wronged enough," the Winter Queen said. "Do not dare attempt to cast blame on the one who should have been Lord of the North Wind."

Snow bowed his head lower. Spring couldn't stand seeing him like this. Sure, the Winter Queen was his... liege or something, but that didn't mean he should have to grovel around her. What kind of person was she?

She's not a person, Spring reminded herself. *She's a fairy.*

But Snow was kind. So was North, from everything Spring had seen. Maybe they were the exceptions instead of the rules? Jack Frost had certainly been a dick.

"You defy me yet again," the Winter Queen said. "Returning to my kingdom without my leave."

"But—" Spring stopped herself as Snow squeezed her hand tighter.

"You were always my most loyal subject," the Winter Queen said.

'Were?' As in past-tense? Was Snow about to be exiled?

"Majesty, I remain loyal." Snow's voice was tight with strain.

"Perhaps." The Winter Queen was silent for a few moments, then said, "Perhaps I will give you a chance to prove that to me. You shall perform penance."

Snow bowed deeper again. "As you decree."

"But he didn't do anything wrong," Spring burst out. It was just too much. She couldn't stand watching Snow being treated this way. "You can't just—"

The Winter Queen spoke over Spring, voice rising. "You may begin your penance *after* you return this woman to the mortal realm. Spin a charm to take her memory of this place, the Fae, and of you."

"What?" Spring nearly shouted.

At the same time, Snow sprang to his feet at last. "Majesty, I beg you—"

"Beg?" The Winter Queen snapped. "You, the Krampus, resort to begging? What has this woman done to you?"

Snow looked at Spring, his expression filled with wonder. "She's opened my eyes, my mind, my heart to a love I never dreamed I would experience."

"She has weakened you," the Queen said.

Snow shook his head. "She's made me stronger."

"I will not have her in my kingdom," the Queen said.

"Then I'll live in the mortal realm and he can visit me there," Spring said.

"Spring…" Snow's voice trailed off.

"I forbid it!" The Winter Queen slashed her hand through the air. Above, the aurora shivered, its green glow cutting out for a moment and throwing them into darkness. The branches shook from a chill wind that swirled around her, then vanished.

How far did Spring dare push this? She looked up at Snow, at the turmoil in his features, and knew she would do anything for him.

She turned back to the Queen and said, "We can find a way to make this work."

"He must prove his loyalty to me and no other," the Queen said. "One world or another. That is his choice."

No…

"Please, all his children are here." Spring couldn't be responsible for Snow being exiled. She knew how that would hurt him. "His family needs him."

"Indeed," the Queen said. "Which is why you must not distract him from his duties. Your paths are different. You must let him go."

"But I can help him, help all of you." Spring dared to take a step closer to the Winter Queen, her voice pleading "Please, haven't you ever been in love?"

The Winter Queen's brow drew down over her eyes, her voice rising as she spoke. "I know all I need of mortal love—fickle and weak. As impermanent as your insignificant lives."

Wait… She was in love with a mortal. Maybe she still is…

It was obvious in the pain that flooded her features, the passion in her tone. What had happened that had hardened her heart? At the same time, she still had warmth toward children. Spring could never hate the Winter Queen, knowing how they both shared that dream of helping others. There had to be a way Spring could make her understand that one hurt—or even many—didn't mean she had to close off her heart.

Begging didn't seem likely to work with her. Plus, that wasn't Spring's style. No, she was going to push this in her own way.

"If we're so insignificant, why bother saving our children?" Spring demanded, crossing her arms defiantly. "They're mortal, too."

The Winter Queen drew herself up taller. "Only when we find them. Once they have joined my court, they become Fae."

"Once you adopt them," Spring said.

The Queen's mouth opened briefly, but then she snapped it shut again. Spring was definitely gaining ground.

"You bring them into your family," Spring said. "Can't you do the same with me?"

"This is what you want, then?" The Queen narrowed her eyes. "Power? Immortality?"

"No." Spring turned back to Snow and said, "I want to be with him. And I want to help people—to help children. I want to stand at Snow's side and support him. To help him in his life's work—the same work I've always dreamed of doing myself. Helping as many children as we can in the best way that we can. Working together to make a better life for them. Can't you, of all beings, understand that?"

Spring looked back at the Queen and her breath caught in her chest. The Winter Queen backed away a step, and then another. Her hand was clutched in front of her heart as if she was desperately trying to hold it in one piece. She shook her head sharply.

In a voice that was barely above a whisper, she said, "I can not."

She looked so lost and alone in that moment, that

Spring's heart felt as though it might break. Whatever had happened to her, this was the crux of it. At the same time, Snow stared at the Queen with wide eyes, his skin drawn and bloodless. He looked... afraid. Terrified, even. What frightened Spring the most was that she wasn't sure what he was afraid of.

The Queen could exile him, but they could make things work in the mortal realm, couldn't they? He had said he had ways of communicating with his people, so they wouldn't be completely cut off. Was he considering erasing Spring's memories of himself?

No. He would never do such a thing. She knew his heart, the goodness and protectiveness there. She hated that the Winter Queen was trying to give him an ultimatum. Spring still couldn't shake the feeling that there was more at stake than he was telling her.

The Winter Queen took a few steps away, shaking her head again, then said, "You have heard my decree. Choose. Are you no longer my Lord Snow?"

"Majesty..." Snow bowed his head. "There is no choice to be made. My heart belongs to Spring. Forever."

Chapter Thirteen

"You choose her over me?" The Winter Queen's voice was low and harsh. "Over your sworn duties as a Lord of the Court of the Yuletide Fae?"

"Majesty," Snow said, stepping forward.

"So be it." Her face became impassive as she stood straighter. "Then you are Lord of Endless Snow no more. You are merely as I found you. The Krampus."

"Wait—" His eyes widened in shock, his stomach flooded with icicles of dread. She couldn't truly mean to turn him back. Could she?

With a flick of her wrist that was as casual as it was cruel, he felt the power of the Lord of Endless Snow leach from his body, summoned back to her. As it left him, curving horns rose up from his head, his shoulders hunched, and claws sprang forth from his fingers. His chin and nose jutted out from his face far enough that he could see them with his own eyes, his cheekbones rising within his periphery as well. His legs morphed and sprouted fur, his feet changed to hooves. All that he had left to cover himself was the tattered remains of his jacket, though his thick fur concealed his skin.

He looked down at his hands, their skin was rough and patchy, sharp, black claws curling at their fingertips. How could he ever hold Spring again like this? How could he let her see him?

He curled away from her, intending to run, but felt her hands on his arm, holding tight.

"Don't even think of bolting," she said, her voice strong and calm. "Look at me. Snow… Look at me."

This was better. Get it over and done with. Let his hope for anything more than this bleak and lonely existence die along with her love for him. He shook his head and turned, standing straighter so that she could see his full, terrifying form.

"Not Snow," he said in a guttural growl. "The Krampus."

Her eyes widened slightly as she looked at him, but only for a moment. Then she smirked at him. That same smirk, filled with warmth and a mystery that no longer bothered him but only drew him in.

"You've always been the Krampus," she said. "I've known that from the start. But you're also Snow, Lord or not. My Snow."

She reached up and cupped his cheek, pulling him down to her. His heart thudded like the thunder of a herd of stampeding reindeer. Did she truly mean to kiss him? Even in this hideous form? She smiled at him—a true smile—just before their lips touched. Warmth flooded him, the same warmth that always filled him when they kissed. Taking great care, he wrapped his hands around her waist, keeping his claws from prickling her clothing or scratching her skin.

She wrapped her arms around his neck and clung to him, moving to his ear to whisper, "I don't care what you look like. I know who you are within. And I love you."

"I love you, too," he said, holding her close.

He looked up at the Winter Queen to see her face a mask of disbelief. Her chest rose and fell quickly with near-panicked breaths. What little color she had had faded from her face and her eyes were wide as she stared at them.

"Very well," she said, composing herself once more. "Since you are so determined to be together, it's only fitting that you match."

The Winter Queen lifted her arms in the air, a terrible energy gathering around them. Bolts of lightning arced through clouds of snow and frost that swirled around her. She raised her hands above her head, the greatest look of fury on her face that the Krampus had ever seen.

He held Spring close, and whispered, "I'm so sorry."

"Elysa!" A loud voice rang through the air, resonating with enough power to make the Krampus stagger.

He held tighter to Spring as they helped each other keep their balance, turning to try to find the source. The Krampus froze as he saw that the fury in the Winter

Queen's face had been replaced with shock and something he couldn't name. Her cheeks flushed pink and her eyes were wide, her lips parted. The energy that had gathered around her dropped harmlessly to the ground and disappeared. She turned slowly, stepping aside to reveal Lord Kringle standing several feet away.

He looked... different. His dark red jacket was replaced with a bright red coat that buttoned on a diagonal up one side. The lapels were lined with white fur and more of the same peeked out from his cuffs. He wore a broad, shiny black belt and matching boots, with darker red pants tucked into them. The buckle on his belt was a platinum snowflake, the symbol of the Winter Queen. His white hair was combed back from his forehead and swept around his shoulders, and his beard had been neatly trimmed.

It was his eyes that were most changed, though. The mirth that usually twinkled in their blue depths was blurred by tears, and deep lines of pain shone in the wrinkles at the corners of his eyes.

"Enough, Elysa," he said, his voice no longer echoing with command. "It's me that you're mad at. Don't take it out on your boys."

"You aren't supposed to be here," she whispered in hoarse tones. "I didn't want... I didn't ever want to see you again."

"I know and I'm sorry," Kringle said. "I stayed away for as long as I could. But I miss you. I miss you terribly."

The Winter Queen drew herself up taller, clasping her shaking hands in front of her as if she was afraid she might reach for him. A day ago, Snow wouldn't have understood. Now... Now, he thought he might have a better idea of what had been going on ever since North had refused to bring the Winter Queen a tribute all those years ago.

"You abandoned me," she said, and power crackled through her words.

Snow pulled Spring closer, inching away from the pair. Kringle showed no sign of fear. Only sadness. He approached the Queen, who arched away from him, though her feet seemed rooted to the spot.

"I was stubborn and single-minded." Kringle shook his head. "I only wanted to feel joy, to focus on bringing more of that into the world. What you wanted—"

"What I wanted was to *help* those children who needed us most," she yelled. "Not simply leave them toys once a year and be done with it."

Kringle's eyes widened. His mouth opened and closed a few times, then shut as he nodded.

"We couldn't..." He paused to clear his throat. "We couldn't help all of them. We still can't."

"That shouldn't stop us from trying to help the ones we *can*," she said, her voice nearly breaking.

"You're right," Kringle said. "You've always been stronger than I. You can look at the ones left behind—the ones struggling and lashing out—and it gives you a sense of purpose. For me, it brings despair that fills my heart and paralyzes me." His eyes shimmered as his voice turned to an intense whisper. "I'm no good to anyone like that."

The Winter Queen stared at him in stunned silence, her own mouth dropping open. A line of frost flowed down her cheek from the corner of her eye, forming a tiny teardrop of ice that softly clinked as it landed on the ground.

This was what had caused them to part ways? Why she had reached out to the Krampus and the Yule Cat to help her with her cause in helping children? No wonder she had lashed out so harshly when North refused. She had already been abandoned once. Now, she thought it was happening again with Snow. But it wasn't. He had to find a way to convince her of that. To show her that they could still help with her mission, but in a better way. With even more resources, especially with what Lord Kringle was saying.

"Kris…" she said.

Kringle dared to reach out and grasp her hands, pulling her closer to him.

"I never meant to abandon you," he said. "I should have faced my fears and shared them with you, not retreated to my workshop and ignored them. I should have supported you and not ignored what you wanted. We could have found a better way to overcome our differences if I only had tried harder. Been less intent on my own goals. But, maybe together, we can find a way forward now."

As he pulled her closer, he whispered, "I swear on

everything I am, I will not fail you again. Please, give me another chance to love you. Properly this time. As partners."

She smiled at him and nodded. "That is all I ever wanted." A tear flowed down her cheek, and this time, it left no trail of frost. She shook her head and said, "I could never resist you."

Lord Kringle and the Winter Queen leaned toward each other, fingers intertwined as they pressed their lips together in a tender kiss. Light spread over the horizon behind them, the aurora above retreating for the first time in Snow's memory. Crocuses burst forth through the white coating the ground, surrounding them with brilliant dots of pale or rich purple and vibrant gold. In the distance, the Krampus heard a songbird pierce the silence of the fallen snow.

Brilliant light spun around Kringle's head as a small crown of platinum and diamonds settled upon it. The light also swept over the Winter Queen, transforming her crown to one that matched his. Her nearly-colorless dress deepened to a rich emerald green that matched her eyes, her skirts became fuller, and an elegant apron appeared tied around her waist. A few wisps of hair loosened from what was now more a bun than a chignon, softening her features as she pulled back and smiled at her husband.

"You're Mrs. Claus," Spring exclaimed. "Mrs. Santa Claus!"

The Winter Queen arched an eyebrow at her. Snow bowed low, tugging on Spring's sleeve.

"Majesty," he said.

Spring grimaced, but then made a quick curtesy. He had no idea that sarcasm could be expressed so eloquently in such a brief movement. His stomach clenched, but the Winter Queen only smiled.

"I suppose I deserve that," she said. She turned to the Krampus and added, "But you don't deserve this. Rise, Lord Snow."

A chill breeze swept over him, snow and ice began wrapping around his horns and claws and disintegrated them with their passing. He felt his chin and nose shrink, along with his cheekbones, and his legs returned to what had become normal to him over the thousands of years he'd spent in this human form. He looked down, patting his body to ensure he was once more himself.

"I'm Snow again," he said, almost giddy with relief. "Not the Krampus."

Spring wrapped her arms around his waist and looked up at him, that smirk he had grown to love firmly in place and her eyes filled with love.

"You will always be the Krampus—my Krampus," she said. "And there's nothing wrong with that."

The breeze warmed, or maybe it was the love he felt for her filling him. The love she radiated right back. He leaned down and kissed her, not nearly as tender as the

Kringles' kiss had been, but filled with all his passion. He buried his hands in her hair, restating his claim, pouring his gratitude and amazement that this incredible woman had chosen him, of every being in all the realms, to claim as her own.

He pulled back to see that the ground around them had thawed, the snow was retreating as he watched. They stood in a circle of greening grass, the bare trees surrounding them were covered in buds that began to unfurl into beautiful petals and leaves popped out along their branches. Birds of vibrant blues, greens, and yellows hopped among them, along with the Redbirds that had been the only bird to be found in the land before. The sun beamed down at them from a clear blue sky.

"My dear," the Winter Queen said, approaching them. "I have behaved so poorly."

Spring shook her head. "I think I get it. You were both trying to find your way. It can be hard to find paths that intertwine, even if you're aiming for the same goal. And the Fae are… passionate and powerful beings." She smiled up at Snow, but then turned back to the Queen, her expression serious. "But listen, no more snatching kids. There's a better way to go about this."

"Oh?" The Queen's eyes widened, her eyebrows rising on her forehead.

A thread of worry wound through Snow's stomach, as he wondered how the Queen would react to being corrected by a mortal. His worry vanished as she smiled warmly.

"Please go on," the Winter Queen said. "I would love to hear your thoughts."

"Well..." Spring looked up at him and he nodded encouragement. "There are systems in place in the mortal realm. Foster care, orphanages. Places that could use more resources and support. Instead of trying to help one or two kids every year, why not send some of your people to work with them and use some of these magic diamonds and stuff to fund organizations that are making a huge difference for many?"

The Queen's eyebrows rose higher. "That is a very intriguing idea."

It was more than an intriguing idea to Snow. It was a fantastic idea. And with his holdings in the mortal realm, he could definitely make an impact. He turned to Kringle, watching the man's reactions carefully as he jumped into the conversation.

"We would have to move slowly," Snow said. "To prevent unbalancing the economic systems we'd be influencing."

"Mortal economies are not my realm." The Winter Queen laughed. She turned to Snow and Spring and said, "But I have a feeling the two of you would be well suited to make strides with this."

Spring's eyes widened and she clutched Snow's arm

tighter. "Us? Me?"

The Winter Queen stepped forward, extending her hands. This time, Spring didn't look to him for encouragement. She stepped right forward, meeting the Queen and clasping their hands together.

"My child, you have done such a great service for my kingdom." The Queen looked back at Kringle, her cheeks turning pinker, then smiled at Snow with such warmth, his heart fluttered in his chest. "For my family. I would ask more of you, though."

Spring swallowed hard enough that Snow saw her throat work, but she nodded.

"Be my agent in the mortal realm," the Queen said. "Stand by Lord Snow's side and help him—and the rest of us—navigate this new path. I can sense in your heart that you have the will, and I can see in your mind that you have the ability."

"I... I don't know what to say." Spring smiled. "Except yes."

"Then there is only one more thing we must do." The Winter Queen smiled back, nodding. "I cannot have a mortal doing my bidding. The other courts would see it as weakness, and we dare not let down our guard."

Spring nodded, her eyes wide. The Queen dropped her hands, but only to clasp Spring's face and draw her close.

"Therefore, I welcome you into the Court of the Yuletide Fae—Lady Spring." She bent forward and lightly kissed Spring's forehead.

A swirl of snow and frost rose around them, coating Spring's skin and quickly soaking into it. She glowed with a beautiful golden light, as bright as the sun, as bright as the heart full of love and caring that Snow knew beat within her chest. Flowers sprang up amidst the grass at her feet, spreading out through the clearing until it was filled with color. The buzzing drone of bees joined in with the chorus of songbirds that trilled their pleasure from the trees.

Two gleaming white deer flew through the sky, their golden antlers gleaming in the sunlight, legs moving as if they were running on the air—Aidan and Sylvia drawn by the light and warmth emanating from the clearing. They landed in the grass, gold eyes wide with wonder as they looked around the clearing, then they turned toward Spring and the Winter Queen and bowed on their front legs.

Spring's hair shone with a lustrous sheen of gold, power radiating from her unlike anything Snow had ever sensed before. The Winter Queen straightened, then pulled Spring into her arms. Kringle stepped to Snow's side.

"Lady *Spring*," Snow whispered low enough that only Kringle would hear.

"We will deal with it should the need arise." Kringle nodded to Snow, before crossing to the women and embracing them both.

Snow's chest felt overfull as he looked at the group

before him. His family. If the Court of the Springtime Fae or any other courts had a problem with Spring's title, Snow—the Krampus—would be ready to protect her. To protect all of them. Though, with the power emanating from her, he doubted that would be necessary.

Spring turned to him, her eyes glowing with the promise of their future and all the good it would hold. All the love. She ran to him, throwing her arms around his neck and pulling him to her for a long, passionate kiss. When they paused at last, he looked into the eyes of his love and said, "I guess spring isn't so bad after all."

Epilogue

Lord Kringle watched as his family gathered together around one of the huge ovens in the Yule Cat's bakery. Elysa was sharing one of her favorite recipes for Chocolate Crinkle Cookies with North and Melanie, the three chatting excitedly about different ways of enhancing the flavor. Snow and Spring had their arms around each other, laughing as Aidan snuck a pinch of raw cookie dough, only to have his hand swatted by Sylvia.

A chilly breeze tickled the back of Kringle's neck. He glanced over his shoulder, then quietly exited the kitchen into the bakery's main room. Jack Frost was lounging in North's favorite window seat, one knee pulled up, his foot on the cushion, the other dangling on the floor. He was drawing little snowmen in frost on the glass.

"Well, that all worked out rather well," Frost said.

"It did indeed. And I thank you."

"Ugh." Frost rolled his eyes. "All this time living among fairies, and you still haven't learned not to thank us."

"Mortal manners are hard to shake," Kringle said, chuckling lightly.

Frost smirked and shook his head. He rose from his seat and crossed over to stand near Kringle.

"Your um 'methods' were not exactly how I'd have gone about this," Kringle said. "Did you have to be…"

"Such a dick about it?" Frost offered.

Kringle's eyes widened and he laughed, his cheeks tingling in embarrassment. "Well, I wouldn't have used that word exactly."

"You are adorable." Frost chuckled, then put his hands on Kringle's shoulders. "And now… you owe me a favor."

A chill swept over Kringle, but he nodded. "That I do. I trust you know that I won't do anything against my nature, however."

Frost placed a hand on his own chest and shook his head. "You wound me." He stepped back, smirk firmly in place. "Now that everything is clear, I'll take my leave." He bowed low and said, "Santa." Then burst into a cloud of frost, tiny particles of ice hovering in the air for a moment before vanishing.

"Everything okay out here?" Snow walked up to Kringle's side, sniffing the air and glancing around as if searching for danger.

"Everything's fine."

Kringle patted his arm and turned him back toward the kitchen. He cast a final glance around the bakery, his eyes settling on the snowmen that Frost had drawn—two full sized, and between them… a smaller one. The trio held each other's stick hands, large, happy smiles drawn on their faces with loving detail.

Kringle's heart warmed and he nodded, thinking of Frost. There was something he could do for that boy. He just needed a bit of time to figure it out. In the meantime, his family had been reunited at last. Lord Kringle—Santa —intended to enjoy every moment of it.

—

Thank you so much for reading *The Krampus!* I didn't intend to write this trilogy, but when the ideas starting pouring forth, I knew I had to capture their magic on the page. It's been such an adventure! Thank you for journeying through the Yuletide Kingdom with me.

There's one more love story that hasn't been told. One that begins before the first whisper of *The Yule Cat*. Of course, I'm speaking of the tale of Kris Kringle and his love, the Winter Queen. When the trilogy of the Court of the Yuletide Fae was written, it didn't feel complete. I knew I had to write her story. Read on to discover the magic behind how this all began.

COURT OF THE YULETIDE FAE

THE
WINTER QUEEN

USA TODAY BESTSELLING AUTHOR
CASSANDRA CHANDLER

The Winter Queen

Court of the Yuletide Fae
Prequel

Cassandra Chandler

Chapter One

Long, long ago...

Light from the hearth glinted along his carving knife as Kris finished the last bit of detail on the wooden toy reindeer in his hand. His eyes ached from so many late nights in front of the fire, but it was too cold to do this sort of work outside during the day. He needed to ration his lamp oil carefully. He had given away perhaps a bit too much of it to the families in town—especially those with young ones to care for. Regardless, his work was done now, and Yule was upon them. With the coming of the Winter Solstice, the days would begin to get longer, and he wouldn't need so much oil to illuminate the nights in his quiet workshop cabin in the woods a bit from town.

Annabelle would love his latest piece. He chuckled to himself as he imagined the little girl hugging the toy close to her chest and spinning in circles as she loved to do, her forest green skirts blooming around her. However, if he wanted to see it in reality, he needed to get moving. The light from the window was fading quickly.

He placed the toy in a square of light green fabric, then folded the fabric over itself and tied it in place with a ribbon. He was sure Annabelle would find a use for both, and if it eased her family's burden, he was all the happier for it. Everyone had been struggling that year. The drought meant harvesting a leaner crop, and it was continuing into the winter. He hoped there was enough snow on the ground to help his team of reindeer pull his sleigh into town. He made sure the screen was in place to keep the fire in the hearth, then heaved his bag over his shoulder and headed out the door.

The reindeer were making happy chuffing noises in their paddock. So happy, in fact, that Kris turned toward them before heading to his sleigh. His cheeks prickled from the cold, but only a thin coat of snow crunched beneath his feet. He pulled his stocking cap a bit lower over his ears, watching his breath come out in frosty clouds.

All of the cold, but none of the snow. If only he was as good at making blankets as toys, the townsfolk would be better off. But his talents lay in wood carving and raising the reindeer that they couldn't do without. Of course, his neighbors did prefer that he raised them far enough away so that the summer winds wouldn't carry too much of their scent into town during the warmer months. Kris chuckled again as he cleared the edge of his cabin. His laughter froze in his chest, along with his breath, when he saw what had his reindeer so happy.

The most beautiful woman he had ever seen stood in the middle of the paddock, surrounded by his herd. They milled about her, nudging her with their noses as she stroked their heads and backs. She was so tall he could easily see her features above the reindeer. A delicate, pointed chin, pert nose, and large green eyes that sparkled like emeralds. Her pale gold hair was loose around her shoulders and cascaded down her back past her waist, a waterfall of wintery light. It was held back from her face with a crown of tall rods of platinum that gleamed like sunshine breaking through the clouds. Her red lips were stretched in a huge smile as she laughed, turning to address the pleas for attention from the reindeer behind her.

She stopped mid-turn as she saw Kris staring at her. His chest burned, reminding him to breathe, though he didn't think he could move otherwise. The reindeer turned to look at him, then bowed their heads and backed away, parting to clear space between the ethereal lady and Kris. Her dress had a silken appearance, the pale blue fabric shifting and shimmering around her, almost as if it had a life of its own. It couldn't be keeping her warm at all, but she seemed completely unphased by the frigid air.

Lights of every color sped from the forest and swirled around the woman, winged pixies, and he knew in that moment that he was staring at a powerful member of the

Fae. All the legends taught that they were not to be trusted, yet somehow, he couldn't worry about the pixies causing mischief among his reindeer. The gentleness with which the woman treated his herd reassured him, and her presence filled him only with wonder.

She rested her hand on the forehead of his largest stag, its antlers rising almost as high as the tips of her crown, and smiled at Kris. His heart pounded as if it meant to throw itself from his chest. His cheeks prickled, and his eyes blurred from unshed tears. He wanted to drop to his knees, but still couldn't bring himself to move. Instead, he forced himself to speak.

"I... I..." He cleared his voice. "Merry Yuletide."

Her smile widened. In a voice that thrummed with power, she said, "Merry Yuletide, indeed."

Warmth suffused him at the rich timbre of her voice. His hand lifted to his chest as if on its own, rubbing the spot above his heart. She turned her attention back to his reindeer as the largest stag nudged her again.

"He's um..." Kris stammered. "He's taken quite a liking to you."

"As I to him," she said. "Your animals are lovely. So well cared for."

"They are very loved." His cheeks heated at her praise, his limbs losing some of their stiffness. "When you remember to appreciate them, the rest falls into place."

"These ones, in particular, are excited," she said,

sweeping her arm over the team he would be using to get into town. With how little snow had fallen recently, he had taken to using a team of eight. They had to work harder to pull the sleigh, and he didn't want any of them being overburdened.

"They know it is Solstice," he said. "The children will sneak them sweet carrots when we get into town with their gifts."

"Gifts?" She turned to him again, her inner radiance catching his breath once more as he stared into those beautiful green eyes.

Finally, he cleared his throat and said, "For the Yuletide celebration." He briefly lifted the shoulder that was supporting his bag. "My team and I always bring toys for the children. I have lumber for their parents and was able to bake a few loaves of bread to contribute to the feast. It's all loaded up in the sleigh, though now that I think on it, I hope I haven't made it too heavy for the reindeer."

"They are strong," she said, turning back to the largest and stroking his cheek.

"Oh, yes, they are. But there hasn't been much snow, and the roads will be slushy or just muddy. I'll be asking quite a bit of them to get us into town."

A tiny crease appeared between her elegant brows, and she frowned. Shaking her head, she said, "That will not do."

She swept her arm in a wide arc over the paddock. Her

smile returned as plump, fluffy flakes of snow began to fall from the sky. Kris looked up, the snowflakes catching in his dark beard, his blue eyes wide with wonder. When he looked back to the woman, she was focused again on his reindeer, as if what she had done was of no significance to her. The flakes were already accumulating on the ground around them.

Kris's mouth went dry, his heart pounding quickly again as he remembered the legends about powerful fairies who could control the weather. Most involved concentration and spells, as well as time and preparation. She had caused an abundance of snowfall in seconds with but a thought.

This was no ordinary Fae. No, this woman held utter sovereignty over winter itself. He was speaking with the Winter Queen.

Chapter Two

"Is that better?" the Winter Queen asked.

Kris had to swallow several times before he could speak again. He nodded at last. "Yes, indeed. They'll have a much easier time of it."

"Then we should be off."

"We?" His heart was thunder in his ears. He must have misheard her.

"I would see this celebration that excites them so."

"I... Well..."

"Is there an issue with this?" She arched one delicate eyebrow, pulling herself up taller.

"No, no. It's just that your appearance is a bit... Well, it isn't what they're accustomed to."

She frowned, then closed her eyes as a white light suffused her body. The snow whirled around her, concealing her completely, then dropped to the ground and she was gone. A sound of dismay rose in his throat, unlike anything he had ever uttered. He staggered forward, leaning against the fence, feeling her absence as keenly as a hole in his chest. He knew the Fae could have such an effect on mortals, but didn't think it could take hold so quickly.

Just as he placed his hand on his heart, as if to hold it in, he felt a light touch on his shoulder. He turned to see the Winter Queen standing behind him, but transformed. The glow that made her skin ripple with light was replaced with ruddy cheeks and a nose made pink from the chill. Her eyes were the same sparkling green, and her golden hair was pulled back in thick braids tucked into each other in a loop, as was the current style. Instead of her soft silks, she wore a thick wool dress in a rich forest green, covered with a matching apron. Red and white embroidery in delicate snowflake patterns adorned each hem.

"Is this better?" she asked, lifting her skirt with one hand and spinning around. He could see sturdy boots covering her feet.

"Much," he said. "Though if you're looking to avoid questions, you may wish to don a hat, coat, and gloves. Perhaps a scarf as well."

She looked him up and down, then nodded. The whirlwind of snow swept over her once more, leaving her in a dark red coat with a hat, gloves, and scarf that matched his own.

"There," she said, smiling. "Now, we're a pair."

His voice seemed to catch in his throat as he tried to respond. The idea of them being a pair, of him being with her, was more than he could dare to imagine. Yet the thought of appearing in town with her on his arm coalesced with a clarity that was matched only by the longing in his heart. Since his voice had abandoned him, he smiled back and nodded.

"Then let's be off," she said.

"Right," he finally managed, heading for the gate to the paddock.

Before he'd taken two steps, she turned toward his animals once more. She swept her arm in another grand gesture, and a wave of snow and wind grew beneath his team. Snorting and stamping, the reindeer turned and ran with the wind, the snow somehow supporting their weight as they ran through the air and over the fence.

Laughing, the Winter Queen followed their progress, dropping her left hand when they were in place before his sleigh. She raised her right, as graceful as if she were in a dance, and the harness for his team rose from the ground and fastened itself to each reindeer perfectly. When she had finished, she clasped her hands in front of her body and nodded.

"I should think that will do," she said. "Let's be on our way."

"Of course."

Kris followed her, wondering if perhaps this was all a strange and wonderful dream. He set his last sack in the back, then turned to help her onto the sleigh. She arched that eyebrow at him once more, but smiled and took his hand as she climbed into the seat and settled herself. He hurried into place next to her, lifting the reins, but taking a moment to calm his heart and breathing. Nervousness would pass through the reins to his team, and the day had been filled with enough surprises.

Sitting next to her felt oddly… not-odd. Not odd at all. He turned to her and smiled before clicking his tongue to let the team know he was ready. They drove in silence all the way to town, watching the trees pass and the snow continue to fall around them, coating the road in a perfect blanket for his reindeer. Even the light seemed to linger a bit longer than was usual, easing their travels.

The sound of laughter reached their ears before the town came into view. The Winter Queen's eyes widened, and she perked up in her seat, angling her head as if to hear it more clearly.

"What is it that we are hearing?" she asked.

"Those are the village children," he said. "No doubt enjoying the gift of this snow."

"It is such a joyful sound," she said.

"Children hold much joy in them."

"Will they also enjoy your gifts?" She half-turned in her seat, reaching out and placing one hand on his arm.

He stammered a bit as he tried to reply, turning the sound into a hearty laugh that shook out his nerves. "That's the hope," he said. "It's been a lean year, but we're all doing our best to give them a joyful festival."

"Hmm." She stared at him thoughtfully for a few moments, then said, "I am eager to see this festival—and the children whose laughter rings so clearly through the forest. Let us hurry."

She turned back to the team and clicked her tongue. The sleigh jerked forward as the reindeer increased their pace, the momentum throwing her against Kris's side. He wrapped an arm around her instinctively to help hold her in place, blushing as she smiled up at him. He felt that he could stare into her eyes forever if she would only let him. And that is how they appeared in the town square, surrounded by all his neighbors and friends. The laughter ebbed as the reindeer slowed and then stopped, the conversation of the adults supervising the children's play also ending. Gretchen was the first to speak, as often was the case.

"Well, Kris Kringle," she said. "When you said you would have many surprises for us this year, you weren't exaggerating. Never would I have thought you'd arrive with a new bride!"

"Oh, that's not—" he began.

"And such a lovely one, at that," Gretchen said. "But come on, now. We should all head inside for the feast. You're the last to arrive."

She clapped her hands, and the children dutifully ran into the town hall, squealing with delight and waving in Kris's direction, no doubt eager to see what he'd made for them this year. The adults who had been out with them gathered around and began unhitching the reindeer and leading them to the barn near the town's inn or unloading the sleigh, smiling and nodding toward Kris and his companion. The men commented on the lumber with appreciation, though they left that in the sleigh for the moment. Looking at his sacks, there seemed to be more in the sleigh than Kris remembered.

"Come now, Kris," the Winter Queen said. "Help me from the sleigh, as is expected."

"Of course." He turned his attention back to her, quickly stepping down, then taking her hand as she followed. Gretchen was immediately at their side.

"Leave that all for the others," she said, gesturing to the sleigh. "Everyone is going to want to meet your new bride."

"Now, Gretchen—" Kris began, but the Winter Queen spoke over him, lacing her arm into his elbow.

"That sounds delightful." More quietly, she said, "Mrs. Kringle. What fun."

Kris felt his mouth drop open and his eyebrows creep up beneath his hat. The Winter Queen grinned at him with a mischievous glint in her eyes. The Fae were known to have a love of sport. Looking into her eyes, his chest filling with warmth, he realized he already trusted her far more than he should. He only hoped he and his town wouldn't come out the worse for it.

Chapter Three

When the Queen of the Winter Court stopped by the paddock filled with beautiful reindeer during her visit to the mortal realm, she hadn't expected to spend time with a group of mortals. Something about Kris caught her interest. It was difficult to look away from his bright blue eyes, the spark within them impossible to resist. His dark hair and broad shoulders also compelled her attention. None of the Fae she interacted with regularly had such physiques, nor did they have full beards such as his. She had the strangest urge to touch it or to bury her fingers in his hair.

Nothing about him was silken or soft. Rough homespun clothes, rough hands, skin that was weathered from the elements and hard work. Each imperfection about him drew her in deeper. He was not a being of light and magic. He was... real.

As they stared into each other's eyes, she corrected her assessment. There was a softness to him. Softness and light. But where the Fae displayed these traits outwardly, his light shone from within. That twinkle in his eye, the gentleness of his touch as he helped her into the sleigh. He was the very opposite of what she was accustomed to—and she wanted more of it.

"Shall we?" she asked.

Recovering himself, he nodded, then led her into the building. The interior was filled with a riot of sensations that nearly overwhelmed her. Fireplaces blazed with warmth and light, and garlands hung festively from their mantles. Candles stood everywhere, creating flickering shadows in the corners of the great room. Huge tables filled the space, chairs and people crowding around them as children darted between, snatching treats and bits of food. The sound of conversation and laughter was near deafening.

"Come and sit here," Gretchen said, leading them deeper into the throng.

Kris let the Winter Queen walk before him, but kept his hand at the small of her back. A thrill coursed through her body, bringing a flush to her cheeks. She glanced at him over her shoulder to see him walking close, but eyeing the rest of the crowd, ensuring that she wasn't too jostled by the merry-makers. Warmth filled her chest at the sweetness of the gesture. No one had ever done anything like that for her before. She would never dare let another Fae close enough to do so.

He caught her looking and smiled down at her. Her heart picked up its beat, and an odd feeling she couldn't name rose within her. She pressed her hand to her chest, hoping to calm herself, just as something crashed into her skirts. Startled, she turned to see a small child before her, eyes wide as she clutched something close.

"Emaline, be careful," Kris said. "Are you both alright?"

The Winter Queen smiled and nodded, then turned back to the little girl. "And you? Are you alright?"

The girl nodded shyly.

"And what do you guard so jealously that you would plunge right into someone in your flight?" the Winter Queen asked.

"I didn't want to miss it." Emaline frowned, then uncurled her fingers to reveal a napkin with half of a small sweet hand pie within it. "There aren't as many as last year. I'm sorry I—"

"Just be more cautious." Kris leaned down and winked at her. "Find me at dessert time, and I'll share mine with you."

The girl smiled brightly and threw her arms around Kris's neck, hugging him tight. Laughing, she disappeared back into the crowd.

That curious feeling rose within the Winter Queen again, strong enough this time to make her throat tighten till no words would come. What magic was this? She had never encountered anything strong enough to affect her so. She needed to understand it.

Kris pressed his hand to her back again, urging her toward a seat at a table close to a large tree that had been brought inside and decorated with ribbons and candles. She recognized some of his bags beneath it next to a bench in front of the fire. He pulled out a chair for her at the nearest table, and she sat, Kris settling beside her.

"Kris, you'll definitely be the talk of the Solstice festival now," a pale-haired man seated across from them said. "How ever did you find such a lovely bride with us all none the wiser?"

"By living outside of town with his reindeer, that's how," another said. "What bothers me is he hasn't introduced her yet."

Kris stammered for a few moments, then said, "You may call her Elysa." He turned toward the Winter Queen and said, "If that's alright with you."

"I prefer Mrs. Kringle," she said, "But do as you will." She hardly cared what they called her. 'Elysa' wasn't her truename, and Kris had been polite enough not to introduce her as if it were so. She nodded toward the men, but her mind kept circling to the little girl. As Kris handled the conversation at the table, the Winter Queen glanced around, noting the size of the plates and the portions that easily fit within, leaving much of the dishes uncovered. If the townsfolk found their feast insufficient, no one let it put a damper on their good spirits. She had never heard such genuine laughter.

When Kris seemed to have endured enough scrutiny from his fellows and was being left alone, she leaned toward him and said, "The girl. She was afraid there would not be enough for her to eat her fill?"

Lowering his voice, Kris replied, "As I said, it's been a lean year."

She frowned, pulling herself up straighter in her chair. This would not do. These mortals had invited her into their domain and shared what food, warmth, and light they had with her. A stranger. She would see to it that they had plenty for themselves as well.

Her magic flowed through her, down her legs and into the ground. Magic of plenty, of wholesome food the likes of which mortals could eat without consequence—unlike most of the food of the Fae. Her magic crept along the floorboards and up the legs of the tables, a fine coat of frost that melted before any could notice. Any but the man pressed against her side.

"Elysa, what are you doing?" he asked. She arched an eyebrow at him. With a sigh, he said, "I mean, Mrs. Kringle."

Smirking, she replied, "I don't know what you mean, *husband*. I'm merely enjoying the revelry." She leaned closer and whispered, "And making sure all enjoy it as well."

His cheeks pinked as she felt a now familiar spark along her skin where they touched. A flush rose to her own face as well. The meal passed in a blur of laughter and joy. The plates were always full of food, no matter how much people partook, the sweets were sweeter and more abundant, and the spiced wine flowed steadily. If anyone noticed how their stores never seemed to diminish, no one mentioned it.

At last, Kris gently touched her arm and said, "It's time to give the children their presents."

She smiled as she rose next to him, taking his arm once more as he led her to the bench near the tree. Adjusting her skirts, she settled on one side, leaving plenty of space for him. He paused, staring down at her with a furrow between his brow.

"What is it?" she asked.

"Nothing." He shook his head and sat next to her, filling the remainder of the bench. "Nothing at all."

"Do we need a larger bench?"

"Well, usually the children do sit next to me, but—" Before he could finish, a brown-haired youth bounded up and plopped himself on Kris's lap.

"Mr. Kringle, what have you brought me?" he asked. "Is it a ship like the one we spoke of?"

With a hearty laugh and a smile that crinkled the skin around his eyes, Kris patted the boy's shoulder, then reached into his bag and rooted around. He pulled out a wooden carving of a ship, its sails perhaps a bit thick, but filled with wind, and loving detail etched into the hull. He handed it to the wide-eyed child.

"Indeed, I did," Kris said.

"How did you... It's like magic—just what I imagined!" The boy threw his arms around Kris's neck, earning another jovial laugh, then turned and bounded away, calling out, "Thank you, Mr. Kringle!"

The evening progressed in the same manner, each child sitting on Kris's lap and talking of the toys they had asked him to carve for them. Some were trickier than others, but the Winter Queen could see where he had spent a great deal of time on each and every one. She could sense his own special kind of magic in them, his caring shining through in every heartfelt detail. The children were delighted, their joy and laughter filling the hall.

The Winter Queen—Mrs. Kringle, for the evening—leaned back and looked around, eager to soak in as much of the merriment as she could before she had to return to her kingdom. Her glance fell upon a group of youths standing near one of the fireplaces. One in particular frowned as he cast his eyes toward them time and again. His face was dirty, and his sweater was more holes than yarn. He wrapped his arms around himself as if striving to keep warm. Some of the warmth left her heart, replaced by a thread of worry wrapping around it.

"What of them?" she asked, leaning closer to Kris.

"Who?" He finished handing out the last toy, beaming at the little girl as she pranced away.

"The older children. Did you make nothing for them?"

He let out a sigh, the spark in his eye dimming. "At a certain age, children become more interested in breaking toys than playing with them."

"How are they to learn to care for things if they aren't given things to care for?"

He blinked a few times, his mouth opening and closing wordlessly before he managed, "I wouldn't know what to make for them."

"Toys and carvings aren't what they need. Look at the holes in their clothing. Especially that one. Children should receive clothes on Solstice. We're heading into the coldest part of the year."

His eyebrows rose, and he stammered again. "*We?*"

Mrs. Kringle shook her head. "You leave this to me."

"Elysa." He reached out and clasped her arm as she rose. Quietly, he said, "You can't work your magic here."

She smiled and leaned close. "Husband, what do you think I've been doing all evening?" With the same wink she'd seen him cast at some of the children, she picked up his empty bag and headed toward the youths.

Chapter Four

By the time they reached the boys standing by the fire, Mrs. Kringle had worked her magic on Kris's empty bag. Each step had seen it grow bulkier, until it seemed full to the brim. The boys snickered as she approached, but as she regarded them cooly, their mirth lessened, being replaced with fidgeting.

"Now, that's better," she said. "I have something for you."

They glanced at each other, as if unsure of how to react. She held up the bag to the closest boy.

"Go on," she said.

He stepped forward and reached into the bag. His eyes widened as he pulled out a hat and gloves spun from a dark blue wool, wrapped neatly in a matching scarf. Smiling at his peers, he quickly bobbed his head toward her and said, "Thank you," before backing away and inspecting them more closely.

One by one, she went down the line of adolescents, each reaching into the bag and pulling out a bundle of warm clothing. If she had thought of it, she would have made sure there were coats within as well. She would simply have to remain as 'Mrs. Kringle' for long enough to furnish them all with coats in a way that didn't raise their suspicion. The laws among the Fae regarding concealing their presence from mortals were strict and bound all the Courts. She would need to add plenty of time to her stay to provide the same for the younger children.

Finally, there was only one boy left—the first she'd noticed. He stood in a corner formed by the hearth, as if that could hide him from her view. Undaunted, she strode up to him and held out the bag. When he didn't reach inside, she shook it, frowning imperiously.

"My Uncle provides for me," he said.

"Your Uncle?" She glanced around, noting that Kris stood a few feet behind her. "Is he here?"

The boy nodded toward a table surrounded by men who were laughing loudly and ignoring most of the others nearby. Through her magic, she could sense that they had pulled more from the barrels of mead than the plates that eve.

"And how does he provide for you?" she asked.

"Gives me clothes. Food. A place to sleep by the fire."

Looking at his garb, the clothes hanging off his slight frame, she didn't doubt they were castoffs from the older man. And judging by his thinness, food was not shared in plenty. Sleeping by the fire… She couldn't bring herself to think on it without a cold fury gusting up inside of her.

Tamping it down, she said, "Never mind him."

Once more, she shook the bag, holding it closer to him. He rolled his eyes, but then reached inside, a look of hope softening his features. They darkened, hardening once more to the scowl that had greeted her.

"It's empty," he said.

"Ridiculous." She shook the bag again.

"It's okay." He straightened a bit, as if trying to show her he could stand on his own. All it did was reveal how gaunt he was. "I'm fine as I am."

The feeling from earlier tightened around her heart, so much less pleasant than what she felt when she looked at Kris or felt his touch. Dark and... cold. For the first time ever, a shiver passed through her. She shook her head, then stepped closer to the child.

"You have to believe there's something in here for you," she said in a hushed tone. "All children deserve kindness. All children deserve to be cared for. You have to believe that as well. I believe in you. You must believe in yourself. Try again."

"That isn't how the world works," he said, his tone as jaded as if he were a dozen years older.

She glanced over her shoulder at the Uncle carousing with others rather than spending this sacred evening with his kin. Turning back to the boy, she stepped closer still.

"Usually, perhaps." She pushed a bit of her magic closer to the surface of her skin, letting it sparkle like sunlight on freshly fallen snow. "But wouldn't it be wonderful if it did just this once?"

His mouth dropped opened, and his eyes widened. She saw no fear in him, though. Only the wonder that was supposed to fill little boys' eyes. He was too young yet to have hardened so.

With a soft smile, she held up the bag once more. "Try again."

He nodded, then reached into the bag. His eyes lit up as he pulled out a dark green hat, gloves, and scarf—the wool the very same color as Mrs. Kringle's dress.

"Well, look at that." Kris stood closer, angling his body as if to block them from view from the other revelers. "You two are quite the pair."

The boy laughed and nodded while Mrs. Kringle merely stared at him, a new magic permeating her bones.

"Child," she said. "Give me your name."

Kris gasped behind her, shifting his weight so that he could stand between them, but she threw up her arm, resting her hand on his chest and holding him back with ease. The boy's eyes widened once more.

"Your name, child," she repeated, voice thrumming with power.

He looked at Kris, who shook his head, his own eyes pinched with worry. She understood their concern. They would grow to understand hers in time.

The boy stood taller once more, squaring his shoulders,

and said, "Eric."

She breathed in the sound, letting it spin through her heart and being. The name resonated in her, amplifying her magic. The name was true.

"Eric," she said, filling the word with power. He flinched briefly, as if startled.

Kris placed one arm around her, leaning down so he could whisper, "What have you done?"

"What I am meant to," she said.

She had grown her court. She had staked her claim on this boy, and now she would take care of him, all the while learning more of the strange magic that Kris seemed to hold within himself, or perhaps bring out of her.

"Elysa, please." Kris turned her to face him. "Eric is part of our town. If he disappears—"

"Why on earth should he do that?" she admonished, holding up the bag and then dropping it so that Kris had ample time to catch it. "Is this not our home?"

Again, he stammered as he rested the bag over his shoulder, his eyebrows shooting up his forehead. "*Our?*"

She turned back to the boy and spoke the truename she had chosen for him, "Eric Kringle." Again, he flinched, eyes growing wide. She reached out and grasped his arms gently, casting a soft smile at him. "Do you accept this name?"

The boy stammered, but then nodded. "I do."

Beaming, she squeezed his arms once more.

"Come along, then." She turned away from Kris's arm around her with some regret. If she had her way, there would be ample opportunities to enjoy his touch later. And she *would* have her way.

She led them straight to the uncle, who leaned back in a chair to the point that it neared collapse. The laughter at his table quieted as the trio stood before him, Mrs. Kringle's hands clasped in front of her above her waist. She said nothing, focusing her magic on the man before her, letting it weave its way subtly through him, so slowly, he wouldn't even feel it.

"Well, then," he said. "What can I do for Mrs. Kringle on this fair Yuletide eve?"

"I am merely letting you know that Eric will be coming to live with Mr. Kringle and me, where he will have his own bed, his own room, and his own food and clothes. In short, he shall have a home."

The Uncle's eyes widened briefly, a flare of anger lighting within that he quickly sought to conceal with laughter. "Sounds fairly good to me. Can I come instead?"

Instead. Not *as well.*

The cold fury coiled around her heart blazed for a moment, feeding into the magic she wove through this callous man. In his soul, she saw that he truly believed there was only enough for one—for himself. That he alone was deserving and entitled. The other men at the table joined in with his laughter.

Eric leaned forward and said, "Mrs. Kringle, never mind it—"

She raised a hand to cut him off before clasping them before her once more. Again, she smiled her sweetest smile at the Uncle. She would not ask his name—did not want it. To give a truename to a ruler of a Fairy Court, or to accept the name given by another, was to join their kingdom. She did not want any connection between herself nor her subjects and this man.

"You see, *my* Eric," the uncle began, a ripple of his own claim resonating in his words, "He's a good lad. Cleans the house and does the wash. Doesn't need much of a firm hand to mind his business. Plus he's family. I couldn't possibly let him go."

"Family." She scoffed. "Do you often show a 'firm hand' to family?"

He shrugged. "Only when it's necessary."

"I quite understand." She paused for a moment, letting her magic creep more deeply into him. "If you would answer one question for me."

He glanced at his fellows, who shrugged to a man, then turned his attention back to her. "I don't see the harm in that."

She smirked as he shuddered, her magic tightening its grip. Their first deal was struck.

"You told me what Eric does for you," she said. "What is it that you do for others? For the town?"

Each action, once taken, created ripples through the worlds. Before she did anything else, she wanted to know how her acts might affect Kris and Eric's home.

The uncle shrugged. "This and that."

One of the other men laughed and the uncle scowled at him darkly. Her magic gave her a truer message. The uncle did nothing for others. He took, and that was all. Fae or mortal, she was acquainted with the type.

"I see," she said. "Then I shall give you the means of acquiring the services of others who can do 'this and that' for you instead of Eric."

The men laughed again, and this time, the Uncle joined in. The sound had more meanness than mirth to it. She couldn't help but compare it to the heartfelt laughter of Kris. His was richness and warmth and theirs naught but hollow echoes. Though she knew his presence at her back was unnecessary, the thought that he was standing with her brought more warmth to her heart.

She reached into her pocket and pulled out a pouch. Opening it, she poured its contents onto her palm. The laughter at the table died as every man stood and leaned closer, their eyes wide with avarice. The light from the candles sparkled and gleamed in the dozen gems she held.

"I can see that you can give him a much better home than I." The uncle cautiously reached out, his eyes locked on the meaningless treasure in her hand.

Mrs. Kringle was loathe to have him nearer. She

quickly poured the gems back in their pouch, but held it out to him, pushing away her distaste. As he leaned in and grasped the bag, their second deal was struck. She tightened her grip, awakening her magic and wrapping them in a bubble of silence. No one would hear what she was about to say, no one would see anything but what she wanted them to see, and if anyone strayed too close, they would feel a chill that would surely drive them away.

"The servants you hire with this will be well-treated," she said. "Your presence will only be a blessing in Eric's life, never a burden. And if you should ever harm another again, I will ensure that you serve the town in a different capacity." She tugged on the bag, pulling him closer. "That of rat catcher."

The uncle began to cough, bringing his free hand to his mouth. The fit grew stronger until he finally coughed up a clump of hair. His eyes widened with fear as he stared at it. Mrs. Kringle only arched her brow.

"Hmm. Ginger tabby," she said. "There are worse forms to take."

He started to back away, though his grip stayed tight on the bag. The magic of their second deal cemented down to his bones.

"This is our agreement," she said. "You shall not break it nor speak of it to others. If you do, I shall know, and you shall begin your new duties immediately—on four legs. But don't worry." She sweetened her smile. "I'll save a place for you in front of the fire. It's no worse than the home you provided for your kin."

She released the bag as the illusion around them dropped. The uncle fell backwards into his chair, the bag held close against his heart, his chest heaving, eyes wide with panic. The spell firmly planted, she turned back to Kris and Eric.

"Well then," she said cheerfully. "Shall we go home?"

Chapter Five

What has happened?

The question kept repeating in Kris's head all the ride home and while tending to the reindeer—without the help of the Winter Queen's magic this time. It continued through welcoming Eric into his house—which was suddenly much bigger than Kris remembered. The kitchen was grand, with ovens that would let them cook feasts for many and a pantry bursting with stores. His workshop had been transformed into his dearest dream, with new tools alongside his favorites, sturdier benches, better light, and everything he had ever wished for at his fingertips.

True to her word, Eric had his own room. It was bigger than Kris's had been, and there were more just like it. How many children did the Winter Queen intend to bring to his home? And did she mean to adopt them, as she had Eric, or…

He shook the thought from his mind, washing up after a final check on the reindeer and packing away his sacks till next year. Walking through the living room, he paused before the fire. A raging blaze warmed the room, though he hadn't built it and didn't remember there being so many logs near the fireplace when he'd left.

The Winter Queen had given him one enigmatic command. She had placed a small rug off to one side of the hearth, barely bigger than a cat, and instructed that they leave it where it was and not place anything on it. When Kris had asked why, she smiled and said she was saving that spot for someone. He had known better than to ask further questions. She had then whisked Eric off to help him prepare for bed, leaving Kris alone in his home. Only it wasn't truly his home anymore. It was *their* home —his, the Winter Queen's, and Eric's. Through a Yuletide miracle, they had suddenly become 'the Kringles.'

Kris knew he should be frightened. A powerful Fae being had decided to play at having a family with him. But the more he listened to her and Eric speak, the more he realized that his only fearful thought was, 'How long do I have with her? How long till she grows tired of this game and leaves?' She might be amusing herself, but she had given Kris everything he had ever dreamed of and more.

He would have been content with his tiny workshop even, to have this family and hope for a future with them. He could have built a new room for their children with his own hands. It wouldn't have been nearly as grand as this, but he would have done everything in his power to fill any home they lived in with love and joy.

He reached out and placed his hand on the mantle. The

wooden frame had been carved with intricate detail. He leaned closer and saw that the etchings were of the toys he had made and given to the children that year. There was warmth in this home. Warmth and care in the magic that she had spun for them. He knew it was probably part of her game. The Fae were not to be trusted. And yet...

He headed to his room, heart in his throat as he wondered what he would find.

The room was cozier than he'd expected. A new wardrobe stood beside his, and the bed was bigger. A washbasin sat in one corner. The windows were framed in colorful tiles of glass depicting winter scenes. His reindeer stood in a snowy field in one. White flakes fell among rich green pine trees in another. It was beautiful and magical. As beautiful as the Winter Queen. As beautiful as his Elysa. Kris sat on the bed, wondering how his life could have taken such an incredible turn.

The door opened, and Elysa stepped in. She closed it softly behind her.

"Eric is asleep," she said, making her way to the new wardrobe.

She opened the doors and stood so that it blocked Kris's view of her. It did nothing to mute the sound of her clothing whispering over her skin. His heartbeat picked up as his mouth went dry.

"He is a good boy," she said. "We will give him the home he needs to grow into a fine man."

"I... That sounds wonderful."

He swallowed hard as she emerged from the wardrobe, wrapped in a thick velvet robe. Sheer fabric peeked around its edges, sending his mind down paths it had no business traveling. She smiled, reaching up to remove the pins from her hair and letting all that glorious pale gold fall around her shoulders. The pins made a light clattering sound as she dropped them in a bowl within the wardrobe, then closed its doors. She approached him quietly, stopping right before him so that she stood between his knees. She reached out and brushed the backs of her fingers along his beard, her lips parting and a flush rising to her cheeks as she did so.

"I am not of this world," she said.

His blood rushed through his ears. Was she about to leave him? To leave *them*? Though she had gifted them with this beautiful home, he would trade it all to have her stay. He reached out to clasp her hand and brought it to his lips, pressing a kiss to her knuckles. He held it in front of his chest, just above his heart, as he stared up into her eyes.

"Children need a mother," he said.

Her chest rose on the slightest intake of air, and her eyes widened. The faintest hint of a smile curved the corners of her lips.

"And a father," she said.

He wasn't sure how long they stared into each other's

eyes, but the warmth he saw blooming there gave him the courage to reach out to her waist and pull her down to his lap. He wrapped his arms around her and held her tight. Names were important to the Fae. He wondered if, even for a little while, she would accept one from him.

"Then it's a good thing we're Mr. and Mrs. Kringle," he said.

She laughed, the sound as musical as wind chimes, then leaned her forehead against his. His heart thundered in his chest, relief coursing through him as he knew that she would stay, at least for a time. And he would treasure each moment she gave him.

"It is a good thing, indeed," she said.

Epilogue

Elysa approached him almost noiselessly, but Kris still knew she was there. He felt her, like a winter breeze cooling him down after a hard day in the reindeer's paddock. Eric and his grandsons did most of the work with the reindeer nowadays. Kris was content to watch them and answer questions that he suspected were more to humor him than anything else. He rested against the fence, watching the grass catch the afternoon sun and counting his many, many blessings.

"Have they finished their work already?" Elysa asked, hugging his arm and leaning upon his shoulder.

"They have. Eric is taking the boys and girls into town for a bit. I would have asked if you wanted to go with them, but you were busy in the kitchen, as always."

She laughed, the sound as musical to his ears now as in the beginning. Her skin was just as smooth, her hair still gleaming gold. Though they tried to explain it away with her being 'from another land,' Eric and their other children must have long since guessed that their mother was special. Time did not touch her, unlike Kris. At least, not physically.

He had sensed a yearning within her. Many nights, he found her standing outside the reindeer's paddock, staring up at the aurora borealis with a distant look in her eye. Though he would always want more time with her, he couldn't be greedy. She had already given him a lifetime— a lifetime filled with love and joy.

"Why didn't you go to town with them?" she asked.

"I'm not quite as spry as I used to be."

"You do seem different." A furrow appeared between her brows as she leaned back and looked at him as if seeing him for the first time. She reached up and lifted a tuft of his white hair between her fingers. "But that's part of the wonder of humans. You change, whereas we…"

His heart felt tight, hearing her speak of her other people. For so many decades, 'we' had meant their family and town. Now, he heard an echo of another meaning in it. Now, he heard 'goodbye.'

She shook herself, then smiled. "I am eager to see what is next for us. Children and grandchildren have been such an adventure. It's much more of a challenge caring for mortals."

He chuckled. "You've excelled at it."

"I have a feeling that change is upon us. What is next for us, Kris?"

Again, his heart clenched, almost strong enough to take his breath away. He rubbed the spot, then patted her hand on his arm. That she still thought of them as 'us' warmed him, but she couldn't follow him on his next journey. She was immortal, after all.

"The next adventure is yours alone," he said. "Though I hope you'll watch over the children and their children and on and on."

"What do you mean?" Her voice was laced with concern.

"It's been over forty years."

She angled her head to the side. "Is that a long time?"

"I am old, Elysa." He knew time flowed differently for the Fae, so he put things more bluntly. "What is next for me is… the end. At least for this body's journey."

"No." Her eyebrows furrowed, and her sweet lips pulled into a frown as she shook her head. "No, I will not allow it. I will restore your youth." She lifted her hands, but he grasped her wrists before she could reach his face.

"Please. Every wrinkle, every crease, every white hair on my head and in my beard holds a memory of our children. Our grandchildren. Of you. I would not change a thing."

"Then I can change you inwardly. You can appear the same."

"Elysa, this is what happens to mortals. I'm at peace with it."

"Well, I am not," she said, an imperious note creeping into her voice. The note surprised him as it quickly turned to pleading. "Come with me to the Winter Kingdom. You will never age and can stay as you are. I'll make space for you in my castle."

"I like my workshop," he said.

"I'll recreate it for you. And give you helpers."

"Elysa—"

"Who will make the toys for children at the Winter Solstice? Who will bring them joy at Yuletide? Your work must continue."

"You have many subjects in your Court. I'm sure you'll find someone."

"I don't want to find someone. I want you. What can I offer? What is it that you need?"

"You've given me everything I've ever wanted and more." Everything except...

"There's something," she said. "I can feel it. Something you wish for even still."

"Your heart."

The words slipped out before he could stop them. She gasped and took a step back, covering her chest as if to protect it. He followed, shaking his head. Gently, he grasped her hands and pulled them in front of his own heart.

"I'm sorry," he said. "I didn't mean to scare you. It's just..." He shook his head, then shrugged, smiling down at her. "I love you, Elysa."

Her lips parted, and her breathing quickened. She snapped her mouth shut and pulled herself up straighter.

He could feel her power gathering around her, charging the air with wisps of cold and frost. All these years, he had managed to avoid offending her. The Fae were quick to anger, deeply passionate beings. But he held passion, as well. He had never loved anyone as deeply.

"Elysa…" he whispered, feeling the power prickling over his skin.

"I accept."

"What?"

"I accept your truename of me," she said.

He gasped, his heart hammering as he realized the implications of what she was saying. She had explained the way of naming among the Fae. He never dreamed in his wildest imaginings that she would accept his name for her, make it part of herself.

"Do you accept me?" Her eyes glimmered, and she angled her head, a stark vulnerability entering her features, the likes of which he'd never seen.

"Elysa, my love, of course I do."

She laughed, then threw her arms around his neck and pulled him to her, pressing her lips to his. The power erupted around them. Waves of light and fluffy flakes of snow swirled so thickly, he could see nothing but white. The cold seeped through his muscles, into his bones. All he could feel besides it was Elysa's lips against his, her hands clutching him close, till their hearts were inches apart. The cold subsided, along with the light, leaving them standing in a field he didn't know. Above, a green aurora rippled through the sky, and a landscape of unbroken snow stretched as far as he could see in every direction.

"What is this?" he asked, his voice laced with wonder.

He turned to Elysa to see a crown of platinum spikes form around her head. His forehead tingled, and he reached up to feel a similar crown on himself. Looking down, he saw that his clothing had been transformed into a bright red jacket with gleaming gold buttons and white fur trim, matching trousers, and shiny black boots. He pulled at a lock of his hair, but saw that it was still white, as she'd promised, though he felt an incredible energy coursing through him.

"My power is now yours, and yours is mine," she said. "Our kingdom is transformed and shall forevermore be known as the Court of the Yuletide Fae."

Behind her, the ground shook as an enormous crystal castle rose from the ground. Lights of every color gleamed in its walls, as well as the green of the aurora reflecting in its depths. More of the lights flew out from the castle, coming close enough that he could see the tiny forms of glowing pixies swirling around them in delight.

"We shall still rule the winter," she said. "But we will fill it with warmth and light. With love and joy. Together."

Kris could scarcely believe what was happening, even with all the wonder that had filled his life up to now, thanks to this amazing and magical woman. His heart was filled with warmth, his mind spinning with ideas for how they could serve the children of the mortal realm as well as the subjects of her kingdom—*their* kingdom.

"I have given you a lifetime in your realm," she said. "Now, I give you my heart. All I ask in exchange is forever. With you. That is my agreement." Her voice became a bit thready as she asked, "Do you accept?"

With a smile that filled his heart with warmth and deepened the crinkles at the corners of his eyes, he drew his wife even closer in his arms.

"I do."

"Then let us begin our eternity together," she said.

And that is just what they did.

—

Thank you for reading this special edition of *The Yuletide Fae!* I hope to make "closed door" versions of many more of my books. If you just can't wait, you can go ahead and read the first chapter of the current, high-heat version of *Court of the Springtime Fae* book one, *Jack Frost!*

Jack Frost

Court of the Springtime Fae
Book One

Chapter One

Sun gleamed blindingly from the boughs of the surrounding trees, catching and reflecting every ray of light. Ice perfectly encased the buds that were just getting ready to open along with their branches, and the few early flowers had a fine sheen of frost on their colorful petals.

Jack Frost sighed, a deep smile pulling on his cheeks. His work for the morning was done. He had transformed the park into a crystalline wonderland—and had probably pissed off at least one member of the Court of the Springtime Fae.

Bonus.

He stretched his long arms along the back of the bench where he sat and surveyed his work. It was so good to love one's job. Spring hadn't quite arrived, so technically, this was still the time of the Yuletide Court. Everyone assumed he was a member, but he skirted the edge between winter and spring. The Winter Queen was certain of his allegiance to her, though Jack occasionally did jobs for the Oak King. It had been a while since he'd interacted with the King of the Warmer Court.

With Ostara—or the Spring Equinox, as most mortals called it—right around the corner, he had a feeling the Oak King would make an appearance soon. This between time, when winter was just fading as spring arrived, was Jack's opportunity to shine.

'*Literally*,' he thought, as he smiled at the sunlight catching and refracting in the ice he had formed on the thin branches of the nearest tree.

The flowers had been pretty before. Now they were magical. The buds weren't so close to sprouting that his visit would cause any actual damage. The area he'd chosen was large enough that he could spread his power out instead of focusing it in one small space.

For a few blessed hours, he could enjoy the warm satisfaction of a job well done. Or rather, the satisfaction of being warm after he used his powers. His smile hardened, mimicking the ice on the trees above.

How long would he have before the cold built within him again, making his skin so frigid that the surrounding air would turn to fog? Would it be days this time? Hours? After all these eons, he still could never predict it. He would just have to find another area to coat with frost. Something higher, perhaps. A building that his powers wouldn't harm.

Or he could call in his favor…

No, he wasn't ready for anything that extreme. Besides,

he hadn't worked out how to word it so that when he asked the King of the Yuletide Kingdom to pay up, the favor would manifest precisely as Jack wanted it. King Kringle might have started out as a mortal, but he had been a fairy for centuries now. Some of their trickery had to have found their way into his heart.

'To experience lasting warmth without losing my powers.'

It was much easier to imagine immediately after expending the energy that had filled him with freezing cold. Jack closed his eyes and tilted his face to the near-spring sun, relishing its warmth. Until it vanished as a shadow fell over him.

Jack looked up to see a young boy staring at him from just the right spot to block out Jack's morning sunbath. Tufts of unruly brown hair stuck out from underneath a knitted blue hat with a pattern that he could only describe as 'white blobs.' Were those supposed to be snowflakes? He wore a similarly awkward scarf around his neck, along with a bulky coat. His thick gloves held a sheet of paper. He blinked his dark cyan eyes a few times, probably to clear his eyelashes of the frost that still lingered near Jack.

"What?" Jack said.

"Why are you dressed like that?"

Jack glanced down at his midnight blue button-up shirt with the top buttons undone and the sleeves rolled up to his elbows tucked into faded jeans that brushed against shiny black boots with very good treads. He was usually walking on ice, after all. No hat covered the even more unruly black hair that stuck out in short waves all over his head, and no scarf disguised the chiseled lines of his jaw or chin.

He looked back at the boy. "What's wrong with being dressed like this?"

"Mister, you're going to freeze out here."

Jack scoffed and shook his head.

"Don't you have a place to go?" the boy asked.

A tendril of cold wound around Jack's stomach, his chest flooding with the feel of ice. It was so soon after using his powers. Too soon. This boy was affecting him somehow.

"Go away." Jack scowled at him. The boy shifted his weight uneasily and glanced over his shoulder, then turned back to Jack. "Does that ugly hat muffle your hearing? I said go away."

"My Auntie made this hat, and it's not ugly. It's…" The boy struggled as if trying to remember something. "It's heartfelt."

Jack scoffed again, leaning forward with his elbows on his knees. His breath came out in little puffs of fog—but just his breath. At least he was warm enough to still enjoy that.

The boy looked down at the paper in his gloved hands and sighed, then clumsily folded it and tucked it into one of his pockets. He turned back to Jack and said, "Mister, you need to get inside."

Jack narrowed his eyes at the interloper. "Didn't your mother ever tell you not to talk to strangers?"

The boy let out another sigh, his hands curling into fists as he stood straighter. He couldn't be more than a decade old, but he managed a surprising amount of moxie.

"My name's Charlie."

Not quite the boy's full truename, but close. He really needed to be more careful who he spoke to. Giving a fairy his name could be very dangerous.

"You're supposed to tell me your name now," Charlie said. "I tell you my name and you tell me yours."

Aside from the incredible rudeness of demanding Jack's name—at least, according to Fae manners—the child's persistence was both confusing and irritating. Especially since it was kind of endearing. Jack wasn't looking for any human pets. He didn't collect stray children the way the lords of the Yuletide Kingdom did.

"What's your name, mister?" Charlie insisted.

"You are annoying. Go away."

Charlie wasn't daunted. If anything, his resolve seemed to grow as he stiffened his spine even more. All Jack wanted was a chance to enjoy what apparently were only going to be the few moments of warmth he would manage from frosting this area. He needed to get this kid to leave him alone.

"It's for a reason." The boy showed no sign of giving up. "What's your name?"

"Fine. It's Jack."

It totally wasn't 'Jack.'

Jack Frost had never told anyone his truename. Not even the Winter Queen. He'd been calling himself 'Jack' for so long, he could trick people into thinking it was his truename. He had even sort of accepted a place in the Court of the Yuletide Fae using the false name. Keeping his truename to himself was the only thing that prevented them from having power over him.

"There," Charlie said. "Now we're not strangers."

Jack snorted as he shook his head and rubbed his hands together.

"Don't tell strangers your real name if they ask." Jack hadn't meant to say that. He wasn't sure where it had come from, or why he was bothering to teach this little brat how to protect himself against fairies.

"Why?" Charlie asked.

"Because you don't know who you're dealing with. They could be a trickster."

"A what?"

"A trickster. Someone who wants something from you and will trick you into helping them get it."

"Are you a trickster?"

Jack chuckled. "Oh, absolutely. One of the worst."

Charlie narrowed his eyes and cocked his head to the

side. "Nah. You're not a bad guy. You're just lost."

The cold that had been spreading through Jack's chest stilled. He held his breath, wondering what was happening to him. Was this really a mortal child? Or some fairy who had found his way into this realm, looking to mess with people? Charlie shouldn't be able to affect Jack's powers. To affect Jack at all. He didn't even have Jack's full false name.

Charlie pulled off his hat, making his hair stand out at even odder angles. He placed the hat on Jack's hands, that were still clasped in front of him. Warmth clinging to the yarn seeped into Jack's skin. It flooded up his arms and through his body, pushing away the cold.

"Don't worry," Charlie said. "I'm going to help you."

The warmth Jack had been enjoying suddenly grew, as if the child had lit a fire in Jack's chest. He sat back, rubbing the spot, brow furrowed as he tried to work out what sort of magic this was—because it had to be magic. Jack had never felt such warmth before.

Charlie leaned forward and clasped the hand that was still resting on Jack's knee. That silly hat encased Jack's other hand, pressed close to his heart. Charlie urged Jack to stand and kept his hold on Jack's hand as he started down the sidewalk, pulling Jack behind him.

"My mom's shop isn't far from here," Charlie said. "It's warm, and she always has snacks. There are even blankets and a cot in the office for when I take naps in there after school, but I don't really do that anymore. She still treats me like a little kid."

"You are a little kid."

Charlie glared up at him briefly, bringing a smile to Jack's face. "I'm not *that* little. Anyway, it's just the two of us, and I think it makes her feel better to kind of baby me, so I let her do it."

Jack's smile deepened. He was really starting to like this kid.

"What about your dad?" Jack asked.

Charlie's grip tightened and his lips pulled into a stern frown. The warmth Jack felt flooding him ebbed a bit.

"He's not around," Charlie said. "But it's okay. We don't need him."

Jack squeezed Charlie's hand. He wasn't sure why. It had been almost an involuntary reflex. But fairies didn't have those kinds of instincts. Did they?

"What's your mom going to think of you bringing home a stranger?" Jack needed them to change topics. This one was making him feel weird.

"We're not strangers anymore, remember? I'm bringing home a new friend."

Jack outright laughed. That sounded just like something he would say. Yeah, he definitely liked this kid.

"Okay, what's she going to think about you making a new friend who's a grown man?"

Charlie shrugged. "She might think it's kind of weird,

but she's always saying we need to help people out whenever we can and that we're all in this together. So, if she says something about it, that'd kind of make her a hypocrite."

"A hypocrite, huh?" Jack smiled down at the boy, who was still staring straight ahead as he led Jack along. "You read a lot, don't you?"

"It gives me something to do. I go to the library almost every day after school."

"It's hard to argue with someone who's well read," Jack said, and meant it. "Lead on, little man."

Charlie glanced up at him with a smile. Jack couldn't help but return it.

—

You can get your copy of *Jack Frost* now! For more of my Paranormal Romances, check out *The Summer Park Psychics* or *Forbidden Instinct*. If you want to explore my other stories, you can go on out of this world adventures with the fated soulmates of the *Cygnian 7* series or check out short, steamy Sci-Fi Romances on a near-future Earth in that same universe with *The Department of Homeworld Security*. And if you'd like a little bit of Scifi mixed into your Paranormal Romance, check out the *Blades of Janus*.

I'd love to keep in touch. Join my newsletter at cassandra-chandler.com to hear about all the adventures happening in Cassland. And if you enjoyed this book, please consider leaving a review at your favorite book review site. Reviews are so important to authors. You can also help by spreading the word among your friends. I appreciate you so much!

Thank you for reading *The Yuletide Fae!*

Cassandra Chandler

About the Author

USA Today Bestselling author Cassandra Chandler uses her vivid imagination to make the world more interesting, spawning the ideas she turns into her evocative Science Fiction Romances and enthralling Paranormal and Urban Fantasy Romances. Fast-paced and funny, lighthearted or filled with suspense, her stories will introduce you to characters you'll fall in love with and worlds you long to explore.